CALL

THE

CANARIES

HOME

CALL
THE
CANARIES
HOME

A Novel

LAURA BARROW

LAKE UNION
PUBLISHING

Published by Lake Union Publishing, Seattle

www.apub.com

Amazon, the Amazon logo, and Lake Union Publishing are trademarks of Amazon.com, Inc., or its affiliates.

ISBN-13: 9781662510267 (paperback)
ISBN-13: 9781662510250 (digital)

Front cover design by Sarah Horgan
Back cover design by Adrienne Krogh
Cover image: ©Wizemark / Stocksy United; ©pixssa / Shutterstock; ©MANSILIYA YURY / Shutterstock; ©Midstream / Shutterstock; ©Elina Li / Shutterstock

Printed in the United States of America

For my daughters and my sisters.
Every girl needs a sister.

PROLOGUE

Savannah

Muscadine, Louisiana
February 1997

I scraped clumsily at the stubborn, sleet-covered earth with Daddy's shovel. Apart from us, it was one of the few things he'd left behind, discarded against the old tin shed as if he had just stopped to take a break for a moment and would drift into view any second, hollering at us to let his things alone. It *clink clink clinked* against the chain-link fence as I worked unsuccessfully to steady the weight of it beneath my knobby frame. Orbs of afternoon sunlight glinted off its worn handle, the blade so dull and encrusted with dried mud that it was barely functional, nearly as useless as my scrawny arms.

Though she wasn't that much bigger than me—all freckles and crowded teeth—Sue Ellen fixed a hand to her cocked hip with all the sass of an angsty teenager. "Let me do it. You might as well be digging with a stick at the rate you're going."

"Fine," I said, one frozen hand shading my eyes against the sun while the other thrust the handle in her direction. "If you think you can do any better." It landed with a metallic thud at her dirty tennis shoes, and she snatched it up, grumbling to herself. Normally I would have shot back with a petty insult, but I had the good sense to hold it inside, because we needed this. It was proof we had once existed here, that we'd breathed in this air, made memories in this place where we had become a family. Before everyone began to leave us.

Rayanne and I watched Sue Ellen take her turn at stabbing the dirt, unimpressed. "You're not doing it right. Put your weight into it," Rayanne said.

"It's too hard." Sue Ellen tossed the shovel aside and smeared a dirty hand down her cheek, her brown hair fluttering like ribbons in the wind, her button nose the color of cranberries. "No way we can dig a hole deep enough for all this junk." Sue Ellen may have believed our memories were junk, but I treasured them each like precious artifacts, stored the ones I still had left tight inside me like the peaches and pickles we faithfully canned every summer with Meemaw. I held on to them for all of us because someone had to. If it weren't for my pestering, all of it would vanish one day like dandelions lost on the wind.

Not ready to give up yet, I called out toward Meemaw in the driveway, where she stood slumped against the old tan Buick, the exhaust sending plumes of gray smoke into the winter air. Bundled up in her pink goose-down overcoat, she took one last drag from her cigarette and stomped it out before trudging over through the gate. She'd been in a hurry all morning to put more than a few football fields between us and the sad little house as soon as possible, but she grunted and puffed and shoveled anyway, until soon there was a respectably sized hole where we could lay our treasure down deep. After she left us to finish our work, we took turns scooping dirt over the little plastic cooler, patting and shaping the earth until it heaped into a tidy little mound.

"Come on, girls. Time to go!" Meemaw's raspy voice called out from the sputtering car, where she sat blowing streams of cigarette smoke out the window.

2

Rayanne and Sue Ellen turned, breaking into a run to meet her, but I yelled after them. "Wait! We have to promise to come back in a hundred years."

Arching an eyebrow, Sue Ellen whipped around midstride and looked at me as if I'd just grown a second head. "That's the dumbest thing I've ever heard. In a hundred years, we're all gonna be lying in the ground with it."

My shoulders deflated, but I picked them right back up and jutted out my chin, doing my best to keep it steady. "Fine then. One year." Would another year be long enough for Georgia to find her way back to us? How much longer would we have to wait?

"Are you stupid? I'm not coming back here in a year to dig up what we just barely put down there," Sue Ellen said. "That's preponderous!"

"You mean *preposterous*," Rayanne pointed out helpfully.

"I *know* that," Sue Ellen said in a voice full of pure spite, her stormy green eyes narrowed to slits. To insult Sue Ellen's intelligence had always brought down the wrath of hell, but neither of us could resist pushing that button when the opportunity presented itself. Especially me.

Rayanne must have seen the fire go out of me, because she moved a little closer and slung an arm around my shoulders. "Let's say twenty-five. That will give us a chance to grow up, maybe have a baby or two of our own to show our things to."

Grateful, I blinked up at her through burning tears. Rayanne had always been softer with me. I figured Sue Ellen was so addled because she was stuck in the middle between us, only a year older than me but just older enough to hold her wisdom over me like a weapon. I couldn't blame her. I hated being stuck in the middle, too, whenever we had to share a bed or ride in the back seat of Meemaw's old Buick together. It was a trapped kind of feeling that made a person want to bolt like an ornery horse.

"OK," I said. The hint of a smile crept across my wind-chapped face. Satisfied, they turned to leave again, but I knew if we didn't make it official, they'd never keep their promise. Sue Ellen had a way of telling me I could have a forgotten toy or a shirt she'd outgrown, only to go back on her word days later when she saw me wearing it and claim she had no recollection of our agreement. Then she'd snatch it back, stretch it down over her belly, and strut around like an overstuffed peacock.

"We have to swear!" I spat into my dirty palm and stuck out my hand, now streaked with rivulets of brown sludge.

Sue Ellen crossed her arms, planting herself like a tree. "That's disgusting. Do you have any idea how many different kinds of bacteria are in your mouth?"

I let myself go limp, plopped my bottom down on the cold ground crisscross applesauce, and started picking slivers of dirt from underneath my too-long fingernails as if I had all the time in the world. Meemaw was not amused. She poked her frizzy head out the Buick's window and yelled over the rumble of the engine. "Girls! Now!"

"Come on." Rayanne tugged at Sue Ellen's sleeve before spitting into her own hand and offering it to her. "Let's get it over with."

Eyeing it with disgust, Sue Ellen put a fist to her mouth as if she might be sick. "No," she said flatly.

"Fine. Then you aren't borrowing my Walkman to play those stupid books on tape from the library." Rayanne winked at me to let me know she was on my side and pulled me up by my elbow. That really peeved Sue Ellen, because she hissed out a puff of air like a rabid raccoon, then spat out a pea-size droplet. After holding out a limp hand, she pasted her eyes shut when we sealed the deal, each of us placing our hands one on top of another in a stack.

After it was done, we cringed and wiped our palms onto muddy jeans. They sprinted to the car, but I lagged behind them, still turning it over in my mind.

Georgia's face flickered in my memory, upturned nose so like my own, blue eyes, and a smile framed by an unruly mop of curly, sun-kissed hair. Over the last few years, I had relied on my older sisters to

4

tell me how to remember her, to fill in the empty spaces of my mind where she used to exist, but these days they didn't seem interested in talking about her anymore. I worried I might forget her face, which was silly, I know, since we were identical. But when you're a twin, you see all the things other people don't see—the amoeba-shaped strawberry birthmark on her left shoulder, the way her dimples were set just slightly deeper than mine, the way she closed her eyes almost entirely when she was caught in an intense fit of laughter. Mama chose our names because she'd always wanted to travel to Savannah, Georgia. She said it was a storybook city with real character. We were meant to grow together as a pair, one never to be without the other. But our story had played a mean trick on us, and here I remained—a lone city without a state. Now that Mama had left us, too, it felt like I'd lost a country. It might as well have been the whole world.

I tried my best to hold on to their faces—Georgia's, and Mama's, and Daddy's. But memories are stubborn little things, like red-eared sliders that won't come out of their shells once you start poking around for them to peek out.

And no matter how hard I tried to remember, I could feel them slipping away.

CHAPTER 1

MEEMAW

March 1969

Marylynn dipped her hands into the rusty basin. Her nimble fingers searched the sudsy water until they landed on Frank's favorite pair of pajamas, the ones with the little trains on them that he'd soiled last night as he lay crying himself to sleep because she had finally forced him out of their bed and into his older brother's room. He was four now, after all, so she reminded herself not to feel guilty about the way his lip had quivered when she'd told him it was time to be a big boy and sleep in a big boy's bed. More importantly, soon there would be a new baby sleeping in the bassinet beside her, and for all their sakes, she hoped it would be a girl. Dennis and Frank had driven her into a constant state of exhaustion with their wrestling and hollering, tearing through the house while she tried desperately to pick up the messes they left behind. How in the world she would ever manage three of them was a mystery to her.

The boys raced between tattered bedsheets, chattering to each other, stopping only every so often to drag sticks through the loose dirt. Shielding her eyes from the sun with one hand, she could almost make out the shape of a little girl trailing close behind them, skipping barefoot, wild blonde hair like Marylynn's own blowing in the wind. She rubbed her belly and mouthed promises to it in soothing tones.

Charlie caught sight of her through the kitchen window and ambled out into the yard to meet her. He placed a calloused, oil-stained hand on her back and massaged tiny circles, then drew her close and kissed her neck, the scruff of his unshaven face scratching her skin like sandpaper.

"Don't do that. I'm sweating like a pig." Stifling a smile, she pulled away and reached again for the bucket of soaking laundry.

"Well, I like your sweat." He brushed a loose curl away from her dripping forehead and smirked, but she'd known him long enough to know that this particular half grin tended to show up only when he wanted something she didn't want to give him.

"What do you want, Charlie? I know it's something," she said, her small but capable hands wringing the fabric out with more force than necessary.

"Can't a man kiss his wife and tell her how beautiful she is without wanting something?" His lips trailed playfully along her cheek.

Pulling away once more, she heaved an exasperated sigh. "Yes, some men can. But you can't," she said through her teeth as she pulled a clothespin from her mouth and tacked the pajamas on the line.

He nodded and dropped his head, then grabbed a yellowed undershirt from the bucket, wrung it out, and secured it clumsily next to the other items. But Marylynn wasn't convinced. Charlie Pritchett did not do laundry. She snatched it off the line and shot him a stern glance before wringing it out again, this time making a point to put her elbows into it.

"Go on. Out with it," she said without looking up from her work.

He pulled a pack of Camels from his back pocket, then lit the end of one and took a deep drag before blurting the words out quickly with the smoke, as if mixing the two together might make her more amenable to the idea.

"Burt's having a game tonight." He held up a hand just as she opened her mouth to comment on this revelation. "Now before you get your feathers all ruffled, it's only a twenty-dollar buy-in. I'd be home before you're in bed. And if I win, I'm gonna buy that baby swing you been looking at." He gave her arm a little nudge, but she only stared at him, her eyes like two hot coals flashing a warning.

"I see." Angling her body away from him, she forcefully plucked another garment from the basin. "So you're just gonna conveniently miss baths and dinner and Frank wailing like a banshee so you can go give all our money to Burt?"

Rubbing his forehead, he squeezed his eyes shut. "Damn it, Marylynn. You know I'm here most all the time or working."

"Sure. When you're not out fishing or hunting or drinking or—"

"Now that ain't fair and you know it." His tone was firmer now, and it startled her. "I help out a lot around here, and every once in a while, a man has to get away for a bit is all."

"And I don't?" She reared back her head, half-disgusted and half-amused at the ridiculousness of it.

"That's not what I meant." His shoulders fell, and he plunged his hands into the pockets of his tattered jeans. "You should take some time for yourself, too. I can take care of the boys."

"Why, yes, I'm sure the boys will be just fine while I go off gallivanting down at the Piggly Wiggly for a few hours. You'd just as soon leave a couple of bowls of water out for them and leave them be in the yard. They're not dogs, Charlie." She swatted at him with a wet T-shirt. "They need supervision. And what about me?" Placing a hand to her arched back, she rested the other atop her bulging stomach. "I'm fit to burst here any second, and I need to be able to count on you."

"And you can." He tossed the cigarette to the ground and stomped it out before pulling her toward him, pressing his forehead into hers. Marylynn breathed in the scent of cigarettes mixed with his sweat and felt herself melting into him as he nuzzled her close. It both amazed and annoyed her that he could somehow always manage to have this effect on her.

"Don't worry, Lynnie. I'm gonna be right here when our little girl comes." He clasped his hand over hers and slid the other down the small of her back, then rocked her gently back and forth. "Right here, baby."

Marylynn studied him from the corner of one eye with a look that said she knew otherwise, but she still let him draw her closer and moved her feet in time with his as he softly hummed a Johnny Cash tune in her ear. Her stomach pressed against his, the two of them swaying as the evening light faded and swaths of cotton candy pink and blue stretched across the sky. "How do you know it's gonna be a girl?" she whispered.

"That's like asking how you know the sun's gonna come up. Can't tell you. I just know," he said, grinning down at her over the crook of his nose. He had broken it in a bar fight, defending her against the unwelcome advances of a handsy drifter who was three sheets to the wind. Since then she had come to see it as a reminder of his love for her, a bend in the shape of his very being that proved he would do anything to protect her.

Charlie was right. It was a girl. But as usual, Marylynn was right, too. Three hours later, she drove herself down to Muscadine General Hospital with two screaming boys in tow, cursing Charlie to the devil the entire drive.

~

At 9:01 p.m., Beverly Jo Pritchett entered the world, squalling like a wild hog and bald as a coot. Unable to reach Charlie, Marylynn had instead called her friend Cricket, who met her straightaway at the hospital and took the boys, giving her a few blessed moments to revel in the miracle of her child.

Before she had children of her own, Marylynn had assumed all newborns looked the same and possessed all the same basic features.

Ten fingers, ten toes, one nose, and two of most everything else. She'd worried that she wouldn't be able to tell her baby apart from another mother's, that perhaps she might leave the hospital with the wrong one. But she'd been wrong. Beverly had the most angelic heart-shaped lips, skinny bird legs, and pointed little elf nose. Marylynn would have been able to pick that nose out of a whole crowd of babies' noses, would have recognized her scent blindfolded. She had still been stroking Beverly's fuzzy blonde head when Charlie arrived, swaying unsteadily in the doorframe, reeking of cheap beer and a losing streak.

"Oh, Lynnie. She's beautiful," he said as he stumbled into the room and reached for her, his sea-blue eyes filming over with tears.

"No, sir. You'll not be holding our baby in that condition." She jabbed a finger at him while keeping a protective arm wrapped around the tiny pink bundle. "You go on and get yourself sorted."

"Now, Lynnie," he said, slurring his words, "don't be mad. I said I'd be here and I'm—"

"Charlie Pritchett, if you don't leave my sight this instant, I'll slap you into next Sunday." Her voice had taken on a steely tone so low and full of warning that she barely recognized it, but she didn't back down. "You are not fit to meet your daughter in that condition, and you'll come back when you can tell your tail from your nose." Still clutching the baby, she held her head high and stared him down, waiting for her relentless gaze to prove too much for him.

Wounded and too disoriented to fight, he slunk out of sight down the hallway. Marylynn smiled in spite of herself. That man would be the death of her, but Lord, she couldn't stop herself from loving him. She knew that when she went home, there would be a brand-new baby swing waiting for the two of them, because he would sell or trade something to make her fall in love with him again. Though he could be impetuous and dim-witted at times, Charlie was as faithful as a Labrador and would sell his own soul to see her smile.

A tinge of guilt crept through her for sending him away so quickly, but in truth she wanted Beverly to herself a little longer. After Dennis was born, she had worried that she could never love anyone as much as she loved her first child. Then Frank came along, and she realized that the space in her heart only expanded by two. But with this baby, it felt as if her whole chest might explode with all the love she hadn't known she held inside her. It scared her a little to know she was capable of loving a person so much, that all that love had been waiting there her whole life, like a dormant seed just aching to get out and grow up into something bigger than the cypress trees in the bayou and the pines that shot up all around her yard.

She would never be able to put it all back inside her if anything happened to this child, this perfect little creature who had stolen her breath and her heart along with all her good sense.

She would never be the same. She had a daughter now.

CHAPTER 2

Savannah

July 2022
Thursday Afternoon

"Look back for too long and you'll end up with a mess of broken dreams and a crick in your neck." That was what Meemaw said after Daddy left. But after thirty-two years on this rock, I'd come to realize that sometimes you had to check the rearview mirror to see the shape of it all and figure out how the hell you ended up where you were—in my case, how I ended up living with Colton Harris in the worn-out tin box we called home.

Sunlight danced across the lake as I fumbled with my key ring in the blazing afternoon heat, then worked it into the camper's lock. Bracing myself against the finicky door, I leaned all my weight against it, the metal burning my skin like a hot griddle. All at once, it gave way, and I spilled inside ungracefully, half expecting to find Colton passed out in front of the TV. Instead, I crossed my arms at the sight of him sandwiched between Wyatt and Trevor as they dug into a foot-long on my still-newish futon, getting crumbs all in its crevices. I sucked in my lips to keep from commenting on this, and he flashed me a sheepish grin. When my best friend, Tammy, had first introduced us after a Keith Urban concert up in Shreveport, I thought Colton resembled a long-lost Hanson brother and was entirely obsessed with his shiny blond hair, which hung loose at his shoulders and sent my stomach fluttering. But it turned out it looked much better on him when he was mysterious and single. It didn't have quite the same effect when he was living on his girlfriend's couch, eating her groceries, and sharing her Netflix password with all his friends.

"Hey, babe." Colton's smile was stuffed with bread. "How was work?"

"Fine," I said, marching the few feet it took to reach our tiny kitchen. Kicking off my grubby black tennis shoes coated in a film of grease, I untied my apron and shoved it onto the sliver of space that just barely qualified as a counter. My pocketbook fell open, revealing a few twenties and some loose change. Lunch shifts at the Salty Pot weren't as lucrative as dinner, but I'd had to rearrange my schedule this week on account of the pact. It had been almost impossible to convince Rayanne to leave her kids behind for the weekend and no less than a miracle that Sue Ellen had agreed to fly in from NYC.

"You working tonight?" He reached for a beer can nestled in a Koozie that read "Hold my beer" and downed a swig.

"No. My sisters are getting in tonight. Remember? I told you about it," I said, opening the refrigerator door.

"No, you didn't. You always work Thursday nights."

I rolled my eyes. Why should he have remembered this when I had mentioned it only about a dozen times before now? "I told you I'm not working this weekend because my sisters are coming in town, and we have that *thing* I told you about?" I lifted my eyebrows, trying to nudge his boozy memory.

"Oh, the time capsule," he finally remembered a little too loudly, snapping his fingers. "That's this weekend?"

I didn't respond, as I wasn't exactly thrilled about Wyatt and Trevor having a front-row seat to my family drama.

Colton scrunched up his nose and studied a finger as if he were trying to work out an algebraic equation. "But didn't you just take time off for that other thing you had to do with Tammy?"

My stomach flipped, and it took me a minute to string together a response. I hadn't exactly told him—or anyone, for that matter— what the "other thing" was. Not even Tammy. I cleared my throat. "Yes, but . . . what does it matter? Besides, family is family." Or at least that was what Meemaw said anytime one of us needed a lesson on forgiving each other.

"Time capsule." Nodding, Trevor wiped a dollop of mayonnaise from his goatee with the back of his hand. "People actually still do those things?"

"Obviously." Wyatt nudged him, then winked in my direction. "Or Savannah Banana wouldn't be digging one up, would she?" He smiled at me in a way that suggested he knew something about me they didn't, and I set my jaw. Wyatt had graciously bestowed the nickname upon me our sophomore year, when we had a hazy two-week relationship that I cannot find words to account for. In any other town, it might have been weird if my boyfriend and an ex-boyfriend were drinking buddies. But in Muscadine, the pickings were slim, and everyone had pretty much dated everyone.

"Don't call me that," I said, irritated that Colton was once again drinking the day away with these two freeloaders, who were still telling the same tired stories they'd told at Muscadine High.

"Yeah, don't call her that," Wyatt said.

Trevor smacked Wyatt on the back of his skull before Colton headbutted the two of them together, shaking the walls of the entire camper and rattling the glasses perched on the coffee table. I cringed. *No coasters.*

"Sorry, babe. They were just about to leave anyway."

"Don't bother," I said, rooting around in the fridge. "I'm staying at Meemaw's this weekend. Just came home to grab a change of clothes." I jerked my head to the side and leveled my gaze at him. "Hey, what happened to the gumbo I brought home from work last night?"

Colton stared at me blankly before blurting out, "Oh . . . we had it for lunch. I didn't know you were saving it. Wait a second." He shook his head as if he were trying to clear water from his ears. "You're staying at Meemaw's? Where you gonna sleep? On the roof?"

I bit my lip, knowing he had a valid point. My old bedroom had been completely lost to Meemaw's things, and the mattress hadn't seen daylight since I'd moved out seven years ago. I figured I would most likely be sleeping on the couch.

Ignoring the question, I blew out my cheeks and slammed the refrigerator door. "From now on, if I put a half-eaten dinner in the fridge, just assume it's mine. Trevor and Wyatt have their own refrigerators, and I'll thank them kindly to stay the hell out of mine."

"Yes, ma'am." Trevor pulled back his shoulders and saluted the wall, pressing two fingers to his bald head.

Still not convinced I could trust them, I rifled through the cabinets and landed on a bag of pork rinds and a can of pizza-flavored Pringles. I grabbed a Sharpie from the junk drawer and proceeded to write my name in thick capital letters on each package before discreetly shoving them underneath the sink. Narrowing my eyes at Colton, I leaned my back against the counter and folded my arms across my chest. "So they've really been here since lunch? I thought you were working today." Though he worked for his father at Harris's Auto Shop, I'd never once seen him spend an entire eight hours there. When he was working, he spent most of his shift in the office blatantly flirting with the female customers, most of whom were bored housewives who looked at him like he was a delicious dessert that wasn't on their diets.

"I was, but . . . Dad had to run a few errands across town, so I took the afternoon," he stammered.

I had heard this before and was not convinced. "What you mean to say is that your father entrusted the shop to you for a few hours, and you thought it was a good excuse to play hooky."

Colton's response came fast and sharp, almost as if he had prepared to defend himself because he knew I'd have a thing or two to say about it. "Oh, so you get to take time off to go digging up stuff with your hoity-toity sisters, but I can't take a mental health day?"

"Spare me." I popped open a cold can of Dr Pepper and took an irritated swig before forcefully setting it down on the counter, then wiped my mouth with the back of my hand. "When you only work three days a week, you don't qualify for one of those."

"Well, he actually had a very good reason," Trevor intervened, no doubt picking up on the dangerous tension brewing between us. "He had to duck out early to help a customer replace a faulty alternator."

I raised an eyebrow. "Oh, really. And this customer wouldn't happen to be a married woman, 'bout five foot two, red hair, and a heaving bosom?" Either Mrs. Henderson had the world's worst luck with alternators, or she had a downright unhealthy appetite for younger men with no ambitions. A few months back, she had started coming into the shop on a weekly basis, studying Colton as if there must be something more behind that baby-faced exterior and shaggy blond hair. It had taken me nearly a decade to learn there wasn't. Then last week Tammy spotted them at the Sizzler, making bedroom eyes at each other in a corner booth. When I confronted him about it, he said they'd just happened to run into each other, that the cosmic forces of the universe had serendipitously placed them in the exact same restaurant at the exact same booth at the exact same time. There had been shouting—mostly from me—and begging and crying—mostly from him. He'd gone through every stage of grief—denial, anger, bargaining. Until finally I was the one who gave in to acceptance when I realized I couldn't bring myself to kick him out. For reasons I could not verbalize, I needed him here.

Colton's mouth gaped, his scruffy, round face the result of three days without meeting the likes of a razor. I could tell he was trying to work it all out in a way that wouldn't make him sound like a jerk.

"She just needed a little help is all. Now what kind of man would I be if I didn't help a woman stranded on the side of the road?"

"The kind that maybe also fixes a thing or two around here every once in a while," I said, thumbing to the kitchen window, which had been lazily covered with a black trash bag and secured with duct tape.

I brought a hand to my temple and rubbed hard. In the beginning, things with Colton had been good. Great, even. Using the savings I'd squirreled away since high school, I'd bought a little plot of land on the banks of Lake Canard, and he'd scrounged up a hideous retro orange camper for us to share, rent-free. It was far from glamorous, but I liked being near the place where Georgia had last been with me—the place where she had vanished into thin air like some sort of strange magic trick no one could figure out. Maybe deep down I thought staying there would make it easier for her to find me if she ever came back. For a time, a part of me believed the song of the water and the birds singing in the branches might hypnotize me into a trance, and I'd suddenly recall all that had happened on our last day together.

Of course, Meemaw said Colton and I were living in sin and that I should never expect a man to buy the goat if he was getting the milk for free. On this one point I had come to realize she was right, but I promised to go to my grave before I ever let her know she was onto something. I was never naive enough to believe I loved Colton, but over time we'd settled into a familiar routine, and it was comfortable . . . enough. I suppose I'd come to see him as a necessary pest in the same way a heifer lets birds eat the flies off her body, though I guessed it must bother her some of the time, because she bats her tail at them occasionally. My relationship with Colton was transactional. I provided food and furnishings, while he provided a warm body and endless commentary on Friday-night football.

It wasn't the life I'd ever pictured for myself, but no matter how many times I'd tried to end it with Colton, he somehow managed to weasel his way back into my life like a stubborn case of head lice. I wondered what Georgia would be doing if she were here. Maybe she would have been the successful half of us and gone on to do something amazing like perform cleft palate surgeries for children or save the whales or solve climate change. But I was all that was left of us. Destiny had seen two identical towheads with bright-blue eyes and had chosen one of them at random.

I wasn't sure it had chosen correctly.

"I'll see you on Sunday. Until then, do not consume anything with my name on it." I went to our bedroom and gathered up my toothbrush, some pajama pants, and a few tank tops, then tossed them into a Save A Lot bag and headed for the door. Before I left, I gave the three of them another dubious once-over before picking up an empty beer can and tossing it in the trash. "And use a coaster."

CHAPTER 3

SUE ELLEN

Thursday Afternoon

After arriving at the airport, I Ubered to Rayanne's house, which was nestled in a gated community of an affluent Baton Rouge suburb. Muscadine was only a two-hour drive northwest from her place, and it didn't have an airport. For that matter, Muscadine didn't have much of anything. When I texted Rayanne that I was flying into her city, she offered to drive. Of course, it had taken her a full twenty-four hours to comment on this information. And I knew she'd seen it because the word "Read" was clearly spelled out next to my message as it hung there awkwardly between us for an entire day.

As soon as we pulled into a driveway lined with grass the color of Astroturf and lilac hydrangea bushes that could have graced the cover of *Southern Living*, my stomach soured. The two-story gray-stone house sat nestled atop a lush green hill and boasted a three-car garage, which I knew from Instagram housed a Tesla, a Lexus, and a boat. I also knew that Rayanne would be about as excited to make this trip as I was. Probably less. After all, at least I didn't have children to worry about while I went wandering down memory lane in our decidedly rural hometown.

I thanked the driver and made my way up the stone path to the front door. After a steadying breath, I knocked tentatively and rearranged my face into something I hoped resembled excitement. After the door swung open, apparently of its own volition, it took me a moment to look down and recognize it wasn't a ghost who had answered but a bare-chested, smaller version of my brother-in-law, Graham. Two trails of green escaped from Tucker's nostrils, dripping precariously close to his gaping mouth.

"Who are you?" he asked, dragging the back of his arm across his nose.

I swallowed hard, trying to ignore what I'd just witnessed. I'd met Tucker only once, a few weeks after his birth, the last time I'd been here. He was the first newborn I'd ever held, and quite frankly I was a bit underwhelmed by the experience. Rayanne couldn't stop going on about his tiny toes and fingernails, his miniature shoes, and that new-baby smell. But the only smell I could make out had brought on an intense bout of nausea, and honestly, I found the whole tiny-hands business to be a little terrifying.

"I'm your aunt Sue Ellen." I smiled and squatted down to face him squarely, careful not to touch his arm glistening with fresh streaks of green.

"You are?" He crinkled his nose and regarded me dubiously. "Mommy says Sue Ellen is a ditch."

Chuckling to myself, I patted the top of his head. I wasn't surprised by the sentiment, but the cussing threw me for a loop. Maybe Rayanne was not as perfect as her Instagram page would have me believe.

"Tucker!" As if on cue, my sister hurried toward us, carrying a babbling Charlotte in her arms, and snatched his hand as if he had approached a stranger, which I suppose wasn't entirely untrue. "How many times have I told you not to answer the door? You're naked, for Pete's sake. Go get dressed."

He let out a bloodcurdling "No, stupid head!" before twisting himself out of her grasp and escaping through her legs into the kitchen like a feral animal.

Rayanne's eyes rested on mine, and for a moment the two of us just stared at one another as if we'd been caught unawares. Even saddled with two children, she looked just as beautiful as she always had, with crystal-blue eyes and a messy blonde ponytail that might have made another woman look tired. On her, it was perfectly on point. Finally she cleared her throat and gave me a defeated smile. "Sorry about that. Normally we do make him wear clothes. How was your flight?"

"Fine." I tucked my thumbs into the pockets of my tapered, cropped pants. "Your house is . . . a lot," I said, taking in the steeply pitched ceilings and sprawling staircase complete with a baby gate at the entrance.

She placed Charlotte on the white wool rug that sat atop the flawless hardwood floors, leading me to wonder why she would choose such an unforgiving color when she had two tiny humans who appeared to excrete bodily fluids like slugs. Charlotte crawled across the toy-littered rug toward a small stuffed pig and promptly attempted to eat him.

"She's adorable," I said brightly, though as I heard the words leave my lips, I realized how unconvincing they sounded. "She's getting so big."

This was the first time I'd ever actually seen Charlotte in person, though I had seen about a million photos flitter across my Insta feed and had received the birth announcement in the mail, a glossy black-and-white photo of poor Charlotte, completely naked and perched in a fetal position on top of a fluffy pedestal. It was totally pretentious, but since Rayanne had married well into a true southern hierarchy of wealth and class, I had expected nothing less from Mrs. Pennington the Third.

"Yeah, well, they do that, you know. Time flies a lot faster when you aren't in the thick of it, but trust me—the days here are long."

I bristled, wondering if that was meant to be a dig at me and the glaring fact that I had no children or husband. And as of four months ago, no boyfriend, either. Unlike my sisters, relationships had never come easy for me. Rayanne always said this was because my standards were too high, that not every man could be attractive, funny, and smart, though it did not escape my attention that Graham ticked all these boxes. For various entirely legitimate reasons, the few relationships I'd managed had all ended before the six-month mark. Until Liam. Remembering this, I felt something splinter inside my heart.

Rayanne gazed at her daughter with a look that conveyed something between bitter anguish and supreme bliss before scooping her up again. For a moment, the morning light streaming in through the windows caught her face, and I thought she could have easily passed for our mother. Before she got sick. I fought back a lump growing in the back of my throat and swallowed.

"Want to hold her?" Without waiting for a response, she offered a slobbering Charlotte to me with expectant eyes. I had no choice but to accept her into my arms, holding her gingerly, the way someone might hold a bomb, completely unsure which way to cradle her wiggly body. Relief washed over me when she started to loudly protest, and Rayanne offered to take her back, then carted her off into the kitchen to prepare a bottle. Perhaps Charlotte sensed I was not mother material—something Liam must have picked up on as well. Not that it mattered. From the start of our relationship, he had been clear about his opinions on global warming and not wanting to add to the problem by creating more people than our flailing planet could support. At the time, I had agreed with him on principle, but now I wondered if he'd shared these opinions with Abby, the junior attorney at his firm who was now sporting a four-carat cushion-cut Tiffany engagement ring. Liam and I had been together for two years and had never once even window-shopped for rings. But apparently three months with Abby was enough to convince him that he couldn't live without her, and last week I'd stumbled upon their engagement photos while casually stalking him online—as one does when blindsided with the news that her boyfriend doesn't love her and needs "space to figure out what he really wants." It turned out what he wanted was Abby. Gazing at Charlotte now, I wondered if he had changed his mind about having children, too, and a searing thought crept in. Maybe he just didn't want to have them with me.

Off to my left, a pair of french doors swung open, and a cool draft swept over me, tousling my hair. "Sue Ellen!" Graham sauntered toward me and pulled me in for a hug. Wearing slacks, a fitted dress shirt, and a gingham pencil tie, it was easy to see how someone like Graham had managed to rise through the ranks of his hedge fund company so quickly. Not only did he look the part, with his dirty-blond hair parted perfectly and slicked back into a classic business cut, but he had a smile that could put anyone at ease, including me. Though at first I'd thought him to be a spoiled frat boy, Graham was sweet—the kind of sweet that knows all about your sad, dysfunctional past and loves you anyway. And he adored Meemaw. "It's been a minute since we've seen you. How's NYU treating you?" He nudged my arm the way I imagine a big brother would.

"Great!" I said, a little too enthusiastically. "Things are busy, but I was able to get my classes covered for tomorrow. You know how it goes. It's tough to get away from the grind."

"Yeah, I get that. It's hard for Rayanne, too." He checked behind him before ducking his head and lowering his voice. "Maybe you can convince your sister that I'm actually a fully grown adult entirely capable of caring for our children while she's away. She doesn't trust me." He'd spoken softly but just loud enough for her to hear him clearly where she stood rummaging around in the kitchen, tossing items into a monogrammed tote.

"I trust you!" she shouted back.

"She's still a little put out about the balloons I bought for Tucker's birthday party last week. It was a whole thing." Speaking softer now, he drew a hand to the side of his mouth, overenunciating the words for my benefit. "Apparently, my actions were—what did she say?—oh yes, 'thoughtless and potentially fatal.'"

Rayanne's voice drifted from the kitchen as if she had heard him perfectly. "They're a choking hazard. And I'm one hundred percent certain I've mentioned this on more than one occasion."

"Well, I wasn't planning on feeding them to him," he countered over his shoulder. "I mean, I know I miss a lot around here, but I do actually know that children shouldn't eat rubber." He winked at me, and my respect for Graham instantly multiplied tenfold. Anyone who could defuse Rayanne's type A personality with humor was a hero in my book. "Guess I'll cancel the tires I was going to cook up for dinner."

He was trying to lighten the mood, but Rayanne was having none of it. Bearing a tight smile on her face and a newly filled bottle in one hand, she returned to the living room with Charlotte pressed to her chest. "I told you. I was just concerned."

"No, you were being all paranoid, the same way you were with the dog, and the Nerf guns, and the nunchucks . . ." His voice grew louder and more accusing with each forbidden item on his list.

"OK, first of all, you didn't ask me about bringing the dog home. Secondly, dog bites are the second-most-common reason for emergency room visits for children. And thirdly, those were real nunchucks! And he nearly knocked out Charlotte's only tooth. Do you want her to be toothless until she's five? I am not the one buying weapons for our children. Stop making me feel like I'm the unreasonable one here."

"Please, when I was his age, I was shooting a BB gun," he said. "Kids are supposed to fall off bikes, get hit in the head with Nerf darts. They're supposed to bleed sometimes. You can't be there to stop every bad thing from happening to them. Right, Sue Ellen?" He looked to me, apparently expecting me to back him up. I shifted between my feet, unsure whom to side with. Graham was making a lot of sense, but I couldn't exactly throw Rayanne under the bus when I hadn't seen her in four years.

"Maybe not. But does it mean I shouldn't try?" Rayanne asked, staring him down.

"OK. So are you planning to follow Tucker to college, deck out his dorm room with surveillance cameras? We have to let them fail sometimes, or they won't know they're capable of getting back up on their own."

I could tell the conversation had left her flustered, because she pinched her nose, and her next words came out stilted. "I can't have this conversation right now. Just . . . keep them alive."

Shoving a fist to his mouth, Graham made a sound that resembled a muffled scream. I winced on his behalf. Knowing my sister, it was a feeling I could relate to.

∼

After we had loaded our bags into the trunk of an immaculate silver Lexus, Rayanne kissed Charlotte and Tucker goodbye, then spent an eternity dispensing instructions to poor Graham.

Finally she settled herself behind the wheel of the car, waving one last apologetic thanks to her family as we drove away. I marveled at the way she expertly maneuvered through the bustle of cars until at last the traffic gave way to a wide-open blacktop littered with the occasional dead animal. We meandered down the interstate, passing vast stretches of pasture dotted by sleepy cows and hay bales until an endless corridor lined with towering pine trees and the familiar bayous of Louisiana sped past us.

I rolled down the passenger-side window, surprisingly relieved to take in the heavy July air. The smell of pine and freshly cut grass summoned memories of every summer we'd spent foraging the earth, catching lightning bugs in mason jars and searching for frogs and box turtles in the ditch behind our parents' house.

Rayanne shouted over the wind as it blew in through my window, scattering my carefully wanded hair every which way. "So how are things with Liam?"

"We're . . . good," I lied. I hadn't yet discovered a classy way of announcing my relationship fail to the world. It wasn't the kind of thing people wanted to read about on Instagram, and I wasn't sure how to spin it in a way that didn't make people feel sorry for me. "What about you guys?" I asked, trying to seem interested. "How are the kids?"

"Great," Rayanne said, not taking her eyes off the road ahead. "Charlotte's almost walking now, and Tucker just started this adorable little soccer league where most of the kids just stand around picking flowers, but it's cute, you know? And Graham just moved up to senior management last year, so . . . everything's great." It didn't escape my attention that she had left herself off the list, and I wondered if she'd noticed.

Approaching a sign that said WELCOME TO MUSCADINE, she glanced over at me and raised an eyebrow, a silent reminder there was no turning back now. We were greeted by hand-painted signs advertising jams and homegrown watermelons along with faded billboards featuring the smiling face of Lonnie LaCrue, a local personal injury attorney who promised to "Cash in your crash!" Poor Lonnie's face was battered now, the giant letters beneath his chin a little worse for wear because, while the rest of the world had welcomed in the twenty-first century, Muscadine had remained perfectly preserved in a mausoleum dedicated to 1984.

After winding our way down bumpy roads lined by forgotten homes that appeared to have all but given up, we could just barely make out the street sign ahead that read POSSUM TRAIL ROAD, marking the unpaved gravel path where Meemaw's dilapidated home rested upon three acres of overgrown weeds.

As we pulled into the dirt driveway, I winced at the sight of the front yard, which had somehow managed to collect even more garbage in the years I'd been away. No doubt the next few days would involve me begging Meemaw to let us haul some of the refuse away, even though I was certain she wouldn't allow any of it to be touched in the unlikely event she might suddenly find herself in need of a rusty dishwasher rack.

Broken toys from our childhood, abandoned tires, and various other undeterminable items littered the yard. To a passerby, it would have been difficult to miss Meemaw's place, since a willow tree trimmed with unexplainable flying horses sat directly in front of it. When the wind blew, the horses fluttered, and a rusted seesaw swayed up and down, letting out a terrifying screeching sound that carried down the road. The entire scene resembled an eerie playground in a low-budget horror movie. It appeared, however, that someone had attempted to inject some sense of refinement into the place, as there were now freshly planted yellow zinnias growing from inside the discarded toilet perched on the lawn. *Classy, Meemaw.* Though I prided myself on an extensive lexicon, I often found myself at a loss for words when it came to this place. And my grandmother.

The humidity assaulted my senses the moment the car door slammed behind me. July in Muscadine was brutal. A warm breeze rustled through the pines but carried with it the pungent stench of sulfur from Lebeaux's Paper Mill. Perhaps it explained why the town population remained at a steady two thousand. Slapping at a mosquito on my neck, I took in the disconcerting scene in front of me—a once-white single-story Victorian farmhouse with half the shutters missing. In a past life, their peeling paint might have been a forest green. A warped wooden staircase led up to the wraparound porch that held a collection of mismatched chairs and stools, all pilfered from curbs and fifty years of garage sales.

"Here we go." Rayanne looked at me, pleading for help, her exhausted eyes wide, as if they were being held open by a speculum. "Just three days. Three days and we get to go back to civilization." It seemed as if she were trying to convince herself more than me.

"You forgot the time warp. Three days in Muscadine is going to feel like three months." I sighed, taking in the broken house that had once held me and all my seemingly unreachable dreams within it. The evening sun caused it to cast a foreboding shadow over us, and my stomach tensed at the thought it might somehow reclaim its hold on me, that it would squelch this slimmer, better version of myself. Sue Ellen 2.0.

My heels scuffed up clouds of dirt onto my black pants as I struggled to wheel my luggage up the drive. Meemaw alighted on the porch steps and held out her arms, fresh tears clouding her eyes. She was wearing a button-down Hawaiian shirt, khaki pedal pushers, and her garden clogs. A slow smile unfolded across her face, highlighting the fine lines that framed her sea-blue eyes. While other women her age had spent years tossing pennies into the fountain of youth, Meemaw preferred to age naturally and didn't bother with makeup or creams. "The good Lord giveth and He taketh away. No point in trying to shovel water out of a sinking boat with a slotted spoon," she had always said. Wild silver strands of hair hung loose just past her shoulders.

"My girls have come home." She pulled us into a fierce embrace and held us there before firmly planting a kiss on each of our cheeks. Given her petite frame, the strength of her hugs never failed to surprise me. But I knew that our grandmother dispensed affection and disappointment in equal doses, and I found myself waiting for the other shoe to drop.

As she tightened her grip on me, I caught sight of Savannah lingering in the doorway behind her and clocked the scant ensemble our little sister was sporting—a black tank top that revealed an obscene amount of cleavage and a pair of shredded blue-jean shorts that just barely covered her underwear, occasionally revealing the rose tattoo that sat just above her hip. Digging her thumbs into her tattered pockets, she flashed me a broad smile, and I did my best to match her enthusiasm.

"I'm glad to see you, too. I've missed you," I said softly into Meemaw's wiry hair.

She pulled back and tilted her head, her eyes searching me as if she weren't convinced. "You didn't think I'd notice it's been weeks since I've heard from you, Sue Ellen? You'd think I didn't have any family at all the way you all treat me. Here I am sick as a dog, and Savannah is the only one who bothers to check on me."

I doubted the part about her being sick. It was a tactical move on her part to garner sympathy—and an annoyingly effective one at that. Like clockwork, every Sunday evening, she phoned to complain about some new ailment before trying to convince me yet again to invest in a Taser gun. The last time she called, I'd been at dinner with Gabriela and a few other college friends at a restaurant that boasted a yearlong waiting list. Guilt crept over me as I remembered how I had discreetly dug my phone out of my tiny, bejeweled clutch and quietly slid my finger across it to reject the call. Three times. She was diligent like that, no matter how many times I'd tried to convince her that texting was a much more efficient way to reach me with my busy teaching schedule.

Like a well-trained actress, Meemaw seized upon this opportunity to cough violently and clasp a hand to her chest as if she were caught in the throes of a sudden heart attack.

I patted her gingerly on the back, making a proper fuss over her until she tossed her hair to the side and straightened her stance, miraculously healed. When she finally appeared to have regained control of her faculties, she cleared her throat before getting right to the point of it all. "I presume they have phones in New York?"

And there she was. The force of nature from my childhood, ready to do battle and guilt me into admitting any number of sins.

Deep breaths. Three days, Sue Ellen. Just three more days.

CHAPTER 4

RAYANNE

Thursday Evening

Once we arrived, I made a quick escape from the car and circled around to the trunk for my bag, eager to put some distance between me and Sue Ellen. I didn't appreciate that she'd seen Graham and me arguing, and trying to talk to her had been like trying to talk to a wall. But my relief was short lived when I spotted Meemaw hovering on the front steps. I had always believed she and Graham's mother would have made the best of friends, since they had both memorized my shortcomings and probably had them laminated, hanging on a wall somewhere. There was no way she would let me get through this weekend without casually bringing up the kids, or rather the lack of the kids on this visit.

I hadn't wanted to come, but Savannah had gone straight for the jugular. "You know Meemaw's still angry she didn't get to see y'all last Christmas, so if you don't want to go getting on her list, you'd better get yourself over here." I was, of course, well versed in our grandmother's list, which ran the length of the Mississippi. It included people with unnatural hair colors, motorcyclists, 4G cell towers, remote banking, and about a thousand other suspicious things she deemed cancer causing. It also included liberals, which I guess meant it included Sue Ellen. Even though Savannah had narrowly escaped the list because, unlike me, she hadn't moved two hours away, I was frequently reminded on my weekly phone calls with Meemaw that she was not exactly thrilled our little sister had opted out of marriage, deciding instead to "shack up" with Colton Harris, who was most definitely, without a doubt, 100 percent *on* her list.

Catching sight of Savannah on the front porch, I imagined her for a moment as that spitfire little four-year-old who once broke into the pantry and ate sugar straight from the bag, Georgia trailing her like a shadow as the two of them tracked grainy prints all over the house. My heart contracted at the memory, and I blinked it away.

Meemaw captured Sue Ellen and me in a firm hug, all the while peppering her with questions. Slipping past them, I was grateful that there was someone even worse than me to take the brunt of her criticism today. I gave Savannah a quick squeeze before venturing into the house. Taking it all in, I felt a familiar, sinking helplessness grip my insides, and I clenched my stomach to brace myself. Beyond the entryway door, a narrow path was formed by boxes that teetered above us, nearly reaching the ceiling, while garbage bags filled with God-only-knows-what lined the living room's perimeter. Straight ahead of us, we were welcomed by a row of stuffed armadillos perched atop the fireplace mantel, unnerving gifts from her neighbor, Sam, who had an inexplicable obsession with immortalizing creatures that ought never have been preserved. One of them was posed in a reclining position and appeared to be guzzling a tiny bottle of Jack Daniel's. Eyeing them distrustfully, I crept farther inside and took in the rest of the house.

Off to the left, the kitchen shelves were filled to the brim with useless appliances—an egg poacher, a George Foreman Grill, a panini maker, three different-size slow cookers—and scores of mismatched plastic Tupperware were stacked precariously along every inch of counter space, while a pile of expired coupons littered the peeling yellow laminate. I inhaled a steadying breath. If the kitchen was this bad, what did it mean for the parts of the house that lay behind closed doors?

In a rare show of welcome, the kitchen table had been cleared of clutter and featured a spread of fried fish, okra, hush puppies, and coleslaw.

"Thought you girls might be hungry after your drive," Meemaw said, motioning for the three of us to take a seat as she reached for a stack of paper plates. Washing dishes did not appear to be a possibility, since the sink was filled with old copies of the *Thrifty Penny* newspaper.

"It looks amazing," I forced myself to say, pulling out a chair next to Savannah. Sue Ellen grimaced as she reluctantly lowered herself into a seat across from us. I could tell she was working out how to avoid eating any of it. Not that she ever needed to, but she'd lost weight since being away. I assumed she was probably on some celebrity fad diet now, but I didn't pry for details.

A strange grunting emanated from the hallway that led to the three bedrooms on the opposite side of the house, and I jolted upright as something on four stubby legs scurried toward us. I let out a stifled scream as a stout potbellied pig appeared at my feet. It was pink with black spots and had beady eyes that made me squirm against my seat. "What happened to the 'no pets' rule?" I stammered, gripping the chair. Our grandmother preferred animals of the dead variety. I was sure I must be hallucinating.

"Bessie's not a pet," Meemaw said, as if she were offended on behalf of the pig. "She earns her keep around here. Tills the soil better than I can with my arthritis and keeps the varmints away, too. And"—she plucked a tomato from a basket on the table and admired it—"I compost her droppings for fertilizer. She's more useful than most people I've met," she said, bending over to give Bessie a pat between her pointy ears. "Smells better, too." Bessie grunted an agreement.

"Perfect," I said, throwing a side-eye to Bessie. *Living in a literal pigsty now.* "Couldn't go with a cat or a dog? Bird, maybe? Where did you even find her?"

"Picked her up down at the Tractor Supply a few months back. She was the runt of the litter, but I fattened her up soon enough," she said, putting a finger to Bessie's snout. "You're next, Sue Ellen." She jabbed a finger at her, and Sue Ellen shifted in her seat, muttering something under her breath I didn't quite catch.

Keeping one eye on the pig, I reached for a piece of fish.

"So how was the drive?" Meemaw asked.

"Not too bad," I said, biting into a fillet. The crust melted in an explosion of flavor in my mouth, and I groaned. I had forgotten the woman could fry just about anything to perfection but had a special talent when it came to catfish. It was one of the few benefits of moving in with her. Mama had been a terrible cook and relied on Hamburger Helper and boxed macaroni and cheese to keep us alive. Still, I would have cleaned my plate every day if it meant she could have stayed with us.

"Except for the restroom we had to use," Sue Ellen added, poking a fork around her plate, trying to separate the greasy crust and pick out the white flesh inside. We'd stopped just once to fill up on gas and use the restroom at the only station that appeared on Google Maps, a filthy Pic-N-Go that boasted facilities worthy of a Stephen King movie and windows secured by steel bars. A rough-shaven apparent cast member of *Duck Dynasty* had handed us a key attached to a set of deer antlers.

"I mean, I'm not a doctor, but I'm one hundred percent certain that someone contracted a severe case of food poisoning or dysentery or maybe even died there," Sue Ellen said, taking a minuscule bite of coleslaw.

"Sounds horrifying." Savannah tossed a hush puppy into her mouth, her voice dripping with sarcasm.

Sue Ellen rolled her eyes.

Bessie grunted and jerked her sturdy head toward my fish with a pleading stare, as if she might will it into her waiting mouth. I shuddered and did my best to ignore her before taking another bite.

"Well, I'm glad you survived," Meemaw said, shoveling a spoonful of fried okra onto Sue Ellen's plate as she looked on helplessly. "I feel honored by your presence." *Cue the guilt trip.* "So. What do you girls have planned for tomorrow?"

"Actually," I said, "we're going to see about digging up the time capsule. You remember when we did that?"

"'Course I remember. I was the one who did most of the work. The three of you were knee high to a grasshopper, barely big enough to hold a shovel, much less dig a hole." She heaved a sigh—the judgmental kind that made me wonder if she was offended by something I had said. "I think it's a good thing for you all. Give you something to do together," she said, offering a tomato to Bessie under the table.

I reflected on the awkward drive with Sue Ellen and the fact that we were going to be sharing a bedroom for the next few nights. As the oldest, it should have been a birthright for me to have my own room. But Meemaw's house had only three bedrooms, and our grandmother had learned the hard way that Sue Ellen and Savannah could not coexist peacefully in confined spaces. Sometimes I didn't think the house itself was big enough for the two of them.

"Right," I muttered under my breath. "That's exactly what we need."

~

The next day we piled into my car, puttered by our old house a few times, and noticed that an elderly, sour-faced woman now lived there. It appeared she had permanently planted herself on the front porch in a lawn chair, observing the activities of the neighborhood children with great suspicion. After we passed by for the third time in less than ten minutes, her eyes followed the car as if her head were attached to it by an invisible string.

"Let's just ask her already. What's the worst thing she could say?" Savannah asked.

Sue Ellen rolled her eyes as I steered the car down Jackson Street and out of the neighborhood, preparing to circle around again. "Sure. 'Excuse me, ma'am, can we dig a giant hole in your backyard to get a bunch of crap we buried twenty-five years ago?' That should go over really well."

"Savannah's right," I said, not particularly enthusiastic to agree with her since she'd been the one to guilt me here in the first place. "Before we go sneaking around, we might as well ask."

"Fine," Sue Ellen said flatly.

I turned the car around and steered it toward the redbrick house and the spindly woman, who was still staring us down. We got out of the car and slowly approached her. The scowl on her face gave me the sense that she would likely not be agreeable to strangers poking around on her property.

Savannah spoke first. "Hello there, ma'am. I know you don't know us, but we actually used to live in this house when we were children." With an unsteady smile, she gestured toward the single-story home behind the woman. It had faded with age, the white trim now a dusty beige, and seemed so much smaller now than when I remembered last seeing it. But I guess it would have seemed bigger to a nine-year-old.

The woman cocked a barely there eyebrow.

Savannah's gaze darted between the two of us as Sue Ellen nudged her forward.

She cleared her throat and continued with a slight tremor in her voice. "See, the thing is, before we moved, we buried a time capsule in this backyard, and we promised each other that in twenty-five years we would dig it up and see all our memories from our old life." Offering a hopeful smile, she pressed on, inching her way closer. "Would it be terribly inconvenient to you . . . if we maybe . . . dug it up? I mean, we'll fill in the hole when we're done," she added quickly. "You won't even know we were here."

With a steely gaze, the knobby woman took in Savannah's tank top, then scrunched her nose and spat at the ground. "What's that you wanna dig up?" She craned her neck forward and squinted hard. In a moment of clarity, it appeared to me that the poor thing might have trouble hearing, which was not unexpected for a person who looked to be upward of eighty years old. I'd worked with plenty of elderly folks in my church's senior citizen ministry, so I stepped forward and spoke loudly, pronouncing each word with precision the same way I spoke to Tucker when I had to remind him for the hundredth time to put his toys away.

"We only need to dig a small hole, ma'am. To recover some personal effects that were left on the property."

"Diggin'?" she bellowed. "No. I don't think you'll be diggin' up anything. I done told them damned companies I ain't sellin' my mineral rights. Y'all may a got the whole neighborhood to sign on to your lies, but I ain't buyin' it. Don't need anyone out here trying to steal it out from under me."

My suspicion about her hearing was confirmed. Though I tried my best to reassure her that we had no intention of stealing any oil, she produced a twelve-gauge shotgun from behind her folding chair and pointed it squarely at my head.

A scream escaped my throat as images of Graham and the kids fluttered through my thoughts. "All right, we're leaving. There's no need for that." I held up my hands in a peace offering, and we backed away slowly. Once we reached the car, I dived behind the wheel, and Sue Ellen jumped into the passenger side. As soon as Savannah stumbled into the back seat, I peeled away from the curb.

"I told you guys," Sue Ellen said with a self-righteous snark. "We should have just done it when she wasn't around."

"She's always around," Savannah said. "That woman has nothing better to do but sit on that porch until she's dead."

"By the look of her, maybe we won't have to wait too long," Sue Ellen muttered.

"I don't know about y'all," I said, "but I've got a family, and I'm not risking my life for your old CDs."

"Not even NSYNC?" Savannah clasped an offended hand over her heart, a wry smile playing at her lips. "Oh, come on, Rayanne. If her eyesight's as bad as her hearing, she probably wouldn't kill you. Maim you, maybe, but you'd live."

"This isn't a joke. I didn't sign on for trespassing and going to jail. And I definitely didn't agree to getting shot." I guided the car to a deserted gas station up ahead and pulled into a parking space, then killed the engine. Mustering my kindest big-sister tone, I turned around to face them squarely. "Look. We tried. We failed. Let's go home." I assumed Savannah would have an opinion about this, but to my surprise it was Sue Ellen who protested.

"I didn't waste my vacation days and leave behind the entire civilized world so I could be pushed around by a senile old bird. We're getting it. Tonight."

CHAPTER 5

MEEMAW

June 1979

Flanked by Dennis and Frank, Marylynn clutched a trembling hand to her chest and held it there to keep from folding in on herself. The boys steadied her by the elbows as she made her way down the aisle, through the back of the church, and out into the blinding sunlight, where she was greeted with tearful hugs and hushed condolences. She'd always known that Charlie would be the death of her. She just hadn't expected it to happen so soon.

Forty-two. That was how many years he'd had, and only eighteen of those had been hers to share. It hadn't been enough, and she was angry. Angry at God. Angry at the cancer. Angry at Charlie for all those years of smoking, even though she couldn't stop herself from reaching for a cigarette now, despite seeing X-ray after X-ray of cloudy lungs. She fumbled with her lighter, then lifted shaky fingers to her lips and inhaled long and deep.

She hadn't known that a person could die inside while the rest of her body kept right on living. For the life of her, she couldn't understand how the sun had come up this morning without his sleepy smile and crooked nose there to meet it. What kind of world would this be without her Charlie in it to torment her to tears, then turn around and manage to make her fall in love with him all over again? Without Dennis and Frank and Beverly, she wouldn't have been able to peel herself out of bed and get dressed this morning. She wouldn't have been able to face the mourners who had come to say how sorry they were for what she had lost and tell her he was gone too soon. Her children needed her, too, and she owed it to them to at least try.

Grinding out her cigarette, she squared her shoulders and acknowledged the other attendees, giving them little nods of thanks as they shuffled past. Her legs wavered unsteadily beneath her, unaccustomed to the black heels that Beverly had insisted she wear this morning. She tried not to hold anyone's eyes for too long, didn't want them to mistake her appreciation for an invitation to linger about. But Penny Dupree was not deterred.

"I can't begin to tell you how sorry we all are," Penny said, crying, though Marylynn could see no tears. "I want you to know that we're all praying for you. Whatever you need. These things are never easy to go through alone, you know." She tilted her head and squeezed Marylynn's arm so hard it felt more like punishment than sympathy. It was the first time the woman had ever acknowledged her existence, though Marylynn had seen her every week for the past ten years in Sister Parker's Sunday-school class and had learned a lot of things about Penny. She knew that all her dresses were homemade, that she wore pearls only when she wore her blue dress, and that she would never be caught dead without a matching kerchief around her neck. But Marylynn felt certain that Penny Dupree did not know a dad-burned thing about her. On more than one occasion, she had made the offhanded remark to Cricket that Penny Dupree was the human embodiment of Spic and Span. Cricket had playfully scolded her and told her that such talk wasn't Christian, but she still chuckled whenever Marylynn referred to her as "Shiny Penny."

Having never been a woman who liked to be on the receiving end of charity, Marylynn swallowed hard to keep the emotion out of her voice. "I appreciate that, but I'm sure we can manage just fine," she said with a shaky nod.

Nevertheless, true to her word, Penny showed up night after night with roasted chickens and casseroles and Tupperware filled with green Jell-O salad. She lingered at the door and pushed her way inside, offering to take Beverly home to play with her own daughter, who was nearly the same age, and volunteering herself to sort and clean Marylynn's house. Marylynn couldn't remember when she had consented to this, but one morning she stood confounded in her nightgown, trying to make sense of the sight of Penny standing in the middle of her living room, all crisp and ironed out, wearing a pair of yellow rubber gloves and brandishing a can of Pine-Sol.

"It's good to clear away the cobwebs and make a fresh start, honey," Penny said cheerfully as she parted the curtains and shook out the dust. She scrutinized the tiny motes that floated free, then pestered Marylynn with questions about how often she vacuumed and whether she owned a lint remover. It was the third day in a row the tiny imitation of June Cleaver had shown up with stiffly coiffed hair, wearing a red gingham apron, and Marylynn had to excuse herself to the garden just to catch her breath. Grieving was not something she wanted to do in front of anyone else, especially someone who seemed to think a little bleach was going to heal the gaping hole in her chest.

Between the squash and turnips, she sank to her knees, hitting the dirt with her fists. Charlie had been the one to suggest the garden, a place of her own not to be trampled by tiny feet. He'd prepared this patch of earth for her with his own two rough hands, the same hands that had taken apart old appliances and put them back together again day after day. The same hands that had cradled her so many nights and traced lazy circles on her back after the kids had gone to sleep. When the children were small and determined to send her to an early grave, the garden had been the only place that gave her any peace. Back then it had been a refuge from the chaos, something to do with her hands when she needed to hear herself think. But even now, when Dennis yelled back at her, or Frank was caught sneaking out with a crowd of ruffians, she came to her little plot of thriving plants and found solace among all the things she could control.

"Mama?" Beverly appeared behind her and placed a tentative hand on her hunched shoulder. "Do you want me to send her away?" She had always been a sensitive child, able to detect the slightest shift in her mother's mood or pick up on which one of her brothers was nursing a broken heart. When she was five, she'd found an orphaned duckling wandering around lost in the yard. They could never figure out how it ended up out there all alone in a puddle, but as soon as Bev found it, she scooped it up, brought it home, and filled the bathtub with water. Marylynn nearly fainted when she opened the door to find her pink-tiled floor covered in bird droppings and Bev crouched down, trying to feed the poor thing mushed-up worms from her medicine dropper.

Marylynn had yelled and told her the only animal she'd have inside her home was a dead one, preferably stuffed and wearing a nice little pair of overalls. Charlie was the one who had helped her build a nest for it and showed her the best places to find night crawlers to feed it. But Marylynn had been the one to help her bury him in a little hatbox out near the garden, holding her as she cried. Men were always there for the fun parts, she thought. Women were always left to pick up the pieces. She cursed him for doing the same thing to her again and wondered how in the world she was going to get up and do this all over again tomorrow.

Marylynn sniffed hard and dabbed at her eyes with the hem of her sleeve, then turned to her ten-year-old daughter. "No, honey. I'll handle it." She heaved herself up and dusted out her hands, breathing in a lungful of the patience she would need to face Penny again. "She means well. I just needed a break is all." Forcing a smile, she tugged Beverly into a hug before pulling back and cupping her round face in her hands. "You have his eyes, you know. Lord, you meant everything to him."

It was true that Beverly was her father's little girl in every sense of the word, a welcomed calm to the storm after the boys had been such a challenge for the both of them. Charlie and Bev had shared a bond that Marylynn was never able to have with her daughter, and in truth she had always been a little jealous of that. It was the horses that did it. As soon as Beverly was old enough to sit atop his shoulders, Charlie had taken her to the racetrack. And on a cloudless January morning, she picked out the prettiest one, a little chestnut filly with white spots, fresh off the trailer. When they came home $500 richer, they had hooted and squealed, drunk off their victory, until Marylynn cornered him, told him to stop putting ideas in their daughter's head and letting her think she would always win.

"It's not right to let her get a taste for that kind of thing. It will only make it that much harder when she loses," she'd said.

But Charlie had waved her off. "It's just a little betting, Marylynn. She knows it's all in good fun."

"She says you're going to buy her a horse when you win the big one. Did you tell her that?" Marylynn brought a firm hand to her waist and stared him down.

"I . . . I may have said something about a pony, but she knows it's a long shot. Hell, we got the land for it. We could use an animal around here to eat the weeds." With an easy laugh, he gestured out to the pasture that sat between the Beauforts' trailer and their own weather-beaten house, which at the moment needed a new roof and gutters.

"That's not the point, Charlie. The point is, you keep filling her head with harebrained ideas, getting her excited for things we can't afford. Don't you see you're only setting her up to be disappointed. Life isn't all ponies and rainbows. It's best she learns that sooner than later."

He hung his head, rubbed his temples, and nodded. The next day he brought home twelve small wooden horses in rich shades of chestnut, midnight black, and creamy white with brown spots. Wrapping her arms around herself, Marylynn had watched the two of them hang them on the willow tree out front and smiled.

"Now you'll have a whole dozen of them," Charlie had said as he lifted Beverly's tiny frame up to reach the branches. "Twelve flying horses. Even better than the real thing because these ones are magic, you see. I got them from an old shaman, who put a spell on them. They come alive in your dreams. That's where they'll live. And the best part is, you don't even have to feed them." He gave Marylynn a little wink, and in return she mouthed a silent thank-you. A gust of wind sent the horses jangling, and Beverly squeezed her little eyelids tight, as if she were imagining them coming to life.

The memory dissipated as a warm breeze rustled Marylynn's hair, reminding her that there was still the matter of Penny to address. "Come on. Let's go back inside," she said, wrapping an arm around her daughter's slight shoulders. They entered the house to find Dennis and Frank zoned out in front of the television, and Penny nowhere to be found. Half-relieved that perhaps she had finally left with her bucket of cleaners, Marylynn shuffled down the hall to her room, where she discovered Penny rummaging through Charlie's oak dresser. In one hand, she held up a fistful of his chambray work shirts, all tattered and stained, his name stitched carefully on the pockets by Marylynn's own hand. The other held his blue jeans, all holey and equally pitiful looking from years of scuffing up against the ground as he stooped over a broken dishwasher or rolled underneath the hood of a dead engine. The bed they'd once shared was now covered in mismatched socks and jackets, a tool belt, and metallic odds and ends he had collected over the years from a thousand different projects he had tinkered with.

How could a man's life be reduced to such simple things? This was all she had left of him in the world, and Penny Dupree was boxing it all up like garbage.

Her mouth went dry, and her heart slowed to an unsteady lull, leaving her limbs numb. "I'll kindly thank you to take your hands off my husband's things," Marylynn managed to say. The words came out stilted, her chest trembling.

"Oh, honey, I'm sorry. I didn't mean to upset you. I was just thinking that you've been avoiding addressing—well—this part of the house because it's so painful for you. I thought maybe it would be easier if I helped sort some of it and get it all donated. Surely you don't mean to keep all this old junk," she said, her cheery tone never wavering. If she had any reservations about going through another person's underwear, she didn't let it show for a moment.

"I think it's time for you to leave." Marylynn felt her composure slipping, and the careful facade she had managed to maintain over the last few days began to crack.

At this, Penny blanched, rearing back her head as if she hadn't heard correctly. "Surely you don't mean—"

"I can assure you I mean it," Marylynn said firmly. "Now, I appreciate all you've done here, but it's time to go." Sweat trickled down the sides of her face, and her fingers shook as she wiped it away.

A confused smile played at Penny's lips. "Well, you're not thinking clearly—"

"Get the hell out of my house!" Much to her surprise, Marylynn's voice shot out like a thunderous bolt, drawing the attention of Beverly, who rushed into the room, breathless. The concern in her daughter's eyes clutched Marylynn's heart, but she had no more energy to keep up pretenses.

"Well, never in my life . . ." In a fit of disbelief, Penny stormed toward the front door and let herself out, slamming it behind her for good measure.

As soon as she was gone, Marylynn set to unboxing every hallowed item, her heart skipping wildly as she fluttered about the room. Maybe she was doing it to spite Penny, but she couldn't bear to let any piece of it go—the nuts and bolts of the life they had built together.

In a world that was determined to forget, someone had to do the remembering.

CHAPTER 6

SAVANNAH

Friday Morning

Rayanne's arms were stiff as branches, her eyebrows scrunched together as she steered the car in the direction of Meemaw's place. I could tell she was trying to work out how we could get away with it without being caught. Or killed. Against my better judgment, I had agreed with Sue Ellen that we should return later that night to get the capsule, and the two of us had worn Rayanne down until she'd come around to the idea of trespassing. I was certain she was regretting it now. And probably silently cursing me for getting her here in the first place, though, to be honest, I had never heard Rayanne say a dirty word in her entire life, especially now that she seemed to be gunning for mother of the year.

"Can we stop somewhere?" Sue Ellen asked, donning an oversize pair of sunglasses and fanning herself in the passenger seat as if she were melting. "I need food."

"Have you seen Meemaw's kitchen?" I scoffed. "You'd think the woman was expecting to feed the entire cast of *Grey's Anatomy*. All eighteen seasons."

"Not that kind of food." She grimaced. "Something that isn't battered or fried or soaked in butter." The way she enunciated the words, as if I were a child asking a stupid question, made me want to slap her. Flexing my fingers, I resisted the urge.

"Fine," Rayanne said, guiding the car onto a side road and doubling back. The closest Walmart was still a good thirty minutes away, so she headed for the center of downtown and parked in front of Lavon's Grocers, which was less a grocery store and more a five-and-dime that offered a smattering of everything from handmade soaps to live bait and tackle. I knew it wouldn't be overflowing with fresh produce.

"Really?" Sue Ellen flashed Rayanne a pointed look.

"What?" she said, shutting off the engine. "You requested food. Behold. Food." She gestured toward the shabby lean-to building decked out with more than a dozen bird feeders and a hodgepodge of signs advertising animal feed, homemade jams, and the "World's Best Frito Pie." It was tucked in on either side by Van's Tractor Supply and Tootie's Treats, which used to be Sue Ellen's favorite place to load up on snacks when we would ride our bikes here. But that was a lifetime ago, before she turned into some highfalutin stick-in-the-mud. Back then she was just a regular stick-in-the-mud. She looked at Tootie's now as if it were diseased.

"Nothing," Sue Ellen said, pushing her way out of the car. "There's just something disturbing about buying a salad from a place that also sells four different kinds of worms."

"Well, that's just not true." I smirked, unable to help myself. "They carry six kinds. And they won't have salad," I added helpfully, following them toward the entrance.

A bell chimed as we trailed into the store, and a familiar greeting emanated from somewhere behind the register. "How you folks doin'?" came Cricket Turnsplenty's soprano voice. Cricket, one of Meemaw's best (and only) friends, had inherited the store from her father and had run it for as long as I could remember. If Meemaw was a prickly person,

Cricket was her equal opposite, always lathering on the praise and hugs to anyone who ventured a little too close to her orbit. I often wondered if she had taken on Meemaw as a personal challenge for attaining sainthood. Though they went to church together, Cricket was more aligned with the promises of the New Testament, while Meemaw stubbornly held on to the hellfire and brimstone of the Old.

"Savannah, hon—" she said, catching sight of me, fixing her fists to her curvy hips. "Well, I'll be." Taking in all three of us, she slapped her knee and popped up off a stool to greet us. Unlike Meemaw, Cricket had always been plump and stout, and she didn't shy away from the finer points of being a woman. She used so much Aqua Net her hair appeared permanently frozen in place, and her fair complexion was the product of too much Mary Kay, which I happened to know she sold on the side if you knew to ask her about it. Her face was framed by a brown-dyed bob, and her blue eye shadow and bright-burgundy lipstick made her hard to miss. Circling around from behind the counter, she squealed and pulled us into her ample bosom, firmly kissing each of our cheeks. Sue Ellen winced through a smile and, when Cricket wasn't looking, tried to wipe away the remnants of her lipstick with the back of her hand.

"I can't believe it. The Guidry sisters here again in my shop!" She beamed at us as if she had just won the lottery. "Isn't this just the best surprise? I'll bet your grandmother is over the moon having you girls home." She nudged my shoulder, and I smiled back at her easily. Cricket's unbreakable enthusiasm for life had always been contagious like that. "Where are the grandbabies?" She searched behind us as if Charlotte and Tucker might suddenly appear, then realized her mistake, and her face fell.

"They couldn't come," Rayanne said in a syrupy voice. Her accent seemed to get a little thicker and a whole lot more fake when she lied. "You know how it is with little ones. It's so hard to keep them on a schedule."

"Of course, dear." Cricket tutted, though I could tell she was disappointed. "I know all about that." Not only had she been an occasional babysitter to the three of us, but Cricket had her own son, who was a good decade older than Rayanne.

"How's Josh?" Rayanne changed the subject. "Meemaw says he's married, and you have a few grandbabies yourself now."

"I do!" she gushed. "And they are just the cutest things!" She fished a phone out of her apron and fumbled with the buttons. "Here." She held it up for us to inspect and seemed to be waiting for us to agree with her. "Aren't they just precious?"

We crowded around her cell, oohing and aahing as she swiped through a string of snapshots until Sue Ellen cleared her throat. "We actually stopped by to grab a few essentials. Where do you keep your produce?"

Cricket drew a hand to her chest, her smile frozen in place. "I don't understand. Your grandmother has a whole garden of fresh vegetables. Surely you can't find anything here she doesn't already have growing in her yard."

"Yes, I know," Sue Ellen said. "But I'm in desperate need of some kale, spinach, maybe some arugula?" She removed her sunglasses and forced a smile.

Desperate need? Give me a break. She couldn't survive one weekend without her organic rabbit food. I nearly pulled a muscle from the epic eye roll I gave.

"Oh, we don't have any of that, but I did just get a shipment of canned peaches in this morning. Joey!" Cricket shouted, causing Sue Ellen to nearly jump out of her skin.

A rail-thin teenager sporting a camouflage baseball cap appeared from inside the double doors at the back of the store.

"Can you show Sue Ellen here around? Help her find some of our . . . healthier options." She smiled brightly.

Joey gestured for her to follow him, and together the two of them disappeared into the next aisle.

Clutching a hand to her heart, Cricket studied Rayanne and me, tilting her head to get a better look. "I'm just so glad you girls are here." Tears glistened in her crinkly eyes, leading me to wonder if I'd missed something.

"Is everything OK?" I asked, hoping she would tell me if something was bothering her. Though she hadn't seen my sisters in years, Cricket and I were still close. The Salty Pot was right down the street, and most days I stopped in to say hello. Sometimes I dropped off leftovers, and Cricket would always push them away at first, claiming her hips didn't need it, but I knew she could never turn down a steaming bowl of shrimp and grits. She would have told me if something was wrong with Josh or one of her grandchildren. Wouldn't she?

"Oh, of course." She waved away my concern. "Don't mind me. I'm just a sentimental old woman," she said, sweeping a tear from her cheek. "Lord, it does my heart so good to see you all together again. I know it means a lot to Marylynn, too." Wringing her hands, she rested her gaze on Rayanne and let it linger there a beat too long. "She misses the children, you know."

Rayanne stiffened and fiddled with her hair, brushing away non-existent strands. "Yes, I know." She cleared her throat and brightened her tone so much that she sounded almost like an entirely different person. "We're planning to spend Christmas with her." It did not sound believable, and I was certain Cricket picked up on the way she couldn't meet her eyes.

"Right," Cricket said, giving her shoulders a firm squeeze. "I'm sure she'll love that." Cricket was one of those people who smiled with her whole face, and when her soft green eyes tugged at the corners, it flooded my insides with warmth. She had nursed Meemaw through Georgia's disappearance and Mama's death, and I knew she loved all of us as much as she loved her own child. For the first time I wondered if Rayanne and Sue Ellen staying away had hurt her just as much as it had hurt Meemaw.

Rayanne's shoulders relaxed when Sue Ellen emerged carrying an armful of assorted foods. I smiled to myself as she clumsily set them on the counter—a few bananas, a trail mix of nuts and cranberries, a couple of protein bars, and a can of water chestnuts. It was worse than I'd hoped.

"Now that won't do," Cricket scolded, inspecting Sue Ellen's items as if they were part of a mystery that needed solving. "No, you all have a seat, and I'll fix you something real nice. Shrimp po'boy?" Without waiting for an answer, she gestured toward a couple of booths near the back. There wasn't enough seating for Lavon's to qualify as a real restaurant, but customers knew that on the weekends Cricket cooked up a few specialty items from an unadvertised menu.

"Sure," I said at the same time Sue Ellen said, "No, thank you." We shared a what-the-hell look with each other, which Cricket took as a solid yes. She darted into the kitchen and returned a few minutes later bearing three plates piled high with toasted bread and a side of pickles. We clambered into a booth just as she set them down before us. I thanked her and made a point to dig in right away, but Sue Ellen only gave a weak smile and picked around the edges of her plate.

She sighed, giving the food another once-over, and said, "Wonder what Meemaw's doing now."

"She mentioned she had some errands to run this morning," I said between bites.

With accusing eyes, Sue Ellen jutted out her chin and scoffed. "You mean collecting more garbage."

"Lay off her. It keeps her busy, and it's not like she's hurting anyone."

"That's debatable," Rayanne muttered under her breath, flashing me a skeptical side-eye.

Ignoring her, Sue Ellen pushed ahead. "I don't know how you put up with it all. How does it not drive you completely insane to watch her do this? She's getting worse, Savannah."

"Easy for you to say," I said with my mouth full. "At least I've been here with her," I shot back before swallowing and washing it down with a hurried gulp of tea. "Someone had to stay. Sure wasn't gonna be either one of you." I let the words trail off, confident I had ended the conversation.

Biting into a pickle, Sue Ellen scowled at me from across the table. I swear, sometimes I got the feeling she hated me. Then again, the more I thought about it, maybe the feeling was mutual.

CHAPTER 7

Sue Ellen

Friday Evening

At sunset, I tugged on a pair of mesh running shorts and a racerback top, then tied back my hair into a ponytail. In the city I had formed the habit of running three miles along the Hudson in the evenings after work, and I was the fittest I'd ever been. It helped that since leaving Meemaw's, I'd learned that fried food was not a legitimate food group. Incidentally, I'd found that I enjoyed living the hipster life of organic smoothies in the morning and fresh salads made with free-range grilled chicken for lunch. I groaned at the realization that I would have none of these luxuries for the next three days and would have to drive a full thirty minutes to find a decent latte. Lavon's had been an absolute desert.

I plugged in my earbuds and headed for the front door, passing the boxes of outdated magazines and newspapers lining the wood-paneled walls of our grandmother's drab living room. While the outside of the house did not instill a sense of welcome, the inside was even worse. The only way to describe the walls, the couch, and the bulky oak furniture that had never been updated was in a single word: *brown*. Boxes filled with old china, carved animals, and other "antiques" rested on the wobbly kitchen table, which had rarely been used for eating. Instead, we'd always eaten our dinners huddled around the ring-stained coffee table that sat directly in front of her old Zenith, watching reruns of *Boy Meets World*.

I headed out the door toward the gravel road, passing Bessie, who was happily rolling about in a patch of dirt. The winding, tree-lined road ahead provided poor visibility for anyone who might drive up behind me, and people here weren't used to sharing the road with cyclists and joggers, but I reminded myself that the nearest neighbors lived a half mile away. Besides, I was desperate to escape Meemaw's house and every person currently inside it. For whatever reason, Savannah had been inexplicably hostile at Lavon's, and it felt as if I'd slipped through a wormhole directly back to our childhood skirmishes.

Though the sun had nearly disappeared behind the trees, the humidity assaulted my senses the moment the screen door slammed behind me. There was no escaping the thickness of the air, which settled over me, pressing down upon my skin like hot car exhaust. My feet crunched over loose gravel as I sprinted past the oaks and pines of my childhood, silent observers who had documented the milestones of my untraditional life within their rings.

I'd been running for less than a mile when a loud and persistent honk interrupted my podcast. I looked behind me and spotted a dusty brown pickup steadily gaining on me. A leathery man with scruffy white stubble and a matching handlebar mustache rolled down the window and shouted, "Get off the road!" as he passed.

Furious, I flipped him my middle finger and shouted back over the offensive rumble of his engine. "Bite me!" If living in New York had taught me anything, it had forced me to cultivate the fine art of not taking anyone's crap. I continued down the road and was rounding the bend of the pond when a familiar cacophonous sputtering returned. My stomach dropped as once more I caught sight of the same brown truck coming from the opposite direction, slowing down as it approached. For a few terrifying seconds, panic paralyzed my limbs. I hadn't packed my pepper spray. Meemaw had warned me a thousand times about the many ways a person could die in a big city, and as much as I hated to admit it, her paranoia had rubbed off on me. Though I hadn't invested in a Taser, I carried pepper spray every time I went for a run or commuted to work. The irony of it all! Now I was going to die in the middle of nowhere at the hands of a pissed-off hick because I had nothing with which to defend myself. In a frenzy, I grabbed the first large rock I saw. Avoiding eye contact with the driver, I maintained a death grip on the stone behind my back. The truck slowed to a stop, and the elderly man behind the wheel rolled down his passenger's side window.

"Sue Ellen? I thought that was you, girl. Haven't seen you 'round here since you left for school." Taking in the sight of me, he shook his head. "You're skin and bones." There was a fatherly concern about his tone that tugged at my memory. "How you doin'?"

My horrified expression relaxed into a smile when I recognized a weathered Sam Beaufort grinning back at me. He and his wife, Shari, were the closest neighbors Meemaw had out here and must have been in their eighties by now. They lived in a double-wide and owned the fenced-off cow pasture adjacent to Meemaw's property. It was fortunate—or perhaps unfortunate—that the two of them should be neighbors, because he held similar ideas about what constituted acceptable outdoor decor. His overgrown yard held a collection of old tires and a few lonely goats climbing aboard forgotten tractor beds.

"Oh, I'm doing just fine." Trying to catch my breath, I leaned over and gripped my side with my empty hand, definitely not fine. "Just out for a run. How have y'all been?" I managed to get out, cringing at my word choice. Though most of my accent had faded over the past decade, sometimes my voice slipped back into the familiar cadences of my childhood, especially when I was home.

His cheeks sagged, and I could sense immediately that I had asked the wrong question. "Oh, well. I thought Marylynn woulda told ya." Tears shimmered in his pale-blue eyes, and he diverted his gaze for just a moment before bravely meeting my eyes again. "Shari passed a few years back. Had a rough go of things for a while there at the end, but it was fast. Pancreatic cancer."

"I'm sorry to hear that," I said, suddenly remembering that Meemaw had in fact called me about Shari's passing some time ago, but it must have slipped my mind.

Perhaps he sensed my discomfort, because he forced a smile and changed the subject. "Heard you got some fancy job up north now. You always were a smart one." He let out an incredulous whistle. "What brings you back to town?"

"Just visiting family," I said, my heart still racing. "Meemaw's feeling under the weather, so I came to check in on her." It was partly true at least. I left out the part about our plans to dig for buried treasure in the dead of night.

"Well, send her my love." His eyes twinkled with a warmth that set my heart at ease, and I felt myself returning it with a tepid smile. "I'm sure she'll pull through just fine. I've always said that woman's a tough old bird. She'll probably outlive us all."

"Thanks, I'll tell her you said hello."

"All right, you take care now, darlin'." He started to roll up the window, then paused and added over the partially opened glass, "Oh, and Sue Ellen . . . next time you're out for a run, take Marylynn's Glock. Pretty girl like you shouldn't be running alone out here. Besides, that rock there wouldn't help you none if I was aiming to hurt ya." He flashed me a wry grin as he rolled up the window and sputtered away, leaving a plume of black smoke in the truck's wake. Coughing violently,

I tried to wave away the cloud, then casually dropped the rock behind my back.

~

I supposed it was a good thing I was in decent shape, because I hadn't anticipated having to make a sprint like the one we had to make on Jackson Street later that night. Though I would never admit this to Savannah and Rayanne, it was probably an ill-advised idea to trespass. I'd forgotten that most people in this town are just as paranoid as Meemaw and probably all sleep with their shotguns underneath their pillows, but it wasn't as if either of them had offered up any better ideas.

Rayanne parked her car a few houses down on the opposite side of the street. Lucky for us, the neighborhood had gone downhill in the years since we lived there and didn't have any working streetlights, so we were able to move unseen through the darkness. Having forgotten to bring a flashlight, we used the light from our cell phones to guide us through the pitch black, toward the house, and over the chain-link fence until we ended up standing in our old backyard.

The house had a lonesome look about it now, and not just because it was swallowed up in the blackness of the night. Tangled vines stretched every which way along the redbrick walls. The flower beds that lined its perimeter were no longer filled with daylilies and yellow roses but had been heaped to the brim with layer upon layer of pine straw and rotting leaves. I wondered how the inside of the home fared and whether the new owners had painted over the lavender walls of the twins' bedroom I'd watched our mother paint as she'd blasted country music on the radio. "Purple is the color of royalty. And you, my dears, are queens," she'd said as she dipped her finger into a bucket and dabbed a little splash of color onto the tips of their noses. Over the years, I had dreamed of this place, but the shapes were always distorted, the dimensions never quite right, like someone had tried to draw it blindfolded.

"I'm telling y'all. It's right here," Savannah whispered, jabbing a finger at a patch of clover-covered earth in the middle of the yard. "I remember because I counted it off from the oak tree, thirty steps."

"Did you ever stop to think that your foot was half the size then as it is now?" I pointed out. "There's no way it was right there. I distinctly remember it being much closer to the back fence. I remember because you were too small to hold the shovel and kept banging it against the gate."

Of course, no one listened to me, so Savannah plunged the shovel into the spot where she stood, pouting, unwilling to give in. It turned out that digging was not a particular talent of hers, and I wasn't willing to sacrifice my leather clogs for the cause. But Rayanne surprised us both when she grabbed the shovel from Savannah's hands and began tossing up dirt like an experienced undertaker. I got the distinct sense it was the last thing she wanted to be doing, but she'd always been a martyr.

Savannah and I kept a nervous lookout over our shoulders until the shovel hit against something hard. Rayanne wiped the sweat from her brow, leaving brown smudges across her cheeks, and a satisfied smile rippled across her face.

"I think I've got it," she said as she bent down, then reached into the hole and retrieved something long and thin.

After a thorough inspection, she brought one dirt-caked hand to her forehead as if she were nursing a migraine, her blonde and normally tidy bun beginning to unravel as sweaty tendrils fell onto her red cheeks. "You were wrong, Savannah. It's not here."

"What do you mean? You just hit something."

"Yes, I did." Rayanne looked as if she might strangle one of us, so I instinctively backed away from her a few steps. "It's the dog."

"Are you kidding me? Are you telling me we just dug up Rusty?" I stammered, unwilling to accept the fact that we had wasted all this time, but also a little smug that I'd been right. "Thank you, Savannah. I didn't think it was possible, but I'm officially the most traumatized I've ever been in my entire life. And that's saying a lot, considering our childhood." A gray-and-black Catahoula mix stray, Rusty had taken up residence in our neighborhood just a few weeks after the disappearance and camped out on our front porch as if he knew it was where he was needed most. Mama had ignored him at first and told us he was filthy and had the mange. She warned us to stop feeding him, but he kept coming back anyway. Then one day, I caught her kneeling on the front porch, stroking his fur and whispering something into his floppy ear, and I knew then that she had fallen for him, too. I think, in a way, we all felt like he was a messenger from Georgia, come to comfort us in our grief. Savannah had been the one playing outside when the car came barreling down the road too fast. And then he was gone, too.

Rayanne tossed a femur and a muddy dog collar at Savannah, who immediately darted off behind a rusted-out shed. When she returned, wiping her mouth with the back of her arm, Rayanne had already begun digging again in the spot I had originally pointed out.

"Can't you go any faster?" I whispered, tightening my arms around myself as if I were freezing, even though the night air was still thick with the leftover heat of the day.

"I'm going as fast as I can." Leaning her weight against the shovel, Rayanne leveled her gaze at me, her stone-cold eyes daring me to disagree. "But if you'd like to trade places, then by all means."

"Fine." I held up my hands in surrender but continued to steal nervous peeks over my shoulder. Try as I may, I couldn't shake the feeling that someone was watching us in the shadows.

"Shh! I think I hear someone coming." Savannah's curls whipped around, and she squinted hard against the night.

I jumped, my heart nearly leaping out of my chest. The darkness had sent my imagination into overdrive, and with every little rustle, the tiny hairs of my arm stood like soldiers at full attention. My stomach unclenched, reassured by the sight of an oak branch scraping against an unlit window.

The rush of blood thrummed in my ears like the steady whir of a washing machine, until finally Rayanne tapped the shovel on something solid again. She dropped to her knees and brushed away the loose dirt before giving us both a quick nod. "This is it."

A warmth rippled throughout my limbs; a sudden surge of emotion filled my throat, making it impossible to speak. It took me by surprise.

Crouching next to her, Savannah smiled, reaching for it. The once-blue plastic cooler was now encrusted with thick dirt, like a forgotten potato that had been growing undetected for all this time. I hoped the little tin lunch box we had tucked inside it was in better shape. Silently, the three of us marveled over the fact that it had survived the years, a mark in the fabric of our lives we had carved into existence.

A screen door creaked open and slammed shut, snapping me out of my thoughts. The three of us stopped cold, simultaneously recognizing the slow shuffle of footsteps steadily creeping toward us from the back porch. Our eyes darted between one another, a telepathic warning that sent my stomach reeling and my head spinning.

"Run!" Savannah snatched the cooler and sprinted for the street just as a blinding light materialized from somewhere behind us. Rayanne took off a beat behind her. Frantic, I trailed them, doing my best to match their pace, but I hadn't worn the right shoes for outrunning enemy fire, and my heels kept getting stuck in the dirt. By the time I made it to the fence, they had already tumbled down clumsily onto the other side into a tangled heap of flailing limbs. Scrambling to the car, Savannah shouted back, "Climb faster!"

"I'm trying!" I mouthed, doing my best to untangle my jeans from a jagged tear in the wire, tugging wildly as my legs dangled on either side like a circus contortionist. At the precise moment they stopped running long enough to realize I wasn't behind them, the three of us locked eyes.

I froze just as a booming crack pierced the stillness of the night.

CHAPTER 8

Rayanne

Friday Night

Flinching at the sound, I whipped around to see the sour-faced woman's birdlike frame illuminated by floodlights, brandishing the same gun she'd pointed at us that morning. Closing in on the edge of the yard, she propped the rifle atop her shoulder and glared at Sue Ellen, who was in dire straits. Chest heaving, I clocked her balancing precariously atop the fence, until finally she toppled over and bolted toward us at lightning speed.

"This is all your fault! Stupid, stupid, stupid idea," she shouted at Savannah, nearly out of breath as they darted into the car, and I stumbled behind the wheel. We tore off into the darkness, leaving a trail of exhaust and a piece of Sue Ellen's designer jeans in our wake.

"I only said we needed to honor the pact. You were the one who insisted on doing it in the middle of the night like a criminal!" Savannah shot back. "I thought you East Coast elites were supposed to be smart or something."

"We're only here because of you!"

"It's not my fault you wore heels!"

"They're clogs! And I didn't expect to be outrunning an armed person."

"It's Muscadine," Savannah deadpanned. "Armed people are pretty much par for the course."

I was doing my best to steer the car down the unlit gravel road, with only the faint glow of my headlights illuminating the blackness a few feet ahead of us. "I can't think with the two of you fighting. For the love of God, just . . . take a time-out!"

Sue Ellen eyed me warily from the back seat, then cocked an eyebrow in Savannah's direction. "Did she really just tell us to take a time-out? We aren't your kids. Don't infantilize us."

Through the rearview mirror, I shot her a warning that looked something like a witch casting a hex. Growing up, I'd always counted myself too mature to entertain her arguments with Savannah and was perfectly content to let them torment each other. But motherhood had changed me, and I couldn't help myself from setting her straight. "Well, if you wouldn't act like children, I wouldn't have to treat you like children. I'd also like to point out that Charlotte and Tucker are ten times better behaved than y'all are, and that's taking into account the fact that Tucker now refers to me as 'stupid head.'" My hands were shaking as they held a death grip on the steering wheel. Taking in a measured breath, I focused my attention on the winding backcountry road ahead. "Now as long as I'm driving, you'll shut up."

A flicker of steel crossed her face, but to Sue Ellen's credit, the car was silent the rest of the way to Meemaw's.

∿

We clambered quietly into the house at an ungodly hour, doing our best not to track dirt all over Meemaw's heirloom rug, and laid our treasure on a pile of newspapers atop my old bed. After prying open the cooler, I tugged out a rusted Captain Planet lunch box and tried to wedge a pair of scissors underneath the thick layers of muddied duct tape that encased it. The signature blue tint of the captain's skin had mellowed into something more like gray, his red suit faded to brown. "Whose idea was it to wrap this thing up like Fort Knox?" I asked, hoping that some of the ice had melted between us.

"That would be me." With her legs tucked beneath her atop the quilt, Savannah looked on eagerly, biting her lip. "I remember reading somewhere that it had to be completely insulated, or water would get in and destroy everything." Apparently the excitement of opening the thing had put her in a good mood.

But Sue Ellen could never dismiss a grudge that easily. She scrolled aimlessly through her cell as she lay on her back on the adjacent twin bed. "There have been all sorts of articles about schools recovering these things, and they almost never come out intact. Which means I ruined these pants for nothing," she added under her breath.

I thought to myself that if Sue Ellen mentioned those damned jeans one more time, I might reach over and finish ripping them for her. I was beginning to remember why she and Savannah had always had such a difficult time getting along.

"You both just left me. I could have died," she reminded us for what I was sure was the hundredth time.

"But you didn't," Savannah pointed out, enunciating the words. "You are still very much alive. Now can you please stop ruining this moment for me? It's not exactly playing out how I imagined it would."

"Oh, it's going exactly as I imagined it would."

I directed all my frustration at the little box in front of me and managed to pry off a significant chunk of tape, revealing the corroded latch underneath.

"We ready for this?" I asked.

Savannah nodded as she watched me flip the latch and work the scissors between the two stubborn sides that had fused together, finally prying it open. Though everything inside was covered in a thin layer of loose dirt, by some miracle, the duct tape had done its job, because no water had seeped through. I blew the dust away as best I could, recognizing a friendship bracelet from my cousin, Katelyn, Uncle Dennis's daughter. We still kept in touch via Facebook, and Uncle Dennis had even given me away at my wedding.

Underneath the bracelet was a copy of Meemaw's *TV Guide* and a ticket stub for *Jurassic Park*, time stamped for a 5:30 showing a little over a year before Georgia went missing. I fingered it gently, remembering how I had beamed when our father announced that I was plenty old enough to see my first scary movie. Even though Mama had disagreed, we'd left her at home with the younger three and headed off together in his red Thunderbird. I remembered the feel of his rough calluses as he squeezed my hand during the scary parts and covered my eyes when he could see that things were getting too intense. Funny how he'd been able to be there for me during a movie but couldn't stick around when the walls of our real world had come crashing down all around us.

Sue Ellen was already flipping through her items: a frayed paperback copy of *Anne of Green Gables*, a stack of school awards, and a mixtape of country music.

"That's funny," she said. "I don't remember putting this in here. Must be yours." She held it out toward Savannah, who snatched it and started reading the songs on the label.

"You used to love this kind of music, too, you know. 'Friends in Low Places' does not get old."

Sue Ellen cleared her throat. "I suppose that makes sense. For you," she added, flipping through the book.

Apparently unoffended by this, Savannah just shrugged. "At least my friends are real. What you see is what you get. No filters."

At this, Sue Ellen sat up a little straighter and cocked her head to the side. "Savannah, you do know there's more to life than Friday-night beer pong and lazing around the lake, nursing a Bud Light with everyone who peaked in high school, right?"

Savannah scoffed. "At least I don't brag about my bougie life using some ridiculous words you assume none of us undereducated folk have the intelligence to comprehend."

"This is how I speak. And it's the correct way, in case you're wondering. I'm sorry if using correct grammar makes me bougie."

Savannah sighed, raking a hand through her curls. "Forget I said anything."

Rummaging around the bottom of the box, I ran my fingers over a yellow square of construction paper that featured three messy handprints, each slightly smaller and sloppier than the next. I plucked it out and slid a hand over the biggest one, a blob of messy purple, and stretched out my fingers, noticing that mine hadn't been much bigger than the other two. Not big enough to protect them. Or Georgia.

Savannah examined a plastic ziplock bag containing three locks of hair and a short stack of pictures. Gingerly, she opened it and began thumbing through the contents as I reached for the snippets of hair.

"Hey, Savannah," I said, changing the subject for their benefit, "remember that time you cut our hair in our sleep without asking?" I grinned as I fingered two slender locks of blonde and one thick chunk of brown.

"Only because I knew you'd never give it to me willingly. Besides, you never even noticed it was missing." A wicked smile spread across her face.

"You gave me bangs." Sue Ellen ran a hand through her caramel-highlighted hair as if checking to make sure it was all still there. "I had to wear headbands for months until it grew out. You didn't do that to Rayanne."

"She never tricked me into thinking my bedroom was haunted."

"Touché," I said, sidling up next to Savannah. "You were pretty terrible to her." I lifted an eyebrow in Sue Ellen's direction. "Telling her ghost stories and hiding under her bed to shake it while she slept."

"What can I say? I had a flair for the dramatic," Sue Ellen admitted with a smirk.

Savannah flipped slowly through the photos, taking space between each one as if she were trying to conjure the day—a snapshot of us at the park, the four of us huddled around Mama on the swings, the twins' piercing blue eyes fixed on each other, laughing about some secret. A candid of Sue Ellen and me—her pulling a sour face while I gave an all-encompassing toothless smile as I held up a fish.

Savannah's eyes came alive when she landed on a picture of Mama wearing her high school cheerleading outfit, surrounded by friends at a football game. The blaze of the stadium lights illuminated her haloed face as she smiled into the camera, completely unaware that I would come into her world in just a matter of months. Our mother had not been able to experience her teens and early twenties carefree and child-less, like we had. She had me when she was just eighteen and Sue Ellen a year and a half later. Before she had time to catch her breath, the twins came along. Bam, bam, double bam.

"I remember leaving this one in here. I always thought she looked like Meg Ryan when she was young." Savannah ran a finger over the photo before passing it to me. "You think she was pregnant with you in this picture?"

"I don't know," I said, staring at Mama's carefree smile and long blonde ponytail. She was so young, too young to become a mother. Knowing how much I'd had to sacrifice for my own children, I felt guilty that I was the reason she had to grow up faster than her friends in the picture. A familiar heaviness settled over me, and I shuddered. "If she was, she probably didn't know it yet. I came along after gradua-tion, right before she had to marry Daddy." The last word caught in my throat. It was strange to call him that now as a grown woman with chil-dren of my own. The title had been a taboo word in Meemaw's home, and on the rare occasion when she'd been forced to speak about him, she'd only ever referred to him as *that man*. After that day at the lake, our father—if you can call him that—didn't bother to come around much anymore. Mama always said it was too painful for him to see the rest of us because we looked so much like Georgia, especially Savannah. But Meemaw said it was because he was a low-down selfish jackass who wasn't worth a sack of potatoes. And though I rarely agreed with her, I tended to concur with the latter assessment.

The last time I'd seen our father was at my wedding, almost fifteen years ago. He had a way of turning up unexpectedly at milestones in our lives. I hadn't invited him, but he'd shown up unannounced and looked genuinely hurt when Uncle Dennis walked me down the aisle. Dennis had been more of a father to me than my own, and he lived in Kansas City, a full eleven hours away from Muscadine, while our father lived just thirty minutes over in the next town.

Savannah looked at the pictures wistfully, as if she could glean some secret from Mama's expressions. I couldn't understand why she was so desperate to relive the past. Maybe it was because she was younger than us and didn't remember how much it all hurt. I was nine when Mama got sick. The cancer had likely gone undetected for some time due to the fact that we never had any decent health insurance. It took her in less than a year.

Unlike Savannah, when I thought of her, I could only see the image of her gaunt face and hollow eyes—not the smiling, golden-haired goddess who made dandelion crowns with us in the yard. In that last year she was with us, I was never sure how much of her pain was from the cancer and how much of it was from the hurt of losing Georgia. And I always wondered if maybe she would have fought harder if it hadn't been for losing her youngest child. It seemed to me like she just gave up after that and forgot she still had three other children who needed her, too. I was the one who made dinner, kept the water from boiling over on the stove when she couldn't get herself out of bed, made sure that Savannah and Sue Ellen had everything they needed for school in the morning. I was the one who kept us all together before she died, and we had to go live with Meemaw in her crazy house full of things. And no one ever asked me how I felt about it.

"I think this was taken on the day we lost her," Savannah said, stirring me from my thoughts. I assumed she was talking about Mama, but as I leaned over to inspect the photo she was holding out, I saw that she meant Georgia. There in the shallow lake water sat two identical towheads, frozen in time as they splashed and squinted away the sun. A searing ache settled into my gut, but I did my best to shake it off.

"It could have been," I said. "We went to the lake a lot that summer, but I do remember you both were wearing those mermaid floaties because you had thrown a fit at Walmart until Mama put them on layaway. And, of course, Georgia had to have whatever you had." I smiled, and Savannah's face lit up at this tiny bit of new information.

Sue Ellen inched over and stared at the image alongside us, her features softening as she shook her head. "It's remarkable. Even I can't tell you apart." The twins wore matching purple swimsuits, tie-dyed with a hole cut out of the center, exposing two identical little tummies.

Savannah was doing that intense detective stare again as she scoured every inch of the photo, like if she concentrated hard enough, she could take the memory and force it inside. We sat in silence for a few moments, and I retreated to the corner of my mind where I had tucked Georgia behind the thin dividing line of before and after. She stayed there, trapped in the before—before my innocence was stolen and I learned how cruel the world really was.

"Who is that?" Savannah tilted her head to one side and squinted at a shape on the far right of the photo, almost out of the frame.

Leaning in to get a better look, Sue Ellen craned her neck. "Who?"

At first it was impossible to know who she was referring to because there were so many people in the background, swimming and floating in the stifling heat of the midday sun. Flecks of sunlight shimmered off the water as it stretched out behind them until it disappeared into the banks of a bustling beach.

"That woman." Savannah pointed to a short brunette standing just where the water met the copper dirt, far enough away that Mama might not have noticed her, but just close enough that she could go unseen while holding her eyes on the girls in the mermaid floaties. It was hard to make out her features at first, and I wasn't sure I would have even noticed her if Savannah hadn't mentioned it. But I recognized her. Perhaps she'd been a friend of our mother's? For the life of me, I couldn't remember her name.

Her hair was cropped short but not in a cute pixie-cut kind of way—more like she had chopped it off herself in a hurry, all shapeless and jagged. She wore a button-up white shirt and khaki pants, camouflaging her so that her drab clothing blended in against the edge of the beach. I had to admit that there was something unnerving about the way she was staring at my sisters. It was the same way I found myself staring at my own children sometimes—a sense of longing and desire to keep them frozen that way forever. But there was something else there, too.

I couldn't be certain, but it looked like pain.

CHAPTER 9

Meemaw

October 1986

"That was the most humiliating thing that's ever happened to me!" Beverly said, slumped against the window in the passenger seat of the Buick. "What is wrong with you? Why can't you just be normal?"

"One day you'll learn that normal is relative, honey," Marylynn said, stoically tapping out her cigarette in the ashtray between them. Beverly seethed, unwilling to give even an inch by looking at her mother, who had shown up uninvited at Christine Dupree's home and dragged Beverly outside by the nape of her cropped shirt in front of the entire football team and half the senior class. Marylynn had to admit it had not been her finest moment, but it wasn't her fault. Sometimes she *had* to do and say awful things just to save her children from themselves. After all, the same God who said "thou shalt not kill" destroyed all those cities full of wicked people and sent the flood, too. She figured spying on her children was just good sense.

Even so, the silence was beginning to wear on her. She rolled down her window and siphoned out a breath of smoke from the side of her mouth. "Bev, do you think I enjoy having to follow you all over town to these filthy places, like I got nothing better to do tonight than ward off pimple-faced delinquents?"

It was the beginning of Beverly's senior year, and for Marylynn at least, it had been the most terrifying year they'd faced together since Charlie died. Without warning, sometime over the course of the previous six months, her awkward and sensitive child had become popular with her blonde hair, sapphire eyes, and mischievous smile that reminded Marylynn so much of Charlie it hurt. She was a cheerleader, too, and a good one. When she'd first told her mother she wanted to try out for the team, Marylynn was firmly set against it. Those skirts were too short, and she didn't see the value of wrecking a perfectly good singing voice by shouting and hollering at the top of her lungs. How on earth would she be able to sing for the Lord on Sunday if she was out abusing her talent on Friday? But after she saw Bev at that first game, saw the way she could get the crowd up and on their feet, hollering back at her, she had beamed with pride.

"That's my daughter out there," she would say as she nudged the person next to her and pointed at Bev all dolled up just like a regular model, her hair bouncing cheerfully behind her as she waved around blue-and-yellow pom-poms.

But after the games ended, when Beverly stayed out late with the rest of Muscadine High, Marylynn would lie awake at night in worried fits. It was different from the worry that came with the boys—she knew that if push came to shove, they could take care of themselves. But Bev was too trusting for her own good, and without Charlie there to steady her, Marylynn wasn't ready for her to face a world of teenage boys and keggers and girls so brutal they'd break a person's spirit just for the fun of it.

That was why she took up smoking an extra half pack a day when Beverly found her place among the most sought-after girls in all of Muscadine High. Shiny Penny's daughter, Christine Dupree, and her gang were birds of a feather—not a breed Marylynn particularly cared for—but they had taken a liking to Bev and had made her one of their own, even encouraged her to join the squad with them. After she'd skittered away from Marylynn's home like a scalded dog, Penny had never given her more than a nod in passing at Sunday services. And for her part, Marylynn didn't mind the slight, as she was only there to save her soul and not to make friends, especially not with someone as starched and buttoned down as Penny. Sometimes she worried that if heaven meant being around a bunch of Pennys, she wasn't entirely certain she wanted to go there.

But Beverly had come to view Christine as a celebrity of sorts. It made it difficult for Marylynn to keep her distance from the Duprees when her daughter was always commenting on what Christine was wearing, and who she was dating, and whether she could get a perm like Christine had. Beverly was floating on air when she was invited to be a part of their group. But for Marylynn, it only reminded her that she was nothing like the Duprees, and if Beverly preferred to spend her time with them, it meant that she had lost her. Those first few months of her daughter's senior year had felt like an endless game of Whac-A-Mole with an ever-rotating door of boys and parties that Marylynn had to keep track of.

Tonight was the second time this month she'd learned about an unsupervised event. Cricket's husband, Officer Turnsplenty, had mentioned to his wife, who had mentioned to Marylynn at Lavon's Grocers, that there was a party going on over at the Duprees' home this evening. The parents were out of town. Nothing too terrible, but Officer Turnsplenty would be keeping an eye on it to make sure there wasn't anything illegal happening. Marylynn didn't wait for a report and straightaway drove herself over to the Magnolia Heights neighborhood in a sweat-filled panic. It was nearly Halloween, and every tidy little house featured cleverly crafted graveyards and skeletons hanging in doorways. Her cheeks flushed at the sight of it. Over the years, word had gotten around town that her home was an embarrassment, a mess that had sent her children out into the homes of their friends like refugees. Maybe it was why Dennis and Frank had abandoned her after high school, put her away like an old shoe, when hadn't she sacrificed everything for their happiness?

After Charlie, she'd had to work at the nursing home while still keeping the boys from going out and stirring up trouble with the wrong crowd. She made sure they finished their schooling, dragged them out of bars when they were teenagers, and chased off a good number of unsuitable girls. But none of it had been enough to hold on to them. The boys had still hightailed it out of Muscadine right after high school. Couldn't get away from her fast enough to go out chasing bigger and better dreams that didn't include her. Each time one had left, he'd taken another piece of herself with him. And it seemed the harder she tried to grab on to them, the more her family was determined to leave and set on their own paths in this treacherous world. They slipped through her fingers like a fine sand she couldn't hold. "You can't keep them small forever," Charlie used to say when Dennis was learning to drive. "You've got to let them go sometime and trust that they know enough to stay out of trouble." But she couldn't. She'd never been able to let them go. Especially not her Bev. With Charlie and the boys gone, she was all Marylynn had left.

Now, with her foot pressed down on the gas, she puzzled over how to slow down time. Was there a way to stretch out Beverly's childhood and keep her from leaving, too? Rounding the corner to her gravel road, she caught sight of a SOLD sign and a two-toned, blue-and-white Chevy laden down with a velour sofa and two mattresses. A red ten-speed leaned against the shoddy ranch-style house with the cracked windows, the one that had sat vacant for close to a year, since the previous family had defaulted on the mortgage and skipped town. It likely had more raccoons and squirrels inside than you could shake a stick at. To Marylynn's surprise, it seemed someone had finally purchased the property. Slowing down as she passed, she couldn't help herself from craning her neck, just barely making out the tiny figure of a child in the lamplight. No, a girl, perhaps? Wearing a pink windbreaker and acid-washed jeans, she sat perched atop the open bed of the truck with her legs tucked up to her chest—reading.

Before Marylynn could comment on this development, she had already made it to the driveway. As the car rolled to a stop, Beverly threw open the door and flew into the house with Marylynn hot on her heels. She entered to hear a door slam shut and Pat Benatar's voice vibrating the floorboards from the room down the hall.

"Beverly!" she shouted, pounding out the syllables with her fist. "Open this door." The music grew louder, and Marylynn knocked harder. "I mean it. Open this door or I will take it off myself."

The door creaked open a sliver, and Marylynn slid her fingers inside, catching sight of her daughter sitting cross-legged on the bed, flipping through a magazine with a half-dressed woman on its cover.

"Well?" Beverly said without looking up through yellow curls that hid her tears.

Careful not to appear as angry as she felt, Marylynn padded softly toward her and sat down on the mattress, her back facing her. "You know I only came there tonight because I care about you, don't you? If I didn't give a lick about you, I would have left you there and let you go on drinking and smoking and doing Lord knows what else."

Beverly folded her arms, her eyes still locked on the pages plastered with women in swimsuits and short skirts and too much makeup. *Why do they always want to grow up so fast?*

"Honey, you're trying to be someone you're not," Marylynn reasoned. At Bev's silence, she prodded further. "Did I ever tell you about the harmless little milk snakes in my garden? They think they're so smart with their bright colors, trying to dress up like their venomous cousins. And just where does all that pretending get them?"

Having heard this analogy before, Beverly drew a hand to her temple and sighed.

"Split in two, that's where!" Marylynn said, finding her strength. "You're lucky, you know that?" she went on, more gently now. "Most of those kids there tonight don't have anyone who cares enough about them to go and bring them home where they belong."

"Lucky?" Beverly scoffed, jostling her shoulders. "I'm lucky because I get to be stuck in this embarrassment with someone who humiliates me in front of the one boy I actually liked? Christine's mother is right. You really are crazy," she muttered through her hair.

Marylynn blinked back indignant tears. How was it that each of her children knew precisely which buttons to push and how much pressure to apply to shatter her? Then again, maybe it was because they'd spent all those months inside her own body, nestled against her heart, that they knew exactly how to break it.

She forced herself to ignore the way her chest burned and steadied her chin. "It's not that I don't want you to have friends, but can't you find some that are little more . . . responsible, that don't drink or smoke?"

Beverly snapped her head up to meet her gaze head-on. "You drink and smoke."

"That's different. I'm an adult."

"Right." She flipped another page and hung her head. "And that worked out well for Daddy, didn't it?"

Marylynn blanched. It had always been easy to dismiss her children when they spouted ridiculous nonsense, when they walked around pretending to know what it meant to be an adult, though they didn't have two nickels to rub together or the sense the good Lord gave them. But every now and then, they would hit on something that held a kernel of truth, and whenever it happened, she felt a stab of guilt in her gut.

Gathering her resolve, she tried to sound casual. "There's a new family that just moved in at the end of the road," Marylynn said, thinking back on the drive home. "The daughter looks to be about your age. Why don't you go over tomorrow and make her feel welcome?"

Beverly rolled her eyes, and Marylynn found herself once more struggling to hold her tongue.

"Look," she said, softer now as she inched closer to Beverly. The springs creaked under the weight of her shifting. "Christine and her friends . . . they aren't the kind of friends that stick around when things get difficult. If the police had shown up tonight, do you really believe she wouldn't have thrown all of you under the bus to save herself?"

A stubborn tear carved its way down Beverly's cheek as she fiddled with her hair. Marylynn cupped her daughter's face in her hands, tilted it up toward the light, and smoothed away the wet strands of hair. "You may not like me very much right now, honey, but I promise you that when the worst happens, I'm gonna be one of the only people left standing in your corner. Friends are nice," she said, with a resolute nod, "but family is family."

CHAPTER 10

SAVANNAH

Friday Night

I knew when I saw the woman in the photograph that I had seen her somewhere before. Of course, Sue Ellen didn't trust my memory after the whole digging-up-Rusty mess—a mistake anyone could have made. But I knew I was right this time.

"I know her. I've seen that woman. Where have I seen her?" I wondered aloud, squinting to make out her features.

"It's not like Muscadine's a sprawling city." Sue Ellen plopped herself onto the bed next to me, lying flat on her stomach, resting her chin in a cupped hand. "I'd venture to guess we've run into most everyone that lived here at some time or another."

She wasn't wrong, but something pricked at the edge of my memory, and I couldn't ignore the familiar, sharp ridges of the woman's chin, the hollow cheekbones and glassy eyes. She was pretty in an undiscovered-model sort of way, but judging from her dumpy clothes, I doubted whether anyone in Muscadine would notice that kind of natural beauty. "No, this is different. I recognize her." I continued absently thinking out loud until the truth hit me like a burst of cold water. I sprang off the bed, and my feet carried me to the hallway, where Meemaw's montage of photographs lined the walls in gilded silver and gold frames, a patchwork quilt of her life in images—Meemaw and her husband, Charlie, in sepia on their wedding day, him wearing a bow tie and a playful smirk that teased the camera while she sported a serious gaze and a simple sheath dress with no frills, her hands clasped peacefully together at her waist. Mama's senior picture, a headshot set against a pink-and-blue laser background that didn't give away her condition, her spotless complexion and dimpled chin resting softly in the palm of one hand. Images of her in diapers with her older brothers, Dennis and Frank, as much smaller versions of themselves, and dozens of photos of her surrounded by the four of us. Until it was just the three of us. In those pictures, there was a shift in her features, a brokenness in her smile that was never mended.

I scoured the dusty faces until my finger landed on a teenage version of Mama surrounded by a group of friends outside the Muscadine Cineplex, which featured a showtime for *Lethal Weapon* in the bright neon lights behind them. Almost all the girls had been posing for the camera, including Mama, who was leaning in, blowing a kiss with one hand while the other rested firmly on her hip. She wore a denim vest over a checkered shirt and a pink-and-orange color-blocked miniskirt that accentuated her tiny form. Her unblemished face still held a childlike quality about it, her features softer and rounder than I remembered them. Mama's entourage wore similar outfits, complete with teased hair and perky ponytails. Everyone looked like they belonged together. Except one person.

To the right of Mama stood a girl with mousy brown hair that reached just past her shoulders. She wore a green jumper that looked as if it were two sizes too big for her and black combat boots laced up to her shins. I was no expert on eighties fashion, but it looked to me as if she didn't quite fit in with this crowd. As everyone else beamed and flirted with the camera, she appeared to be shrinking in on herself with an unsure half smile and pale, gangly arms crossed awkwardly over her chest.

"This is the same woman. I'm sure of it," I said, pointing to the girl in the frame as I carried it back to the bedroom. Scrunching up my eyebrows, I placed the two photos side by side on the bed. "I knew I wasn't imagining it." Her hair was much shorter in the lake picture, but it was her.

"I remember her." Rayanne took the photo and studied it casually. "I think she came to the house a few times when we were small," she said, before handing the photo back to me, unimpressed. "I can't remember her name, though."

My heart sank. I couldn't believe the two of them weren't taking this more seriously. "She was there," I said, almost to myself. "Maybe she saw something."

They passed a worried look between each other before Sue Ellen said, "Let's not do this, Savannah."

"Do what?" I asked, feeling heat rush into my cheeks. "Say her name?"

"You know what I mean."

"Actually, I don't."

Rayanne heaved a sigh and glanced over again at Sue Ellen, as if she were trying to enlist her support. "We're not even sure if this photo was taken on the same day. Even if it was, she would have already told the police everything she knows." Placing a concerned hand on my knee, she softened her gaze. "I know it's always been harder for you, but you have to stop self-sabotaging. Listen, I didn't think I needed a therapist, either, but Deborah is amazing. I think she even takes clients over the phone. I have her number here somewhere, so . . . just hang on a sec." She rummaged around inside her oversize purse, pulling out hand sanitizer and baby wipes and a Tide pen. Apparently Deborah had come highly recommended from someone in Rayanne's mom group, which I had secretly renamed "Bored Housewives Anonymous."

I waved her away and shook my head. "I don't need a therapist."

"Maybe not, but you need someone to talk to. Reliving all of it again isn't healthy. Besides"—she paused and fixed her gaze on the photo of me and Georgia again, her eyes glistening with fresh tears— "we know what happened. Finding out who this woman is—it's not going to change anything. It won't bring her back."

"She's right," Sue Ellen said with more tenderness in her voice than I'd come to expect from her. "They got him. Just because we never found her doesn't make it any less true. He confessed. What more proof do you need?"

A wave of nausea washed over me, but I pushed it down. Nearly five years after the disappearance, a man named Levi Morrison was arrested in Tennessee for the rape and murder of a sixteen-year-old girl, Marissa Jenkins. When police discovered he had once rented a houseboat in Muscadine on Lake Canard, they questioned him about the details of Georgia's abduction. Eventually he confessed, though he stubbornly refused to reveal what he'd done with her body, leaving everyone to speculate that she was likely at the bottom of the lake or in a shallow grave somewhere along an abandoned stretch of highway. Everyone except me. Even now, the words didn't ring true in my ears.

Rage bubbled up from my toes, burning in my throat until the words spilled out of me like hot bile. "You don't know that he did it. We don't know anything. She could still be out there somewhere!"

Sue Ellen shook her head and let out a scoff. "This is exactly why I didn't want to come here. You've never been able to let her go." She sucked in a deep breath and held it there before letting her chest sink. "She's dead, Savannah, and it's sad, but at some point . . . life goes on. You grow up. You get a job—a *real* job—a real relationship, and you move the hell on."

My body thrummed with rage, and I balled my fists. "I have a real job."

Closing her eyes, Sue Ellen pressed two fingers against her skull and rubbed hard. "Savannah, you're thirty-two and still waiting tables at a place that doesn't even qualify as a restaurant. Bouncing around from one crappy service job to another does not equal a career." She said this as if the very act of repeating the words were physically painful.

"They weren't all crappy," I fired back, indignant. "I almost made management at Dillard's."

"Weren't you fired from that job?" Sue Ellen furrowed a perfectly shaped brow.

"Technically, but it was totally unfair." I'd actually loved that job, especially dressing the mannequins up like life-size dolls. It wasn't my fault that prude of a store manager hadn't been able to catch my vision. The display had been tastefully done, and we'd sold loads of lingerie that day. I'd also been a grocery store clerk and the worst smoothie maker known to man. Then there was that awful two weeks when I got tangled up in a pyramid scheme selling skin-care products that were later banned by the FDA and resulted in a monthlong rift between me and Tammy. I didn't know then if she'd ever forgive me for the way her face had swollen up like a tomato after she'd contracted hives from something labeled "Blackhead Destroyer." Sure, those were all probably lateral moves, but I didn't care what Sue Ellen thought. At least I told myself I didn't care.

"Look, this isn't about me. It's about her. If it had been either of you"—I fought against the tears, desperate for them to agree—"I'd want to know the truth. Leave no stone unturned. Wouldn't you?" A telling silence hung between us, and I bristled. "So what?" My face reddening, I went on working myself into a righteous fit. "We just give up on her? Forget she ever existed? Because it's more convenient if you don't have to explain to your friends that you have another sister who may or may not be dead?"

"Yes!" Sue Ellen snapped. "Is that so bad? Is it wrong to want this to all be over? Why can't you just let it go?"

My heart in my throat, I bit back the tears burning in the corners of my eyes. "Because it could have been me. It could have been me, and y'all would have just gone on with your lives and forgotten all about me." My voice cracked with the realization that maybe I should have been the one whisked into thin air that day instead of her. I snatched up the photos and started for the door. "What does it matter, though?" I said, turning back to face them. "I'm still here, and you forgot me anyway."

"Savannah, wait!" Rayanne called after and followed me down the hall until we were both outside. After I climbed into my truck, she planted herself in front of my door, blocking my escape. "We didn't forget you. We're just . . . busy is all. You know you're always welcome to stay with Graham and me, don't you? We've always been there for you."

"But you're not here," I shouted out my open window. "That's just it. When you left home, you left me. And don't pretend that's not what happened." I had tried for so long to keep up the weekly phone calls, but everyone had been so busy, and I'd let it slide. Until eventually one day it hit me that I couldn't remember the last time I'd had a real conversation with either of them. Aside from liking and commenting on their Instagram feeds, I knew next to nothing about them. And it was becoming more obvious that they knew even less about me. Especially Sue Ellen.

"You don't call, don't text. Sue Ellen hasn't even commented on the fact that I graduated, that I have a *degree* now." I emphasized the word in her direction, where she hovered near the porch steps. I hadn't intended to bring it up, but I'd let my emotions get the better of me. When I posted a photo of me in my cap and gown a couple of months ago, Rayanne had at least called to congratulate me and sent a check for a hundred bucks in the mail, but apparently Sue Ellen had been so busy that she never acknowledged it. Not even a like. Of course it was only an associate degree in hospitality management, so maybe she hadn't thought it worth the effort, especially considering that it took me more than ten years to take the plunge into higher education—something Sue Ellen had harped on me about for as long as I could remember.

"I'm sorry. Congratulations," Sue Ellen stammered, halfheartedly, almost as if the word were a question. Not ready to forgive, I let the heated charge hang in the air between us.

"OK," Rayanne said finally. "Let's find her." Closing in on the truck, she leaned her elbows against the window frame, then took the photos from my hands and gave me an encouraging nod. "Look, I'm sorry we haven't always been there for you." She glanced over her shoulder at Sue Ellen, who didn't appear eager to agree with her. "Right?" An awkward silence passed between them before Sue Ellen nodded a beat too late. "But we're here now. And we're going to make it up to you. Starting with finding this woman." She shrugged as a reluctant smile tugged up the corners of her mouth. "Besides, it might be nice to meet someone who knew our mother, someone who remembers what she was like." The way her eyes glimmered with sadness softened my heart around the edges, but I did my best not to let it show. I knew she didn't want to be here, that she didn't want to waste any more time away from her real family, going on a wild-goose chase to satisfy her fickle-minded sister. But for the first time in a long time, I was excited about the possibility of finding something real for me. Because as much as I hated to admit it, Sue Ellen was right. Unlike her rocket ride to success, my career path had been more of a winding trail with switchbacks and steep hills and deep ditches filled with steaming piles of manure. Maybe Rayanne had a point about the whole self-sabotaging thing.

It was a long shot, but maybe now this woman in the photo could give me some answers about what happened at the lake that day. At the very least, maybe she could tell me something—anything—I didn't already know about our mother. About our past. About me. And maybe if I found her, I could finally have some peace of mind and go on with my life instead of being stuck in this job and in this rut again with Colton.

For the first time since we'd lost Georgia, I sensed something tugging on the other end of the invisible thread that tethered the two of us together. It wasn't a feeling I could explain to Rayanne and Sue Ellen, but it was there just the same. My sister was not dead. Because as soon as I saw that photograph of the two of us, it was as if I heard a familiar voice calling out, as clear as if she'd been standing right next to me.

Come and find me, Savannah. It's time.

CHAPTER 11

Sue Ellen

Friday Night

I'd finally changed into my pajama pants and settled onto the blue paisley-print quilt that graced the twin bed adjacent to Rayanne's identical one, when my phone buzzed with a text from Gabriela.

Celebrity sighting! Guess who I saw today?

Like me, Gabriela was not from New York, and while I had often felt like I immigrated there from another country, she actually had. She'd been admitted into Yale from Mexico via their international scholarship program, had earned an MFA in creative writing, and was now working as an assistant editor at a major printing house in the city, which was amazing, because we could still meet for weekly lunches and play the celebrity-sighting game we invented in college—one of our favorite pastimes when we were broke, living on ramen noodles and wandering around Grand Central Station to people watch.

Though my childhood could not compete with Gabriela's when it came to surmounting obstacles, she was the only other person who knew what it meant to be from a small town—and not the kind of small town that people say is small when they really just mean quaint and ordinary, but the kind of small that makes people strain their eyeballs trying to locate it on Google Maps. Gabriela was also the only person who knew about my history. My real history. Not the one I had filtered for Liam and my colleagues.

Who? I texted back.

> Lucy Liu! Strolling through a Walgreens and buying her TP just like a regular person! Guess what brand she bought.

Charmin? Something tells me generic isn't good enough for someone who can afford an apartment in Manhattan.

> Angel Soft!! They really are just like us. Soooo . . . How goes the sisters' weekend? Your grandmother shoot anyone yet?

No. But I did almost die. Will call later with deets. Always knew this town would kill me. I'm suffocating. Send help!

> Hang in there. And send celebrity sighting ASAP!

Does cast of Duck Dynasty count? If so, I forgot to take his pic. But it was magical.

> Totally counts. BTW Think I've got a lead on a place for you. My old boss is subletting a basement in Midtown. Interested?

Disappointment settled in my gut. Though it was ridiculous, a sliver of my soul still hoped Liam would change his mind and invite me to move back in with him. If I was being honest with myself, it was probably why I was still crashing on Gabriela's couch even though she already had a roommate, and my presence there was becoming a heated topic of debate between the two of them.

Sure! Send me the info.

I dropped my phone, then sank into my mattress and made myself comfortable with Virginia Woolf, while Rayanne checked her voice mail for the umpteenth time in hopes of another pointless update from Graham. For a moment it seemed as if nothing had changed since we were teenagers—my nose in a novel as Rayanne cradled a phone to her ear. With my addiction to books and lack of any apparent sense of fashion, I had never been popular in high school. But while the puberty gods had seen fit to punish me, they had smiled upon Rayanne early and blessed her with a tiny waist, slender legs, and pouty lips. I took more after our father with my dark hair, green eyes, and the grace of a linebacker, but Rayanne was a smaller, nearly identical version of our mother. Her sandy-blonde hair set against tanned skin with sapphire eyes and an elfin nose had been a dog whistle for every boy within a twenty-mile radius. Of course, they couldn't really date her, because our grandmother had tended to make herself an unwelcome third party in any relationship Rayanne attempted.

She set down her cell and plugged it in to charge, then reached beside the bed and rummaged around in her purse before producing an orange bottle. After popping a tiny white pill onto her tongue, she fell back into her pillow. Her eyes were closed, and her chest heaved unsteadily with every rise and fall. A swath of pink crawled up her neck as she let out shaky breaths. For the first time, I noticed her hands were shaking, too.

"Everything . . . OK?" I asked cautiously.

She didn't answer but forced her eyes open and seemed to have fixated on a point in the wallpaper.

"Are you having a panic attack?"

"No," she snapped. "It's just a little anxiety. It'll pass. Just . . . give me a minute," she said, clutching her stomach. Rayanne had always been a little high strung, and I assumed that perhaps all that worrying and the need to take care of everyone else had followed her into adulthood. But I didn't know if this was something that happened often or if she took medication for it. That would be hard to gauge from her Instagram feed. Maybe it explained the tense conversation I'd unwillingly witnessed between her and Graham.

Testing the waters, I made an effort to take her mind off whatever was bothering her, which I supposed was our near-death experience. "How are Charlotte and Tucker?"

Wiping away tiny sweat beads from her forehead, she chuckled, almost maniacally, as I looked on, a bit bewildered. "So you're interested in my kids now?"

As I reflected on my behavior from earlier tonight, my voice gave way to a softer tone. "I'm sorry if I came off hostile before. Of course I care about the kids."

"Yeah, well. It's fine. That makes two of us. I can't believe we did that." She propped herself against a stack of floral-shammed pillows and stared at her screen as if it might suddenly ring again.

I proceeded cautiously. "So everything's fine at home?"

"Graham's there loading them up on sugar and TV, so I'm pretty sure they're happy I'm gone."

I detected a hint of annoyance in her tone. "Come on. That's not true. I'm sure they miss you."

Sitting up a little straighter and clutching a pillow to her chest, she said, "I'm a terrible person. I mean, it's not like I *want* things to be difficult for them when I'm not there. It's just nice to feel needed every now and then, like the sacrifices I made for our family actually matter. That they mean something, you know?"

"I get it," I said, searching for the right words. "Everyone needs to feel validated every now and then. I'd be pissed if someone walked into my job and managed it effortlessly. Especially since most days I feel like I'm drowning in all the things I don't know."

Rayanne looked up at me, appearing almost surprised. It was rare for me to admit a weakness—to her, anyway. "Really? But you always seem so sure of yourself. So . . . fearless."

This time, it was me who laughed. I wasn't ready to divulge the fact that I was camping out on my best friend's couch, but I could at least try to meet her halfway. "Seriously? I'm terrified every day that someone will find out I don't know nearly as much as I should, especially one of these pretentious kids who come to me from private boarding schools and grew up with au pairs and weekend homes. But I feel like if I just pretend to be a professor long enough, then one day"—I pulled back my shoulders and jutted out my chin—"I'll feel like I deserve the title." This was entirely true. Though I'd grown accustomed to life outside Muscadine, sometimes it still didn't feel real. There were moments when I worried that maybe I'd been admitted to Yale only to meet a quota for underprivileged students, or that maybe I got the job at NYU because of Liam's connections. My first week teaching last fall, I read a book about impostor syndrome and promptly diagnosed myself with it. But before long, I began to wonder if I was one of the few who truly didn't have the skills to back up my reputation. Did that make me an impostor to impostor syndrome? The daily mental pep talks I had to give myself were exhausting.

Rayanne's breathing evened out, and her face relaxed into a genuine smile, the first I'd seen from her since coming on this godforsaken trip. I took it as a sign that maybe the next couple of days held some potential for repairing things between us, or at least making the drive to the airport less awkward.

"So what do you think of Savannah's theory?" I asked. "Do you think this woman will have any information, if she's even willing to talk to us?"

"I don't know." She heaved a sigh, drawing a hand to the back of her neck. "But maybe if we find her, it will finally give her some closure. I worry about her."

"Me too," I said, surprised to learn I wasn't lying. "So? What next?"

"As much as I hate to say this, I think we have to ask Meemaw. She's our best bet for getting any information about that day or Mama's high school years."

I pursed my lips. Our grandmother had a steel-trap mind. Our birthdays and Social Security numbers, along with every indiscretion we had ever committed, were tucked safely away in that stubborn head of hers, often spilling out unprovoked at the most inconvenient times. And she hated our father. As children, anytime we asked her questions about our mother, Meemaw would either conduct a monologue on the many faults of Jack Guidry or get misty eyed and excuse herself to take a nap. "I think I need to rest my bones for a minute or two, and then we'll talk," she'd say as she shuffled down the hall, into her room, and closed the door. But we never did, and I always felt a pang of guilt for dredging up the past when it hurt her so much to relive it.

CHAPTER 12

Rayanne

Saturday Morning

Meemaw cooked a breakfast that could have easily fed my church's entire youth ministry—biscuits and gravy, bacon, scrambled eggs, and a large pot of grits topped off with way more butter than I allowed myself in a day, much less a single meal. By the time Sue Ellen and I stumbled, zombielike, into the kitchen, an annoyingly chipper Savannah was already at the table piling food onto her plate, thickly laying on the charm with Meemaw. Apparently sleeping on the couch had agreed with her.

"This looks amazing," she said. "Any plans for today?" Her voice was tinged with a strange, sweet lilt that made me do a double take in her direction.

Meemaw licked a finger and continued thumbing through the morning's copy of the *Thrifty Penny*. "Well, there's a couple of estate sales down on Floyd Street if anyone would like to come with me today." I winced, realizing that today was Saturday, and in Meemaw's world that meant estate sales. Children are supposed to love Saturdays, but we hated them because we knew she would be hauling more junk into the house before we'd even wiped the sleep from our eyes.

Of course there were the dreaded few occasions I'd been forced to tag along as punishment. Because being alone with a boy was explicitly forbidden, if any of us broke this holy commandment, we found ourselves grounded for an unspecified length of time. I should note here that being grounded by Meemaw was different from the boring weeks at home our friends experienced. It meant that we were never left to our own devices, not even on Saturday mornings, when she made her rounds all over town. It was a special kind of torture. Meemaw had towed me all over Muscadine and forced me to lug portraits and drapes and broken appliances into the back of the old Buick on account of her back pain, which tended to show up only when something heavy needed lifting.

"Dottie Burnfield passed a few weeks ago," Meemaw continued, with a regretful shake of her head, "and her children are selling everything from the china to the bedsheets. Don't think they're keeping anything at all from the woman. Just a shame, I tell you, a damn shame. I hope to heaven that you all won't do that to me when I go, that you'll at least keep something to remember me by. I only save all this for the three of you." She took an agitated sip of her coffee, then waved a wrinkled hand toward the boxes that sat teetering atop one another along the wall.

"Don't worry. I don't think we're gonna have any trouble remembering you." Savannah flashed me a wry smile, secret code for something that only the three of us could ever truly understand about our grandmother's sense of logic. Over the years, Meemaw had come to rationalize her hoarding by claiming that "all of this" was for us. Little did she know, the idea of having to sort through a mountain of useless crap after her death crippled me with anxiety. It also made me question whether our grandmother had ever truly known me. If she had, she would know that bequeathing her collection of stuffed armadillos to my children would not bring me peace, though I supposed it would certainly remind me of her. But at what expense?! No, it would all be going to the Salvation Army, and that was that. I hadn't the time or slightest interest in trying to keep any of the mess. Some things were not meant to be salvaged.

"Well, I suppose I'll just have to ask Sam to bring along his truck. There's no reason to let perfectly good furniture go to a landfill. The only thing around here that came in its original packaging is me, and I mean to keep it that way." She now pointed a finger at Sue Ellen, who had walked straight past the artery-clogging spread and plucked an apple from the fruit basket on the counter. "You know, for as much as you blabber on about global warming, I'll have you know I'm doing my part to save the earth. Waste not, want not, I always say."

Sue Ellen rolled her eyes, as she always did when our grandmother resurrected this tired argument. "You are not going to save the ice caps by filling this house from floor to ceiling with everyone else's junk. The idea is for people to buy less in the first place." She said this as if it were something so painfully obvious it didn't bear repeating, then stared intently down at the screen of her cell.

"And I'm sure that phone you're so attached to isn't wasting any natural resources at all. You millennials or whatever the hell they call your generation"—she inserted air quotes around the word *millennials*—"have to buy a new one of those things every four weeks, and what do you think that does to the earth, huh? You think there's a farm somewhere that just regrows precious metals? Not to mention all the cancer those things cause," she added under her breath. I could tell by the way her neck muscles had tensed that Meemaw was only just getting started. "No, these days, they don't make things that last. Hell, they want 'em to break so you've got to go out and buy another right after the warranty runs out. But my icebox is just as good as it was when your granddaddy brought it home fifty years ago."

Sue Ellen's gaze landed on the appliance in question, zeroing in on a screwdriver jammed into one of the holes where the handle should have been. "Meemaw, that thing is falling apart. And it's yellow." And not the bright sunny shade of yellow that calls to mind images of marigolds or lilies in the spring. If there had ever existed a shade of paint named "Dusty Vomit," it would have accurately represented the exact shade of Meemaw's prized Frigidaire.

"Which just so happens to be my favorite color," she declared proudly, flipping another page in her newspaper without looking up. Though he had died long before any of us came into the world, Charlie Pritchett's legacy had been preserved through Meemaw's colorful stories about him. According to her, their marriage had been a whirlwind affair, love at first sight, followed by nearly two decades of petulant arguments, each one followed by him making some sort of grand gesture as penance. I assumed the fridge was one of his many offerings and glared at Sue Ellen to drop the subject.

"Speaking of junk," Meemaw said, then licked a finger to turn another page, "I heard quite the ruckus last night." She shot me a probing glance from the corner of one eye. "Did you find your buried treasure?"

"We did." I coughed into my elbow at the memory of us nearly getting shot and wondered how much she knew.

Sue Ellen bristled and straightened herself against the counter where she leaned.

"Though I did most of the work," I pointed out.

"Well"—she stared me down from behind her newspaper, waiting—"what was in it? Hopefully not any food. I had to convince Sue Ellen that Moon Pies wouldn't keep, and she cried a river when I took them out."

Sue Ellen pressed her eyelids shut and grimaced.

"Just . . . junk," I said. "Movie stubs, bracelets, a few pictures—that kind of thing."

Savannah took a seat at the table, clutching the framed photo of Mama and her friends to her chest. "Meemaw, we were looking at some of the pictures last night, and we were wondering . . . Do you know who this is?" she asked, carefully sliding the photo of the movie night onto the table in front of her, then tapping her finger underneath the mystery girl.

Squinting behind her bifocals, Meemaw scrutinized the image until a spark of recognition flickered in her eyes. Her face went slack, and I could tell she'd gone somewhere else.

Gingerly, she lifted the frame. "That's Celia Peters," she said. "Your mother's friend. Not the most popular girl in their class, that's for sure. Not that I thought there was anything wrong with her," she added. Her lips settled into a joyless smile as she traced a finger over Mama's face. "She wasn't like my Beverly." At the mention of our mother's name, her eyes searched the room before glassing over and fixating on the weathered frames on the wall in front of us.

"What else can you remember about her?" I asked gently. "About Celia, I mean. How did she come to be friends with Mama?"

"Well, now, that's an easy one. I was the one who suggested it," she said proudly before knitting her eyebrows together. "A lot of good it did her, though, since she still ended up with Jack." She spat out our father's name as if it were bitter coffee, and I knew that I was going to have to redirect her attention to the matter at hand instead of letting her fall into the endless pit of regret that is Jack Guidry. "I'll never understand how that man managed to weasel his way into her life and leech on to her like a fat tick," she pressed on, seeming to have completely forgotten the question. "Sucked the life right out of my child."

She railed on as if the three of us had evaporated from sight and began listing off the many ways in which our disappointing father had ruined her life—and those of everyone else who'd ever had the misfortune of meeting him. "I know the Lord isn't supposed to make mistakes, but that man is as close as it gets." After a while, she appeared to suddenly become aware that the person she was denigrating happened to share a significant amount of DNA with the three of us, and she tried to make us feel better about this unfortunate fact. "Oh well, I know you girls aren't like him at all, though. Not my girls. Luckily, the apple fell far away from that rotten tree."

There was no telling how long this could go on. I took a breath of fortitude and tried gently to bring her attention back to the matter at hand. "But what do you remember about Celia? Can you tell us anything about her?" I pressed.

At this she went quiet and drew a fist to her chin.

"That was so long ago. I just remember she was . . . different." She shrugged. "A little homely, you might say. They were new to the neighborhood. An only child. Her father had died recently, and I suggested that your mama befriend her, help her find her place, you know? To tell you the truth, I was glad she had a friend like Celia. I worried about her being lonely after she had you all."

"So they remained close?" I asked. "Even after high school?"

Meemaw nodded. "Yes. Celia was there for Beverly after each of you were born. I'm sure she helped change all your diapers at some point or another."

"And what happened to her?" I asked. "Where is she now?"

"I'm not sure. I seem to remember her taking a job somewhere out west, though Bev never really said where. I think she grew tired of being stuck here, still living with her depressed mother while Bev and everyone else had moved on and started their own families." The creases framing her eyes deepened, and she frowned. "Her mother died a few years back, all alone. Don't think Celia even came back for her funeral, so I always suspected they hadn't ended on good terms. Never could put my finger on what it was about that woman, but something wasn't right with the mother."

Savannah couldn't help herself and asked the question I knew she'd been holding back. "Meemaw, did you know that Celia was at the lake that day?" *That day* had only ever meant one day to all of us—the day the first domino in our lives had fallen.

"I didn't know that," Meemaw said, her voice sounding distant and small. A stillness settled over the room, until Meemaw cleared her throat. "But there were so many people there, so it's hard to remember," she said, brushing a tear from her cheek.

Guilt swept over me as I watched her smile crack. I could sense I'd asked too much. "Thanks." I scooped a spoonful of grits into my mouth, melted butter and all, and swallowed it down. If Sue Ellen wasn't going to eat, it meant I needed to at least try to put a dent into the spread before us, or we'd never hear the end of it. Bessie trotted underfoot, scavenging for crumbs and making horrendous slurping sounds that made me cringe. Meemaw offered her a biscuit and patted her head, which led me to wonder if pigs were supposed to eat table scraps. Shuddering, I shook the thought away.

"Thanks for breakfast." I cleared the table and started down the hall to get dressed and phone Graham.

"You know you could look for her journals, though," Meemaw called after me. "I know they're somewhere around here. The thing is, I can't rightly remember where I stored them, so it might take some digging."

I crossed my arms victoriously and cocked an eyebrow at my sisters. "Well, lucky for all of us, I happen to have a knack for that."

CHAPTER 13

MEEMAW

January 1987

A sliver of light spilled through the cracked bedroom door, where Marylynn caught sight of the two girls, Celia sitting statue-like and Beverly all business, a serious crinkle in her brow as she brushed careful strokes in the orange glow of the vanity. The stool swiveled full circle, bringing Celia face-to-face with her reflection. She studied herself as if for the first time, gently pulling back her stringy brown hair to finger her new complexion.

"Just remember: blush is your friend." Smirking, Beverly extended a compact case and closed Celia's fingers around it. "Here. Keep it."

"Thanks. But I don't think I can do it on my own," she said, pushing it away. "How'd you learn to do all of . . . this?" she asked, still locked on her own image, turning her head every which way like she was trying to figure out a stranger.

"Christine." Beverly sighed, running a brush through her hair. "When she was still speaking to me. Before my mother went postal and ruined my social life. I mean . . . no offense," she apologized. "I like being with you, too. It's just . . . she has a way of making my life a living hell."

Marylynn reflected on this from her place in the hallway, remembering the way Beverly had yelled at her after Christine's party, told her she'd never speak to her again. Despite the January cold, her garden was in full bloom this season, because the house had been even colder. At least her herbs didn't shout back at her when she talked to them calmly, and they didn't mind when she trimmed them down occasionally.

"Now Christine is obsessed with Tim Clearhaven. They got together the night my mother dragged me out of her house like a child," she said, emphasizing the last word. "And now they sit around talking about how my crazy mother ruined her party and got everyone grounded. It's all over school."

Marylynn was not surprised and had to fight back the urge to shout that she had been right about that girl, that Beverly should count herself lucky to have discovered the truth before she wasted any more time on such a person.

"At least your mother cares where you are," Celia said softly, tearing her eyes away from the mirror.

Smart girl. Marylynn was liking her more by the minute. It had been a pleasant surprise the day Beverly had taken her advice and brought Celia home after school three weeks ago. Beverly never brought anyone into their home. From what she could tell, unlike the mile-high hair club, Celia didn't seem to harbor any interest in boys or drinking and usually showed up on her ten-speed without a stitch of makeup. In the beginning, Marylynn had wondered what it was that made Bev want to reach out to someone so far outside her social circle; eventually she'd decided that it must have been all those years of dragging her to church by her ears. In a way, she was proud that she had helped bring this friendship about.

"Please. You are so lucky." Beverly plopped down on the bed. The springs squeaked under the weight of her, jolting Marylynn back a step.

"Do you know what I would give to have what you have? Your mother lets you do whatever you want. You're practically emancipated."

"Yeah. Well . . . my mother isn't . . . she's not like other moms."

"Neither is mine. Has yours ever spied on you, read your journals, had other people in town report on your whereabouts, that kind of thing? I mean, we're talking full-on stalker stuff." She animated the point with her arms, punctuating each word. "Last week she showed up to the theater and parked herself behind me and Tom Harris and coughed whenever he tried to put his arm around me. This is my life now. She's suffocating me!"

Celia lifted an eyebrow. "To be fair, you can do so much better than Tom Harris."

Exactly! The boy had a tattoo. And not just any tattoo but one of a snake that wrapped clear around his scrawny biceps. Marylynn could tell those arms were not working arms. They would never be able to do the heavy lifting required of a husband to support a family; they were nothing like Charlie's. It had been a blessing that he hadn't asked her out again, and one day Bev would see it.

"She's certifiable." Beverly pressed a bright-red tube to her lips before smacking them together and approving of herself in the mirror. "First thing I'm gonna do after graduation is get as far away from here as possible."

The words landed like a stone in Marylynn's gut, and she gave a little gasp before quickly reining herself back in so as not to be discovered. Collecting herself, she straightened her spine and rapped on the open bedroom door, startling the girls.

"Is Celia staying for dinner?" she managed to get out.

"If that's all right with you, Mrs. Pritchett. I'd love to."

"Of course," Marylynn replied brightly. "But maybe you should just call to let your mother know. You've been spending so much time here. Not that I mind, dear." And she didn't. In fact, Celia's presence created a buffer between her and her hostile daughter. None of her children's friends had ever wanted to set foot inside her home, and it was nice to have someone appreciate her dinners or comment on the originality of her finds. But she often wondered what went on in the Peterses' home and why it seemed Celia always wanted to be here instead of there. Perhaps Celia's family didn't own a TV, because she sat glued in front of Marylynn's for hours, fascinated by *Growing Pains* and the heartwarming adventures of the Seaver family. When evening came, she never seemed especially thrilled to head out on her bike, and Marylynn hoped everything was all right at home.

"Oh, that's OK." Celia straightened and offered a nervous smile. "I know she'd be all right with it. Can I help you with anything in the kitchen, Mrs. Pritchett?"

"Oh no, honey. It's all ready. You girls just come on out when you're done here." Marylynn lingered in the doorway, trying not to appear nosy. "Are you sure you shouldn't call her?"

Beverly's shoulders went slack, and she rolled her eyes. "Mama, she doesn't have to call over every little thing. Her mother isn't a jailer."

Stung by the barb, Marylynn pulled the door shut and shuffled toward the dining room, on her way trailing a finger over the oak credenza, a find that she had stumbled upon months ago on the side of the road, discarded like trash when all it needed was a good sanding and a little polish. Stroking the intricate, hand-carved maple-leaf patterns on its drawers, she couldn't shake the thought of Celia's mother, sitting at home waiting for a child. It was a feeling Marylynn knew all too well. She tugged the drawer open and heaved out the phone book. Her finger traced the names as she scoured the list for Peters until, eventually, it landed on one that seemed promising. She reached for the telephone and dialed the numbers before the line rang. When it continued to ring with no signs of a message machine, she wondered whether she should just hang up. But as she moved to place the receiver back on its base, a sleepy voice emerged on the other end.

"Hello?"

"Hello. Mrs. Peters?" She cleared her throat and brightened her tone. "This is Marylynn Pritchett. Beverly's mother," she clarified. Though she lived just down the street, the two women had yet to meet, and Celia always had some flimsy excuse at the ready for why this was. "I just wanted to call and see if it's all right that Celia stays for dinner tonight. We'd love to have her."

"Celia? Yes, that's fine, honey. Stay as long as you want."

"No. I think you misunderstood me. I'm not Celia. I'm Beverly's mother," she said a little louder.

"I don't understand. Is Celia in some kind of trouble?" The voice carried a note of annoyance now.

"Oh no. No trouble at all. She's just as delightful as can be. We'd just like her to stay for dinner is all."

Silence hung between them so long that Marylynn shifted her weight back and forth between her feet, eyes lifted to the ceiling as she prayed for some sort of response. She'd always prided herself on having a sixth sense about people, and something was not right about this woman.

"Tell her to lock the door when she comes home." A click followed by a busy signal sounded in her ear.

Poor Celia. To have a mother like that, a woman who couldn't be bothered to ask after her own child. It was no wonder she'd rather stay here. Marylynn had tried to stay out of her daughter's affairs since the debacle at the Duprees', but perhaps she should look into Mrs. Peters and see what this woman was about. Then again, she'd finally begun to recognize that spark in Beverly's eye whenever Celia was around. It reminded her of the sensitive child she used to be when Charlie was still alive.

Maybe just this once she would let sleeping dogs lie.

CHAPTER 14

SAVANNAH

Saturday Morning

After breakfast my phone buzzed with a call from the restaurant. Hoping it was a mistake, I declined it and finished off the biscuits and milk gravy that Meemaw had made for us. With matted hair, Sue Ellen dragged herself into the kitchen and plucked an apple from the fruit basket on the counter.

"You're not going to survive under this roof on cucumbers and qween-wah." Meemaw tutted without even turning around as she fished out a coffee mug from the cupboard. "If I can't pronounce it, I can promise you that I will not be making it."

The table vibrated as my phone danced across it once more. Gritting my teeth, I answered and heard Eddie's voice grating in my ear.

"I need you to come in," he said, not bothering with formalities.

"I can't today." I cupped a hand over my mouth to mute the sound. "Lauren's covering my lunch shift. We marked it on the schedule."

"Lauren called in sick this morning, which means that either you find someone else to cover it, or I'll see you at eleven." After three years of working for Eddie, one might come to expect a little understanding, but the gruffness in his voice did not encourage me to push him any further.

"I'll figure something out," I said, though I knew I wouldn't. No one was going to give up a Saturday afternoon in the summer at the last minute. My fingers busily texted everyone I could think of without any luck. I knew they were all pretending not to notice my messages, because it was exactly what I would have done. Finally I admitted defeat.

"I have to bail for a few hours," I said between hurried bites before gulping down the rest of my orange juice.

"Excuse me?" Sue Ellen stopped midchew, bits of apple rolling around inside her mouth. "I'm only here because you begged me to come, and now you're leaving?"

"I can't help it. It's my job. And if I want to keep it, I have to go in for a bit. Don't worry. We can meet up for a late lunch with Meemaw."

"Maybe this is a good time to reflect on some other possibilities when it comes to your career?" Sue Ellen took another bite from where she stood leaning against the yellowed Formica counter. "If you had something a little more stable, you could have more vacation time, maybe a decent health care plan." If the same words had come from anyone else's mouth, I would have considered them, might have even pulled out a notebook and made a chart of pros and cons or written my goals in big curly letters at the top of the page. But the way Sue Ellen discussed my life made it seem less like a kind gesture and more like I was a problem we must all put our heads together to solve, like litter on the street or potholes in the road. *What will we ever do about Savannah?*

"No, thank you. I happen to like my job." It was a lie. Working for Eddie was the equivalent of shoveling manure, and my new favorite pastime had become daydreaming about quitting in a very public way, really sticking it to him for the way he had passed over making me an assistant manager so that he could hire outside help—a man-child named Paul who possessed no relevant credentials and lingered uncomfortably close behind me whenever I entered my orders at the kiosk. Fed up with the way he seemed to find every opportunity to brush against me, I'd once "accidentally" jerked back my shoulders, sending him fly-ing into a tray of fried shrimp. Ever since then, Paul and I had not exactly been simpatico. In my mind's eye, after my award-winning per-formance telling Eddie to shove it, I would go on to open a competing restaurant right next door, something trendy and modern—as modern as one could manage in a place whose downtown storefront included one of the last Kmarts still in existence. I would call it "Savannah's Staples" or "Country Comfort." Maybe "Beverly's Place."

~

The kitchen bustled with the clamor of aprons swishing past one another and the clinking of steaming plates. Behind a tower of glasses, I ran a finger across the chalkboard calendar, searching for my name. When it landed on the following Friday night, I read the name "Tessa Thompson" where my name should have been. Barreling through the double doors that led to the tables, I scanned the room for Eddie, whom I quickly spotted standing with Tessa herself at the hostess stand. She couldn't be more than twenty and had been hired only six weeks ago. Completely enthralled with whatever he was saying, her big doe eyes framed by thick, dark brows locked onto his as she twirled a finger around a strand of box-dyed blonde hair.

Ignoring her, I dug into him. "Why did you give my weekend night to the hostess?"

"As of tomorrow, she's no longer a hostess. Waitstaff in training," Eddie said, running a hand over his bald, tattooed head and throwing an adoring smile back at Tessa.

"And who's going to be training her?" I crossed my arms.

"Funny you should ask. She'll be shadowing you starting Monday."

I strained forward, putting a hand to my temple. "So let me get this straight. I'm training my replacement so she can steal my Friday-night shift? That's my best night, Eddie. I have regulars. People expect me to be here. Besides, you can't just throw her into deep water on her first night alone. She needs more experience."

"Savannah, I don't make the schedule. If you have a problem with it, you know who to talk to." He thumbed toward Paul, who was currently out of his depth, red faced and sweaty, shouting orders at the salad-line staff. Eyes forward, I steeled myself for a heated conversation and marched across the floor.

"Paul, I need Friday nights. I can't pay my bills on lunch shifts," I said, leaning against the sneeze guard of the salad station.

"Everyone needs weekend shifts, Savannah. I can't give you special treatment just because you've been here the longest." He said the last word as if it were something to be ashamed of as he shuffled bowls around and squinted to read the little paper receipts that were nestled atop each one. "This is wrong, Sal! I asked for a house salad, not a Cobb!"

Idiot. "We don't have a house salad." I sighed. "Customers just assume it's the Cobb because it's the best. Look, my liquor sales are stronger than anyone else's, and clearly I know this place backward and forward. If you'd just let me help out with the schedule, I could make your job a little easier. I have a degree in this sort of thing and loads of ideas to increase business that—"

"I don't care if you have a degree in rocket science. You were hired to wait tables. Besides, I can't keep accommodating your requests. I seem to remember someone asking off for a trip last weekend, too, and now you suddenly *need* weekend shifts again?" He flashed me a what-are-you-gonna-do-about-it look, and I balled my fingers into fists to keep myself from slapping it off his face. "Oh, and we don't have a busser today, so you'll have to clean your own tables." He pulled a wet rag from his shoulder and tossed it to me, then hoisted a tray atop his shoulder. "By the way, table thirty-two is yours," he said, jerking his head in the general direction of a couple of cheapskates in the corner who I knew from past experience would not be leaving a tip.

Biting my lower lip, I ambled over to greet a fiftysomething gentleman wearing a button-up plaid shirt tucked into a pair of crisp blue jeans. The blonde woman seated across from him was dressed to the nines, sporting a fresh set of nails and a Marc Jacobs handbag resting beside her on the seat cushion. Pulling a pencil from my ponytail, I opened my receipt book and tried to sound friendly. "Welcome to the Salty Pot. What can I get for you today?"

"Not quite ready yet." He sniffed from behind his menu, which he was studying with a bushy, furrowed brow and the focused intensity of someone deciding which car to buy. "We'll start with two waters and the free rolls." He said the word *free* slowly to drive home the point, a gesture I took to mean that I should fill the basket to the brim.

Tapping my pen, I flashed him a plastic smile and headed for the kitchen. I wondered what my sisters were doing right now. Sue Ellen had flown more than a thousand miles to be here, and Rayanne had been so nervous to leave the kids, yet here I was at the mercy of two middle-aged penny-pinchers who were going to determine my income today.

When the lunch crowd had thinned and all the other tables had left, table thirty-two was still taking their sweet time picking over the remnants of a slice of pecan pie. In a hurry to leave, I made one last attempt to speed things along. "Can I get you anything else? A to-go drink for the road, maybe?" I smiled warmly, trying to communicate the words *please just leave* without actually saying them.

"No. That'll be all." He tapped the closed black receipt book that I had placed conspicuously near his drink and moved to exit the booth. When they were out of sight, I flipped it open and zeroed in on the tip line, which was glaringly blank.

Normally I would have cursed, called him some clever, derogatory name, and commiserated with the other servers. But not today.

Something snapped inside me, so loudly I could almost hear it. Before I knew what was happening, my feet had carried the rest of me into the parking lot, and I found myself face-to-face with Mr. and Mrs. Free Rolls.

"Hey!" I called out to him as he waddled to his truck, no doubt feeling the effects of all the food I had so graciously served him free of charge. "Excuse me, Mr."—I looked down at the receipt and squinted to find his last name—"Mr. Williams. I believe you forgot my tip." I waved the receipt book and a pen over my head in case he hadn't heard me. But I was sure he had. I yelled it loud enough to draw attention of other soon-to-be customers who were exiting their vehicles.

He stopped cold and turned to face me. His cheeks had flushed the color of turnips, but his eyes were hard. "Well, now, that's because I didn't leave one."

"Were you unhappy with your service?" I asked. "If so, please enlighten me so that I may uncover the secret to serving your fish-and-chips in the most professional way possible."

By now Eddie was in the parking lot between us, calmly explaining to Mr. Williams that he would comp his next meal and that he would deal with me directly.

"Is this how you treat your customers?" Mr. Williams asked him. "Let your staff chase them out and harass them? The customer is always right." He jabbed a finger at me, punctuating each word.

"I got news for you, buddy." I leaned forward and pointed to his name on the receipt. "I've got your name. And now"—I dug into my apron and produced my cell phone, then snapped his photo—"I've got your picture, too."

"Savannah, get inside!" Eddie shouted, but I couldn't hear him over the rush of adrenaline pumping in my ears. By now I was drunk on power.

"Now anytime you go out to eat, every server from here to Alabama is gonna have your name and your picture, and you'll have to wonder from now until Judgment Day if one of them licked your fork. So"—I leaned back on my heels and crossed my arms, satisfied with my quick thinking—"eat slowly. How's that for a tip?"

It was only after Eddie had escorted the man to his truck, showering him with apologies, that my head stopped spinning. All at once, I was painfully aware of what had happened here. Bracing myself for what I knew was coming, I tried to think of something, anything, that would absolve me but came up empty.

"You're fired," Eddie said, brushing past me.

It was not the way I had planned to quit.

CHAPTER 15

Sue Ellen

Saturday Morning

Savannah's old bedroom closet was filled from top to bottom like a precarious Jenga tower. Every piece of misshapen pottery, every scrap of abstract artwork, anything our hands had touched was jumbled together in a sea of randomness. Mason jars filled with buttons, marbles, and loose change had been crammed together in shoeboxes, while Tupperware bins filled with various holiday decor and incomplete sewing projects balanced atop one another in no apparent order. Carefully, I pried out a box from the shelf above me, trying to ignore the falling debris.

Rayanne tapped the screen of her cell. "Still nothing on Celia. Zero social media presence. What kind of person doesn't at least have a Facebook account?"

"Meemaw," I replied helpfully. As shameful as it was to admit it, I was immensely grateful that our grandmother harbored no interest in social media, because if she had, Facebook and the world at large would have been ill prepared to handle her musings on current affairs.

Drawing her eyebrows together, Rayanne fired off another phrase into the search engine. "Maybe she got married and changed her last name."

"The patriarchy strikes again," I said, heaving a bright-green bin onto the mattress. I smoothed away a layer of dust from the lid. Inside sat four large volumes wedged on their sides, surrounded by a collection of photo albums and a handmade scrapbook bound in cracked brown leather. Gingerly I pulled it out and opened the cover. "This was hers."

Rayanne inched closer to me as a rush of emotion filled my throat. "I've never seen this. Have you?" she asked, taking it from my hands.

"No." I choked back unexpected tears as she flipped through the heavyweight pages, which had been carefully plastered with stickers and cropped photos of our mother and her friends. Something about seeing her so carefree, so young and beautiful, sent a stab of pain through my chest. I wished this were the version of her I remembered.

"That must be Christine Dupree." Rayanne pointed to a tall red-head standing arm in arm with Mama in front of a row of baby-blue lockers, the same lockers we'd all used at Muscadine High to store away our Trapper Keepers and plaster foldouts from magazines. "Meemaw said she was the ringleader of the crowd she ran with." Her matching eyebrows were expertly plucked in a thin arch and caked in thick blue eye shadow, her glossy lips resting in a *Mona Lisa* smile, as if she knew a secret.

"You think she was jealous of Mama?" I asked.

"What makes you say that?"

"Because, in my experience, that's what these kinds of girls do, isn't it? It's who they are. Popular, beautiful, vindictive." I mimicked a pretty spot-on Valley girl accent as I added, "The *Oh-my-gosh-let's-be-best-friends-until-I-stab-you-in-your-back* kind of girls." Not that any of that was ever my scene, but I did go to the same high school as my sisters, so I knew a self-obsessed airhead when I saw one. "God, can you imagine how she reacted when Mama befriended Celia? It must have set her perm on fire."

Gingerly I fingered the pages, noticing that some of the photos appeared to be sloppily pasted in, as if someone had torn them out and glued them back down. "Celia's not in any of these." I snapped the book shut, then reached for Mama's senior yearbook and began flipping through toward the Ps. I traced my finger down the list of alphabetical last names until it landed on Peters. Eagerly I scanned the row of horizontal images, but when I reached the box intended for Celia, there was no headshot, just an inscription that read, "No photo available."

"Guess she missed picture day. Maybe she was in a club or something."

I scanned the rest of the pages. "Not there, either."

At this Rayanne's face lit up, and she snatched the book from my grasp. "If they were really friends, she would have signed it." She flipped to the last few pages at the back, which had been left blank for autographs, then scrolled down until she stopped and read aloud: "Bev, I wish you and J the best. You'll always be my best friend. Love, Celia."

"That's her." I ran my fingers over the inscription, tracing the loops in the signature.

"A lot of good it does us, though. We still don't know anything about her," she said. "'J' must be referring to our father."

It occurred to me that Mama had never spoken about high school much, at least not to us. Muscadine was a tight-knit town, so she must have kept in touch with at least some of the girls she'd once called friends, though for the first time I realized that I didn't know any of them. She never took us to church, and we could never have afforded any extracurricular activities, so most of the time it was just us, with Daddy off at all hours of the day and night. Until that moment, I'd never understood how lonely she must have been.

"I guess that's that," Rayanne said. "As far as I'm concerned, Celia doesn't want to be found. Maybe it's for the best."

"Maybe not," I said, arching an eyebrow. "Haven't checked obits yet." I hadn't considered that she could be dead, but it would certainly put the matter to rest for Savannah if she were.

"Nice job, Professor." Rayanne smiled, then checked her watch. "If we're going down to the library, we should go now. Savannah's shift will be over soon, and I promised Meemaw we'd take her to lunch."

Reaching for her purse, she jerked her head toward the door and stood to leave.

"One request." I held up a finger, then pressed my palms together, mustering the most genuine smile I could manage. "Can I drive?" Living in the city meant that it had been years since I'd sat behind the wheel of a car, and I missed it. As a bonus, one of the perks of living on the edge of civilization meant that there would be hardly any traffic.

Rayanne glared a warning at me before reluctantly tossing me her car keys. "Fine. But don't you dare put a scratch on it. Graham would kill me."

~

I had made it nearly halfway to the library when I noticed the flashing lights in the rearview mirror. Rayanne shot up, her spine ramrod in the passenger seat.

"Stay calm. Don't make things worse," she was saying in measured tones, her face devoid of all color as she glanced back and forth between me and the police cruiser on my tail. She fumbled around in her purse, presumably searching for the little orange bottle I'd seen last night.

I guided the car to the side of the interstate and rolled down my window. My mouth went dry as I watched a stocky but lean officer make his way toward the car, then stoop slightly to inspect me. His chiseled jawline was interrupted only by the deepest dimples I'd ever seen, and he had dark eyes with just a touch of gold flecks that gleamed against flawless brown skin. He looked so familiar, but it didn't feel like an appropriate time to ask him if we'd met before.

"Hello there, ma'am," he said, his voice softer than I'd expected. *Ma'am?* I waited for Rayanne to answer until it hit me that I was the *ma'am* in question.

"Do you know how fast you were going back there?"

"I'm afraid I don't. I'm sorry, Officer. We're just on our way to the library." As the words left my mouth, I realized it must have sounded as if I were sucking up, and I didn't want him to think I'd offered up this information to get special treatment for being studious.

"You were going ninety in a seventy-five. I'll need to see your license and registration," he said, apparently unmoved by my riveting performance.

"I'm so sorry. I had no idea," I said, digging into my purse. "Here's my license. And it's actually my sister's car." As I passed my license through the window, my mouth continued spouting all kinds of information he hadn't asked for. "I don't remember seeing a sign. Was there a sign somewhere? I don't actually live here. I mean, I used to but not anymore. Do you live here? I mean, of course you live here. Stupid question. I meant, Do you live nearby?" *Why? Because you're planning a visit? Please make it stop!*

With my license in hand, he scrutinized my face, then squinted as his eyes flickered between the two.

"Sue Ellen?" he asked, tilting his head. "Sue Ellen Guidry?"

"Yes, that's me. Is there a problem?" I asked, looking around stupidly, as if he might possibly be referring to a different Sue Ellen Guidry.

"You don't remember me, do you?" he went on, his features softening into a sheepish smile. "I'm Derrick . . . Cunningham." He thumbed to his chest, but I was still at a loss. "Aliyah's little brother."

All at once my memory came to my rescue, and I gasped. "Of course! I remember you." Though we weren't really friends outside of school, Aliyah and I had been in history and chemistry together and had once crammed before senior finals at the Cunninghams' home. I'd been more than a little miffed when she managed to beat me out as valedictorian, but I couldn't deny that she deserved it. I remembered Derrick as the flustered, nerdy kid a couple of grades beneath us, who couldn't seem to manage more than a few syllables in my direction when I was in their home. Though he was standing right in front of me, I couldn't picture Aliyah's baby-faced younger brother holstering a gun, escorting hardened criminals into the back of a cruiser. Though I had to admit he didn't look so little anymore. "How's Aliyah doing?" I asked, doing my best to seem unaffected by the way he was smiling at me with impossibly gorgeous teeth.

"She graduated with a degree in finance and works over in Baton Rouge now. She's married and has two little girls. I get to see them every so often when they come up to Mama's house."

"Well, I'm glad to hear that," I said, suddenly very aware of the fact that we were making small talk while he was holding my license, preparing to write me a ticket. He must have sensed my discomfort, because he pushed away the registration papers I had extended to him, then pursed his lips and squinted an eye at me. "How about we call this a warning if you promise to slow down out there, Danica Patrick." He scribbled something on his notepad, folded the sheet in half, and handed it to me.

"Thanks, Derrick." I felt undeserving of his charity but accepted it graciously. "It's been a while since I've driven, and I think I'm going to need some more practice."

"I'll second that." He cocked his head to the side, and his lips tugged up at the corners. "Did you know your license is expired? Might want to get that renewed." He tapped it with a finger and passed it back through the window.

"Of course. Absolutely. First thing I'm going to do when I get home." My face flushed so hot I was sure he could feel the warmth of it radiating from my skin.

"How long you in town for?"

"Just a few days," I said, grateful for the change in conversation. "Our grandmother is sick, so I'm just making a quick trip to check on her." No way I was going to tell him the real reason—that I'd traveled more than a thousand miles to dig up a piece of junk I'd helped bury when I was eight years old.

"I see." Hands on his hips, he nodded approvingly. "Well, I hope she's better soon. Your grandmother is a"—he paused thoughtfully before blowing out his cheeks and shaking his head—"formidable woman. Hard to imagine anything taking her down."

"Do you know her?" I asked, unable to hide my interest.

"Let's just say she's a . . . bit of a legend in my book." The way he said this made me think it wasn't in a good way. Knowing Meemaw, it probably wasn't. I looked up at him, confused, my eyes searching for more of an explanation, but he didn't offer one. "Hopefully we won't be meeting like this again." He winked at me and made a clicking noise out of the side of his mouth.

"Definitely not," I said a little too enthusiastically. He saluted me with two fingers, and after he left, I let my head fall back on the seat rest.

"Oh my God. Can you believe that?" I cringed, pressing my fingers against my eyelids. "Did I sound nervous?"

"What the hell?" Rayanne shoved me, knocking me out of my celebratory daze.

I shoved her back harder. "Don't push me. It's not like I did it on purpose."

"Driving with an expired license? Get out of my car," Rayanne ordered.

Taken aback, I let out an indignant scoff. I couldn't believe she was being serious.

"Don't you mean Graham's car? It's not like you paid for it or anything," I heard myself say, instantly regretting it.

She narrowed her eyes at me. "How dare you. You know, maybe I don't get a paycheck, but I do a lot for my family, which is more than I can say for you."

"What's that supposed to mean?" I wasn't sure where exactly things had gone wrong between Rayanne and me, but I guessed it was most likely around the time I left for college. I couldn't remember her ever congratulating me on my scholarship or acceptance letter to Yale, and deep down I'd always wondered if she resented me for it, especially after she dropped out of college herself.

"It means that maybe you're secretly jealous of me. That maybe success isn't defined by how many degrees you have or how many five-star restaurants you go to with your uptight boyfriend."

Before, I had simply declined to mention the fact that Liam and I were no longer together, but after that dagger, there was no way I was going to admit the truth to her now. "Well, it's also not defined by how much Prozac you have to take to survive your boring life in white suburbia," I shot back before I could think better of it.

An uncomfortable silence hung between us. In my gut I knew I'd taken things too far with that last quip. I was just about to apologize and take it back, but she cut me off before I had the chance. "Bitch," she mumbled as she unclasped her seat belt.

"I'm sorry. What did you say?" I reared back, feigning surprise, though somewhere inside I had suspected all along that this was what she thought of me. "You may think you're the perfect soccer mom, but you should know your toddler called me the same thing. Maybe you should be more careful with what you say around your children. Your therapist wouldn't approve."

"Tucker didn't say that." She waved the idea away. "He wouldn't."

"He did," I said smugly, putting a finger to my temple. "Except I believe he said *ditch*. Yes, 'Mommy says Sue Ellen is a *ditch*.' Kids say the darndest things, don't they?" With a sardonic smile, I snapped my fingers.

"Fine." She shrugged, rearranging the shock on her face to something more like acceptance. "Maybe I did say it. It's true, though. Savannah agrees with me. Meemaw knows it. Hell, we all know it. You're so stuck on yourself that no one can tell you a damn thing you don't know."

I supposed it wasn't untrue, but it still hurt to hear someone else say it. "Fine then. Maybe I am. But maybe I had to be to get where I am. I'm not ashamed of it. Shout it from the rooftops for all I care. Sue Ellen is a bitch!" I shouted so loudly that Rayanne stared at me with her mouth agape. It took me a moment to realize she wasn't staring at me anymore.

Derrick tapped the partially open window, jolting me out of my performance. "Sue Ellen?"

"Yes?" I cleared my throat, which now felt coated in sand, and rolled the window down the rest of the way, casually. Slowly. So painfully slowly.

After choking out a noise that sounded like a cough, he said, "Just wanted to tell you ladies to be careful. There were reports last night of suspicious activity in the area—some trespassing and strange folks hanging around. Nothing too worrisome. But you should keep an eye out just to be safe."

Somehow I managed a nod and something that resembled a thank-you.

Ambling back to the cruiser, he flashed me a cryptic grin over his shoulder. I sank down behind the steering wheel and waited for him to disappear so that I could do the same.

As soon as he was out of sight, Rayanne gasped and shoved me again. "He knows! About last night. He knows what we did!"

"That's ridiculous. He doesn't know anything. He was just being nice."

Reaching over me, she snatched the paper he had given me and unfolded it in a hurry. As her eyes trailed over the words, she groaned and made a face. "I can't believe this. He likes you."

"That's ridiculous." I tried to dismiss her but felt my cheeks pull my lips into a slow smile.

With a deadpan stare, she tossed the scrap of paper into my lap. "Unless he gives out his phone number to everyone he pulls over, he totally likes you."

CHAPTER 16

Rayanne

Saturday Morning

Doing my best to ignore Sue Ellen, I guided the car into the weather-beaten parking lot of the library—a single-story ranch-style building that gave off a distinct *Brady Bunch* vibe. Like most government establishments in Muscadine, it hadn't seen the likes of an update since the seventies, which didn't make me hopeful that we would find anything helpful there. As we entered the main doors, the earthy smell of books decaying on dusty shelves called a picture of our mother into my thoughts that stopped my feet. In the half memory, she was sitting in an overstuffed chair with Georgia and Savannah on her lap while Sue Ellen and I sat on the alphabet rug centered in front of a puppet show theater. The twins were tossing back their heads in laughter, their movements mirror images of one another as the frog prince danced across the tiny wooden stage.

A woman with silver hair and a thick Arcadian accent greeted us at the circular desk, and I shook the memory away. "Can I help you ladies with anything?"

"Yes, we're looking for obituaries," Sue Ellen said, cutting me off before I could even open my mouth. "Do you know if the library subscribes to any online databases of newspapers?"

Her eyes crinkled at the corners as she scrutinized us from behind her thick-rimmed glasses. "Wouldn't be much of a library if we didn't." Giving us a thorough once-over, she lifted her chin and said, "You're Marylynn's granddaughters, aren't you?"

"How did you know?" I asked, trying to place her among Meemaw's friends, of which I was certain there weren't many.

"Look just like her," she said, flatly. "She's in my Bible study group. Talks about you all the time." Ignoring Sue Ellen, she lowered her glasses in my direction. "Says how much she misses those grandbabies."

I cringed at the realization that Meemaw had probably made me out to be the villain whenever she explained to her friends why her great-grandchildren never came to visit. "I'm aware," I answered through a tight smile.

She waved for us to follow her, and we obeyed, trailing behind her to the back of the building and into a tiny room lined with filing cabinets that nearly reached the ceiling. "This here's our genealogical section. It's nothing fancy, but you should be able to find whoever it is you're looking for." Pursing her lips, she gave me another dubious once-over before adding, "If they're dead. You ladies holler if you need anything."

After she shuffled back to her desk, the two of us sidled up next to each other in front of an ancient-looking HP screen and modem. Brushing against her arm, I flashed Sue Ellen a side-eye to let her know I hadn't forgotten about the petulant way she'd behaved in the car, and the unfair—if not somewhat accurate—way she had described me.

"Well, this does not look promising," she said, surveying the beige keyboard and stretching her fingers over it. But after just a few keystrokes, she was able to pull up a list of obituaries for four women with the name Celia Peters. She shook her head as she scrolled. "None of these women match her approximate age. And I don't recognize her in any of the photos." She sighed, running a hand through her dark curls. I could tell she was about to say something I wouldn't agree with. "Don't you think something's . . . wrong with her? I mean, why is she obsessed with knowing every morbid detail?"

"She's just"—I cast my eyes on the ceiling as if the right word might be written up there—"incomplete. I mean, maybe it's harder for you to remember, but seeing the two of them together was like . . . magic. Even when they weren't talking to each other, you could tell they were passing secrets. To have it ripped away—well, I don't blame her for wanting to have that back." My voice caught on the last word. As a child, I assumed that my little sisters would always be there to pester me. Until the day I saw Mama break into sobs as she told the rest of us that Georgia was lost. *Lost?* The word didn't feel right. I thought of one Christmas when I'd gotten a Polly Pocket that had inexplicably disappeared the next day, though I eventually discovered she'd become an unwitting victim of the twins' mud pies. When I finally found it, I washed away the dirt and restored every piece of plastic clothing that had been buried alongside her. But what did it mean when a person was lost? Would I be able to fix Georgia when we found her? If we found her.

Shaking her head, Sue Ellen let out a resigned sigh. "Yeah, I guess so. Hey, wait a minute." Squinting at the screen, she dragged the mouse over a headline and enlarged the article, then read the words aloud.

Celia Peters passed away on November 21, 2019. A dedicated wife and mother, Celia was a light to all who knew her and leaves behind a legacy of kindness to everyone who had the privilege of meeting her. She leaves behind a daughter, Evangeline Wright, and two granddaughters, Cora and Matilda Wright. Services will be held

on November 25 at the First Baptist Church of
Midland, Texas.

Skipping over the text, my gaze landed on the accompanying
photo. The black-and-white image of her face left no mistake, and I
recognized her instantly. Celia was older, with short brown hair and
sweeping bangs. A few fine lines fanned out at the corners of her eyes.
In the photo, she clutched two little girls with matching dark ringlets
and chubby cheeks, one on each knee. And though she was smiling, I
wasn't entirely convinced she was happy. There was a weariness behind
her eyes. My chest sagged, heavy with the realization that she had been
young when she died, only around fifty years old.

"That's sad," Sue Ellen said, her shoulders sinking. "But I guess
that settles it."

She printed the article, and we listened to the hiccup of the machine
as it spat out a copy.

"I guess so." I hadn't ever believed that finding Celia would lead to
finding Georgia, but the news still pricked at my heart, and the only
thing I could hold in my mind was Savannah's face.

This was going to crush her.

~

When we returned from the library, we rolled up to find Sam Beaufort
single-handedly attempting to unload a pink, tufted love seat from the
bed of his truck while Meemaw supervised, offering the occasional word
of encouragement. "Easy now. You'll dirty the fabric. That's it! Hold it.
I said hold it! Now bring it down nice and slow."

With his white beard and unkempt mustache, Sam resembled a
much older version of Kenny Rogers, albeit a skinnier one with a lot less
hair. Sweat trickled down the sides of his face as he struggled to lower
one end of the faded furniture onto the ground. Once he'd managed

that much, he ambled back into the bed of the truck and pushed from the other end until the whole thing landed in the dirt with a heavy thud.

Meemaw rushed over to inspect the damage and drew a hand to her lips. "Well, now you've ruined it!" she cried. "I'm sure I heard a crack."

Setting himself down on the open tailgate, Sam tucked his thumbs beneath the straps of his overalls and struggled to catch his breath. "That's the least of your concerns right now," he said, wiping his glistening forehead with the back of a sunspotted arm. "The real question is how we're gonna get it through there." With a shaky finger, he pointed toward the front door. Anyone with eyes could see it was too narrow to accommodate her newest find.

Meemaw only tutted. "I'm sure you'll figure something out. You always do."

By now Sue Ellen and I had made our way over to them, and I had to clench my jaw to keep from commenting on the scene playing out before me.

Sue Ellen just shook her head and mumbled something I couldn't quite make out.

"Hi, Sam," I said, trying to ignore the couch resting in the driveway behind him. The fact that it didn't seem out of place here made me cringe.

"Well, look who it is." He leaned in for a hug and drew me close. "Aren't you girls a sight for sore eyes," he said, taking us in.

"We were just about to take Meemaw to lunch. Savannah's meeting us at Shane's." It hadn't escaped my attention the way he'd always been so helpful to our grandmother, and for the first time, I wondered if there was something more between the two of them than friendship. "Would you like to join us?"

"Of course he wouldn't," Meemaw answered for him matter-of-factly. "He has to figure out how to get this thing in my house."

~

After the four of us shuffled through the buffet line and settled into a sticky booth, Sue Ellen broke the silence. "So what's the deal with you and Sam?"

"Sue Ellen!" I shot her a look.

"What? I'm just asking. I mean, he's a widower. She's a widow," she reasoned.

"That doesn't mean they're . . . ya know . . . together. Don't be ridiculous."

Savannah dragged a french fry through a puddle of ketchup. "I mean, it's not ridiculous." I narrowed my eyes at her, but she only shrugged. "What? She's a woman. She still has . . . needs."

"Oh, for heaven's sake," Meemaw said, lowering her voice, "he's just a friend."

Savannah scoffed. "In my experience, any man who offers to move furniture free of charge is more than just a friend. Especially a man as . . . seasoned as he is."

"She means old," Sue Ellen clarified, zeroing in on Meemaw. "Look, no one is saying you can't have a fling, but can't you choose someone with a longer shelf life? You still have a lot of years ahead of you. If you take better care of yourself," she added.

"I will not indulge in that kind of sordid talk. In my day we knew to keep that sort of thing sealed between your ears, where it belongs." Meemaw gave a resolute nod, putting the matter to rest. I was grateful when she changed the subject. "I suppose I should thank you girls for letting an old coot like me join you. Especially when I'm sure you have more important things to do than hang around your sick grandmother." Her shoulders shook as she sputtered a cough; then she picked at her mashed potatoes and heaved a sigh. "Of course, one o'clock is a little late for me to be eating lunch, because of my blood sugar, but I don't expect you girls would know about all that." She stated this fact as if it didn't trouble her at all, but the sweet lilt in her voice had an edge to it that told me otherwise.

"I'm sorry," I said finally, though it pained me to give in to her theatrics. "We had a few things to take care of this morning, but I can think of nowhere else I'd rather be than right here." It was a lie. Shane's offered a generous spread of everything from roast beef to Asian stir-fry, but the food was only a slight step up from that of a hospital cafeteria, and the table bore the remnants of sticky, cheap cleaner along with the fingerprints of about a thousand patrons before us. "Also, I'd appreciate it if you stopped acting like you're dying all the time," I added.

"We're all dying, dear," she said casually, waving around a chicken leg. "I'm just much closer to the end than you all. None of us can predict when the Lord will call us home." She took a bite.

"Actually, some people can," Sue Ellen said, stuffing a forkful of dry salad into her mouth. "They're called doctors, and I'm pretty sure yours said you could live a lot longer if you gave up your Virginia Slims."

Meemaw had been a chain-smoker for the entirety of our lives, and her voice held the raspy tone of someone who was a decade older. I was certain the cough she'd been experiencing had more than a little to do with that. Still, I didn't think it was time to be planning her funeral. Besides, she'd already done that for us. Though her home was a mess, her funeral had been tidily squared away, right down to the dimensions of the coffin and the three of us singing "I'll Fly Away," though I strongly protested this since none of us sang.

Meemaw dismissed Sue Ellen with a wave of her hand just as a family with three young children trailed in and piled into the table adjacent from us. She offered them a broad smile and continued gazing at them far longer than it was socially appropriate to do so. "You know Cricket has four grandchildren now," she said to no one in particular, but I knew it was directed at me. "Four!" She held up her fingers to drive home the point. "And they live right down the street from her, so she sees them all the time. They have Christmas morning at her house, too."

I knew where she was going with this, but once she started down the path of indirectly shaming you, there wasn't much one could say to stem the tide. Maybe she was right, and I would regret that I hadn't brought Tucker and Charlotte on this trip with me. Would there come a day when my children would ask me why I hadn't tried harder to keep Meemaw in their lives? Maybe. But bringing them here meant making them a part of everything I'd left behind. I wasn't sure if it was Muscadine or the possibility that our family had been cursed, but I worried that somehow it might be contagious. The very idea of bringing the kids here sent my heart skipping a few beats faster, and my words came out sharper than I'd intended.

"I already told you. Charlotte would have been a nightmare in the car, and Tucker has a soccer game today. Besides, he's still potty training." There was some truth in this. I thought we had crossed that bridge months ago, but lately I'd been finding mysterious puddles around the house and Tucker hiding underneath a blanket somewhere, sucking his thumb. I suspected this had less to do with his bladder and more to do with the fact that Graham and I had been arguing more than usual.

"Well, I don't know what all the fuss is about," she pushed. "I never catered to that kind of nonsense when it came to my children. Just tossed them into the car, and if they felt the urge to relieve themselves, we pulled over and they pissed on the side of the road like any normal person would do."

At this, Sue Ellen choked on her water, and I became painfully aware that the adjacent tableful of children was staring at us with newfound curiosity. I hated when people looked at us that way.

"Listen"—I lowered my voice, hoping Meemaw would follow my lead—"you can't honestly want them here. What happens when they knock over one of your . . . valuables? The rusted junk in the yard is a safety hazard, not to mention all the boxes that could tumble on top of one of them. Do you even know what's in half of them? I just think,"

I said, straightening my shoulders and gripping the table, "that maybe you ought to think about their safety." It was a low blow, and I knew it.

Of course I was grateful to her for taking us in after Mama died, but I never understood the woman's obsession with things—scraps of paper, porcelain dolls, ceramic figurines, wooden carvings, and the unexplainable roadkill taxidermy. How many nights had I lain awake worrying that it would take only one of her cigarettes left smoldering on the couch to send the entire mess of it up in flames? When I was a kid, I once made the mistake of trying to organize it all. Even now I could still see the worry creases in her face as she paced from room to room in search of various items she feared had been lost to her forever. "These are my things!" she had shouted through angry tears, her voice quivering. "Don't you ever do anything like this again, Rayanne. Do you hear me? You are not to touch my things!"

Aside from all that, I wasn't sure I wanted my own children exposed to her unpredictable temperament. None of us could ever forget "the incident" at Sue Ellen's tenth birthday party. Those kinds of things can scar a child.

Meemaw put down her chicken leg and pushed away her plate. Dabbing at the corners of her mouth with a napkin, she hardened her gaze at me. "I'm ready to go home now. I think I've had quite enough," she said, reaching for her purse and moving to leave.

That makes two of us.

CHAPTER 17

MEEMAW

March 1987

That evening was the first time Marylynn laid eyes on Jack Guidry, and the experience was underwhelming. He blew through in an old Pinto the color of dirt and didn't bother getting out of the car to walk the girls up the drive. Marylynn slipped a hand between the curtains and studied the scene out the corner of one eye—an arm draped around her daughter in the front seat, the outline of what she was certain was a fully grown man pulling her into him for a long kiss, a flustered Beverly slamming the door. Celia emerged from the back seat, following after her friend, and the two of them waved goodbye as they scurried up the drive in the darkness. The sound of his engine grated against Marylynn's eardrums, and the car raced out of the drive, kicking up a tornado of smoke and dust. Dread settled into her bones. If anyone had asked her—and they didn't—she would have said that two girls traipsing around at night with a grown man was just asking for trouble.

Before the girls could slink unseen down the hallway and into Beverly's bedroom, Marylynn called out to them from where she sat brooding at the kitchen table, her arms crossed, her face hard as concrete, illuminated by the brass chandelier.

"I thought Celia was driving tonight."

"She was." Beverly's cheeks flushed pink, but she answered as if nothing were amiss as she crossed the kitchen, making her way to the cupboard. "But she had car trouble, and Jack was just giving us a ride home. Please don't make it a thing."

"You have car trouble, you call me. Not some . . . some man who can't be bothered to come to the door. Do you even know anything about him? Because it sure looked like the two of you were mighty friendly with one another."

"He's a good guy. Ask Celia if you don't believe me," she said, nudging the poor girl at her side, who startled at her touch.

"You have nothing to worry about, Mrs. Pritchett," Celia stammered. "I was there the whole time. You know I'd never let anything happen to her." But her pale cheeks had turned the color of strawberries, and Marylynn suspected she had been coached to say as much.

"I know that, dear. It isn't you I don't trust."

"It's me," Beverly said to Celia, though she leveled her gaze at Marylynn. "She doesn't trust me."

"Of course I do," Marylynn shot back. "It's everyone else I don't trust."

"In that case, would you rather we walked home? In the dark? Alone?" Beverly cocked her head to the side for effect before pouring herself a glass of water.

Sensing Bev pulling away from her again, Marylynn stopped herself from saying the thing she knew would send her stomping off to her room. Parenthood meant throwing all kinds of things against the wall to see what stuck, and most days she was grasping at straws. The thought occurred to Marylynn that perhaps she could head things off differently this time, try honey instead of vinegar, make Beverly realize what a mistake it was to be with someone like him. There was more than one way to skin this cat.

~

Jack Guidry was not a handsome man and, as far as Marylynn could tell, must have been an ugly child, too. While she knew some people might mistake her honesty for rudeness, she had been commanded by the Lord and Savior, Jesus Christ, not to bear false witness against her neighbor. She didn't make the rules, but she was determined to follow them to the best of her humble abilities.

He was tall—too tall for someone as petite as Bev, and his eyes were too close together. Like a predator. Dark, greasy curls hung stiffly at his shoulders in a mullet cut. His sturdy frame seemed to take up all the space in her home, lumbering about like an unwelcome giant. Though he was only two years older, he was too much of a man for her eighteen-year-old to date. Marylynn had always believed it was imperative to be blessed with good genes or a quick wit, but poor Jack seemed slap out of luck on all fronts. As far as she could tell, he wasn't smart or funny or interesting. In fact, she didn't rightly know what had attracted Bev to him in the first place. Maybe it was the fact that he had a car, or maybe it was because he was older, or maybe it was because she didn't have the self-esteem to shoot for anyone better. Yes, she strongly suspected it was that.

Beverly sat nestled against his broad chest on Marylynn's floral wingback sofa, every so often stretching her neck up to whisper something in his ear. With his foot propped atop her coffee table and one arm slung around her doe-eyed daughter, Marylynn thought him slovenly and disrespectful. She bristled at the way he couldn't stop touching Beverly, massaging her shoulders, running his lips over the top of her head. At least when Marylynn was young and in love, she and Charlie had the decency not to do that sort of thing in public. But Beverly lapped up the attention like a starved puppy, completely ignoring her mother and regarding her as if she were a piece of the furniture. With Charlie gone and the boys away, it had been strange to see a man in her home again, especially one who thudded about it as if he owned the place. Eyeing the size eleven shoe on her table, she squeezed her fingers into her palms to keep them from swatting it away.

"Mama, Jack knows all about cars," Beverly said, lacing her slender fingers through his. "He says you should sell the Buick and get something more modern. He could help you pick something out."

"Did he?" Marylynn smiled, not tearing her gaze from his for a second. Beverly had often told her that she had a talent for making people uncomfortable, and if there was ever a time to utilize this unique skill set, it was now. "Your father bought me that car, and I wouldn't sell it if the good Lord himself asked me to."

Jack gave a nervous laugh as he took note of the boxes lining her walls. It irked her the way he kept glancing around as if he expected a rat to jump out. Her house may have been a bit cluttered, but it wasn't filthy. There was a difference.

"I noticed you have a few loose floorboards there in the hall," he said, changing the subject and gesturing toward the ground. "You should get it checked out and make sure there isn't any rot under there. A rotting floor is dangerous, especially with so much"—he paused and cleared his throat—"with so many valuables. Better to nip it in the bud." He made a little swordlike gesture. When Marylynn said nothing, just continued to gaze at him intently, he flashed a flustered smile and tightened his grip on Beverly's shoulder.

Perhaps he had only been trying to be helpful, but it did not escape her attention that he hadn't offered to fix it himself, just felt it was his God-appointed duty to call attention to what was amiss in her home. The only thing that needed to be nipped in the bud around here was this relationship, and she would figure out how to accomplish that soon enough.

From the corner of her eye, she scrutinized the shape of his head, the color of his yellowish-green eyes, as if he were a wild animal, an unfamiliar creature who had yet to state his intentions here. It was still entirely possible he might prove to be a serial killer and murder them both in their sleep. Even so, she nodded attentively as he discussed how he had dropped out of high school last year, gotten a job down at Lebeaux's Paper Mill, and was making more money than any of his friends who had graduated. Apparently this decision had not been the kind of success his parents had wanted for him, and they kicked him out, leaving him on his own for the better part of a year.

Taking all this in, she struggled to hold in her thoughts until, finally, she gave up trying. "I hope you won't mind my asking," Marylynn said, though her tone made it clear that she did not, in fact, care at all, "but where are you living?"

Scratching his head with two fingers and leaning back into the sofa, he would not look at her directly. "Well, I'm still trying to work that out. Lived with a friend for six months until he got married, and now I'm waiting on a buddy of mine to get half the money for a deposit on a rental out near the mill. It's a nice place, or at least it will be once we get the raccoons out." He gave a nervous laugh.

"I'm sorry," she pressed on, ignoring Beverly's silent rebuke with her eyes, "but you didn't answer the question."

He ran a hand through his gelled hair, which hardly moved when he shook it. "Truth is, right now I'm a . . . well, I'm sleeping on a friend's couch. But it's only temporary," he added quickly, holding up a hand.

"I see," Marylynn said through gritted teeth. Though she couldn't see anything clearly anymore. What could Beverly be thinking taking up with the likes of Jack, who didn't seem to have a plan past this very moment? Things were getting entirely too serious between them. Someone had to slow down this train.

It might as well be her.

CHAPTER 18

SAVANNAH

Saturday Afternoon

Still nursing a bruised ego, Meemaw settled into her worn leather La-Z-Boy and made herself comfortable in front of reality court TV while Bessie snuggled in a blissful heap at her feet. For someone so adamantly opposed to plastic surgery and sex outside of wedlock, it defied logic that our grandmother should be so invested in the twisted, seedy plots that dragged on into eternity in her soaps and daytime television.

It didn't take long before she began dozing along to the soundtrack of *Judge Judy*. Rayanne pulled me out onto the porch and gave me that motherly look that made me feel like I was six years old again. The three of us settled ourselves into rickety rocking chairs, and I fanned myself against the sweltering afternoon heat.

After a while Rayanne steepled her fingers together and drew in a long breath. "We found Celia."

The words slammed into me, and I felt my heart tick up speed. "Where is she?"

Sue Ellen wrapped her arms around herself, unable to meet my eyes, then handed over a folded piece of paper. "She's dead. She passed away a few years ago in Texas," she said, pushing her hands apart. "And as hard as it is to hear it, this just confirms what we already knew. The reality is . . . Levi took her. And you need to make space for what that means."

Rayanne reached out for my hand and squeezed it. "This is all for the best, Savannah. We can't change what happened."

I'd known there was a possibility we might not find Celia, but learning she was gone felt wrong in my bones. Tearing my hand away, I tugged open the folded paper and spread my fingers over the creases to smooth it. "This is her," I said, almost to myself. My gaze drifted to the little girls on her lap, and my skin prickled with goose bumps. "Do you think these are her granddaughters?" I looked up at Sue Ellen, desperate to gauge her reaction, but she only shrugged.

"Probably. The obituary says as much."

Something about those little faces clutched my heart, and I couldn't believe they hadn't seen it, too. "They look like us," I said, unable to tear my eyes away from their freckled faces and curly hair, my voice thin, almost a whisper.

Sue Ellen stiffened. "What are you talking about?"

"The girls. They look just like you at that age," I said, more confidently this time. "The hair, the freckles. And the dimples just there . . ." I brushed a finger over their cheeks. "They look like mine. Like . . . Georgia's." Something in my chest told me this wasn't just a coincidence.

"So?" She shrugged, casting a confused glance at Rayanne, who looked equally baffled.

"So . . . Celia was possibly there on the day Georgia went missing. And now there's a photo of her with two kids who look like us. Her granddaughters . . . what if they're . . ." I couldn't bring myself to finish the sentence.

Sue Ellen's mouth fell open, and I immediately regretted thinking this aloud. "You've lost it." Shaking her head, she gave a sardonic laugh. "This is unbelievable. We already know what happened to Georgia."

"That's just it! We don't know anything!" Still brandishing the article, I flew up from my seat, sending my chair teetering backward.

"I know enough," she shot back. "And I know that you're never going to be happy unless you let yourself move on. She's dead, Savannah." This time I knew she meant Georgia, and a flush of heat swept over my face.

"You could be wrong."

She sighed and squeezed the bridge of her nose. "I'm not. I know it's not what you want to hear, but this is where the road ends."

"No." I shook my head. "Maybe Celia is dead, but that doesn't mean Georgia isn't alive. This could be proof." Lowering my gaze again, I ran a finger over the girls in the photo.

"We tried." Rayanne touched my shoulder. Her eyes were wet, and I had to look away from her to keep from crying, too. "You have to accept it."

My arms crossed and fists clenched, I shook my head. "I can't do that, because I know Levi didn't do it."

"How can you know that for certain?" Rayanne pressed gently.

I pulled at a few loose strands of hair that had escaped my short, curly ponytail and began twisting them into knots.

"Because he told me."

The two of them locked eyes with me, and I froze.

"He did what?" Rayanne stuttered, wide eyed and blinking.

"I asked him, and he told me," I managed to say matter-of-factly, as if speaking to a convicted murderer were an everyday occurrence.

"You mean, you wrote him a letter, right?" Sue Ellen asked, staring me down, her mouth still hanging open. "Because you aren't dumb enough to actually meet that monster in person. Are you?"

I shrugged her off and steeled myself against what I knew was coming. "Why not? I mean, he's just a person, a sick and demented one, but we were separated by bulletproof glass and surrounded by guards. I was never in any danger," I reassured them.

"Because he's a psychopath, Savannah. And the last thing you need is for some narcissistic murderer to get inside your head," Rayanne continued, her words coming higher and faster. "I'm pretty sure Deborah would agree with me when I say that this kind of behavior is not conducive to your mental health."

"It was fine." I rolled my eyes. "In case you haven't noticed, I can take care of myself. Besides, he isn't the first narcissist I've met. I've dated more than a few." I smirked, desperate to lighten the mood. If there was one thing both of them could agree on, it was my taste in men.

Sue Ellen appeared to be on pins and needles and lifted her eyebrows in a frozen state of anticipation. "Well? What did he say?"

"It doesn't matter what he said." Rayanne shut her down, lowering her voice as she kept a lookout for Meemaw. "The man is a murderer. You can't believe anything he told you. Just forget him."

I took a deep breath, remembering the way Levi's eyes had never left mine when he spoke the words, the way he had spoken them as if he needed me to believe him. Maybe I needed to believe them, too. "He said he'd never seen her before." I let the words hang in the air between us and watched as they both tried to make sense of what I'd said.

Looking back, I suppose I should have felt safer knowing that a person like Levi was penned in like a rabid dog behind barbed wire and thick concrete walls, separated by miles of highway. But it was the uncertainty of it all that haunted me, the uneasiness that came with wondering if her body might be in a place that I passed by every day. Could she be in a field somewhere, held at the bottom of the lake by heavy stones, or buried in an unmarked grave in the same dirt that I'd trodden over day after day? Had I crossed paths with Georgia and not recognized the energy of her spirit there? What kind of a twin would that make me?

My voice grew thick, my hands sweaty. "I don't know why, but it just felt like it was time. I needed to hear him say it." This summer would mark twenty-eight years since I had last seen Georgia. Twenty-eight years following a winding path that looped in and around and around in dizzying circles until it brought me back to the same emptiness I felt now. Standing on the beach day after day, staring out over the horizon, like she might suddenly drift into focus. And I realized that it would always be this way for me as long as her spirit lived in the in-between.

"Meemaw doesn't know about it. I told her I was going out of town with Tammy." Looking at my sisters' tortured faces, I cleared my throat. "But I may have stretched the truth a little."

~

Visiting Levi had brought back the same sinking pit in my stomach I'd felt when I had visited Mama at the hospital in her final days, when her body was at its weakest and her spirit fractured. Neither was a place where I thought a person should ever want to live. Or die. The thickly set prison walls were painted an institutional blue, and the white-and-gray-speckled tiles beneath my feet reeked of fresh bleach so strong it burned my nostrils.

I didn't allow myself to be afraid or let my knees buckle beneath my weight, but pushed my body forward to the sound of my feet padding along the floor in steady thuds as if they belonged to someone else entirely—someone braver.

As a child, I'd studied his photograph printed in black-and-white newspaper clippings, so I was surprised when I didn't recognize him at first sight. The years had not been kind to him, and though he was in only his midfifties, his yellowed teeth and shrunken body bore the evidence of a smoking addiction and questionable dental hygiene. As I mechanically took my place in a cold metal foldout chair in front of him and picked up the telephone attached to the wall, his leathery, pockmarked face settled into a sinister grin that was missing a tooth or two. I tasted the bile rising in the back of my throat but willed myself to swallow it down and say something. Anything. But the words had left me, and the only thing that remained was an uneasiness in my gut.

Leaning back in his chair, he locked his fingers together behind his head, the top of it a sweaty ball surrounded by stringy black sprouts along the sides. His snakelike eyes narrowed in on me as if I were a hidden-image puzzle he might solve. It seemed he found my presence amusing, and I guessed I was probably the most interesting thing that had happened to him all day, maybe even all year.

That morning, I had traded in my shorts and tank top for a long-sleeve cotton shirt with blue jeans and sneakers in spite of the glaring fact that it was the middle of summer. But even though I'd covered every inch of myself, the thick glass between us still wasn't enough to protect me from his wandering eyes. I tried to ignore it but felt suddenly haunted by Marissa Jenkins. As morbid as it seemed, as a teenager I had pored over her case, wondering if maybe whatever happened to her had happened to Georgia, too. But their cases had been so different. For starters, Marissa was a runaway, a sixteen-year-old whose parents reported her missing. Months later her body had been found in a shallow grave in Tennessee, strangled and broken. And traces of Levi's DNA had left little doubt that he was the one who had committed the crime. Marissa Jenkins was the reason he ended up here. Not my sister.

I tried to shake the knowledge of what he had done to her, but as I opened my mouth, my voice cracked, and I quickly closed it. In the weeks before, I'd rehearsed this moment again and again, but now that I was finally here, my body betrayed me, and I couldn't seem to ask the one question that I'd been asking ever since that day at the lake: *Where is my sister?*

We'd given Mama a proper goodbye, but there was never any funeral for Georgia, no lifeless body to bury in the cold earth. Instead, we held a "Ceremony of Remembrance." As I stared out over the sea of sorrowful faces lit by candles, I figured since no one had called it a funeral, she couldn't really be dead. Maybe there was some sort of magical power that came from all those people remembering her that would be enough to bring her back to us. Maybe she was like the swamp canaries that flittered about in our bayous, traveling the world for a season but always returning to build their nests in the hollows of the trees. And maybe when she returned, she would tell me all about her adventures flying high above the dull canvas of brown and green where we lived in the muck.

I steadied my breaths and kept my eyes fixed on Levi, though the sight of him made me wish I could scrub him from my body, watch the grime of him circling down the drain. I cleared my throat and righted my shoulders, though my hands shook as they gripped the phone a little too tightly, sweat making it slippery in my grasp. "I came here to ask you something," I managed to get out.

He strained forward and furrowed a thin eyebrow as if suddenly entirely fixated on every word I had to say. Keeping one eye on him, I reached into my back pocket, then pressed a photo of Georgia against the cold glass—one that had been of the two of us smiling sweetly, wearing matching pink-plaid jumpers as we sat in a sea of black-eyed Susans, but I had folded myself out of the photo.

"Did you take this girl?" I studied him carefully and silently hoped that he would reveal some tic that would give him away. His eyes, which seemed to be smirking, kept a firm hold on mine, never once glancing at the picture.

"You know, I'm not so much interested in talking about the past as I am in talking about the present. And you, darlin', are quite the present." He whistled and scanned the length of my body, tilting his head back to get a better view of me through the glass.

My heart pounded faster, so hard that I could feel the pumping in my toes. I pressed my feet into the floor to stem the flow and drew in a shaky breath. All at once the words came tumbling out of me, tripping over each other and falling all over the place.

"I need you to remember. Did you take a little girl from Lake Canard in the summer of 1994? I need to know. Our family needs to know. Can't you do this one thing for us after you've taken so much? If you did it, I need you to tell me where she is."

He cocked his head to one side, then clicked his tongue against the roof of his mouth. "Seems pretty important to you. I just wonder . . . how important?" Leaning forward, he spat into his palm and slid it across his greasy black comb-over.

My stomach turned at the thought of him. All at once, fear gave way to anger, and I found my footing. "Let me spell this out for you." My voice was shaking now, but there was an edge to it that I had never heard before. "You're in there, and I'm out here. I don't really think you're really in any position to be making demands, do you?"

"Well, that depends on the value of my information, doesn't it? And how badly you need it."

"Trust me," I scoffed. "I don't need anything that badly." I moved to leave, but as my fingers retrieved the photo, my eyes rested on Georgia's face, and my limbs suddenly felt heavy, like they were trapped in concrete. On the drive here I'd played this scenario out in my mind and wondered what I could possibly say to him to get him to open up to me. I didn't exactly have any leverage. He would rot in prison until he was executed. As I turned to leave, Meemaw's face floated into my thoughts, and a sudden hope pooled in my chest, giving me courage.

"Mr. Morrison, do you believe in God?" I heard myself say. I wasn't naive enough to think he was a religious man, but spending the better part of his life locked away in a cell, inching toward the end of his life— it would give a man time to think about things like that.

"Ain't no Bible-thumper, if that's what you're asking," he said, setting his jaw and casting his eyes to the side.

"You must have some theory on what happens after you die, though, whether or not there's some higher power up there who's watching us all and keeping score."

He shifted in his seat and tugged at his chin. I hoped that I had struck a nerve and might be able to find some shred of decency that still existed within him. After all, even someone like Levi Morrison had a grandmother somewhere. And I hoped to God she had the moral righteousness of Meemaw.

I continued, choosing my words with precision. "You can't undo the past. What's done is done. But if you tried to make amends, tried to help a person like me after all the wrong you've done . . . well, I like to think that at the end of the day, that counts for something."

He sniffed hard, and I thought I caught a hint of shame in the way he diverted his eyes from mine before locking in on them firmly. He muttered so softly that I instinctively leaned forward in my chair to make out the words.

"It was late. They questioned me for hours." He frowned. "Had receipts that put me in the area, but that was it," he said, shaking his head. "So I happened to be working a job nearby, but does that make me guilty?" His voice had risen to nearly a shout. "Not a shred of evidence. Just their ideas. Wouldn't even give me a bathroom break or a decent cup of coffee." Crossing his arms, he narrowed his eyes at me, sending a numbness all the way through my feet. "So maybe I confessed, but I don't remember. Not that it matters." He scoffed. "They gave me the needle anyway. But it's like I told them in the first place." He nodded once at Georgia's picture, then swung his gaze to me and held it there without wavering. "Ain't never seen that little girl."

Closing my eyes, I let out a shaky breath. There was something in the way that he spoke the words with such disgust that made me think he just might be telling the truth.

"Satisfied?" His eyes were hard and unfeeling, but I was desperate to believe him.

I nodded slowly, tried to get my bearings, and cleared my throat. I'd gotten what I'd come for, and there was really nothing left to say. I went to replace the receiver onto its base, but he called out to me before I could.

"You really believe all that? That me helping you's gonna save my soul."

Stunned, I sat in the silence for a moment, trying to make sense of the words. Still recovering from the daze I was in, I shook my head.

"How would I know? That's between you and God." I put down the receiver and carried myself toward the exit, my head held high but spinning as I thought about what all this could mean.

Before I reached the heavy double doors, I turned once more to face Levi, who was staring back at me like a wounded dog, then walked out into the sunlight.

CHAPTER 19

RAYANNE

Saturday Afternoon

"I don't understand why you're so upset," Savannah said, brushing me off as she paced the length of the porch.

"Because you put yourself in danger. You're so stuck in the past you can't see what you're doing to yourself. To all of us."

"Oh, get over yourself, Rayanne. It had nothing to do with you or anyone else. I did it for me."

"It was irresponsible and stupid." Checking behind me, I lowered my voice to a whisper, hoping our grandmother was still asleep. "Can you imagine what Meemaw would do if she found out?"

"She's not going to find out," she said, hardening her gaze at me.

"God, you are so selfish. Have you forgotten how much it crushed her when we found out the truth? I haven't. And she took all of us down with her into her paranoia. The hoarding got twice as bad. I'm not going to watch her go through it all again because you need closure."

"Ease up on her," Sue Ellen said, making me do a double take in her direction.

"Oh, you of all people are taking her side?"

"I'm not taking anyone's side. I just think you need to calm down." She pushed out her hands smoothly, which only made me want to slap her.

"Right, because I'm the unreasonable one." When neither of them responded, I scoffed out a laugh. "Excuse me. Am I the only adult here?" I asked, drawing a hand to my chest. "Am I the only one who can see how irresponsible it is to go traipsing around prisons with murderers?"

"She made a mistake," Sue Ellen reasoned.

Savannah shook her head. "I didn't make a mistake."

"And just because you have kids," Sue Ellen continued, "doesn't make you more responsible than us, so please stop throwing it in our faces."

I gave an incredulous laugh. I could not believe she was going there again. "What is with you? I don't think I'm better. You think your life's better because you have the freedom to do what you want? God, you never were able to see past yourself."

She drew herself up, fixing her gaze on me like a predator eyeing its next meal. "No. I think my life's better because I don't have to medicate in order to survive it." She said the next part under her breath, but I heard it loud and clear. "It's not my fault you didn't finish college."

Stunned, I stared back at her open mouthed, trying to make sense of her words. Only a few people knew that my first pregnancy had ended in a miscarriage, *after* I'd agreed to marry Graham and dropped out of classes. When we lost it, I felt guilty that the thing I felt most about it all was relief. Afterward, it took us ten years to conceive Tucker, and I wondered if it was some sort of punishment for not being more upset about it. "I can't believe you would—"

"I'm sorry." She screwed her eyes shut and cringed. "It just came out. I don't know why I said that. I didn't mean—"

"I can't do this. I cannot stay here." With no thought for where I would go, I headed for my car.

"Wait!" Sue Ellen called after me, but by now I was a woman on fire.

Ignoring her, I settled myself behind the wheel and threw the car into drive. Steering down dusty roads lined with thick brambles and honeysuckle and wild blackberry bushes, I passed Linda's Diner and Jasper's Bar, marking the edge of town, but for reasons I could not explain, I kept going. Mindlessly, I followed a nameless country road until it met the interstate and steered the car down the exit ramp. By the time I entered Porter's Trailer Park, I couldn't quite recall how I'd made it there. I parked the car in front of a rusty, two-toned double-wide with aluminum-covered windows and slowly lifted myself out of the car.

Staring up at the sorry structure, I debated whether to make the climb up the wooden steps, hesitated for a moment, and turned back for my Lexus, which stuck out like a sore thumb in this place. But a gravelly voice called to me from behind, and my feet stopped as if they'd been caught in thick mud.

"Rayanne? Is that you?" A screen door slammed shut and a shrunken ghost of a man emerged, stooping on the doorstep. His curly, graying hair was too long, and it looked as if he hadn't shaved in days. I turned toward him, and his green eyes met mine. It was too late to leave.

"Hi, Daddy."

~

I hadn't planned to see our father, but when I promised Savannah I'd come home, the thought did cross my mind. Porter's Trailer Park was only a thirty-minute drive from Meemaw's. At first I thought I'd just stake out the place, see where he lived, and maybe catch a glimpse of his pathetic life through the window. I'd seen photos of the woman he was currently living with—Kathy Something, who seemed nice enough but hadn't aged nearly as beautifully as our mother would have, her leathery skin the product of a few too many trips to the tanning bed. At the sound of his voice, I scrambled to think of something to say. I'd had the entire drive over and twenty-five years to prepare something, yet there I stood, unable to form complete sentences.

"You look . . . well," I finally said, trying to sound as if I meant it.

"I do?" He smiled weakly. "That's not what Kathy says. She says I look like death run over twice."

"She's right. You look like hell," I said deadpan, still not ready to let him feel comfortable.

"I'm glad you came. I wasn't sure if you got my letter. Figured maybe Marylynn had given me the wrong address on purpose. Sounds like something she would do." He laughed nervously, then let out a shaky cough. I'd received his letter a few weeks ago, asking me to pay him a visit. Though Graham had told me I was being unfair, I suspected it had to do with money, as he knew we were well off. According to Meemaw, she'd heard through the grapevine that he had a bum knee and was living off disability checks.

"Well. I'm here," I said. "I don't know why." I surveyed the trailer park and took in the lots filled with overgrown grass and too many cars crammed in front of each neglected structure. It was the kind of seedy place I would have been hesitant to drive through at night, especially with the kids.

"You want to come in?" With hopeful eyes, he motioned toward the front door, but I stayed firmly planted on the gravel drive, digging the ball of my foot into the rocks.

"No. I'm fine here."

"Right." He gave a curt nod before descending the porch steps and limping toward the car to meet me. Maybe he wasn't lying about the knee. "I'm so glad you came. Kathy said you'd come, but I didn't believe her." Stuffing his hands into his pockets, he chuckled. "Shoulda known. She's usually right."

"Well. Here I am." I couldn't quite bring myself to look him in the eyes and stared up at the trailer, where I caught a glimpse of Kathy in the window as she moved about the kitchen. What was it about her that had been enough for him to stay?

"Why exactly am I here?"

He hesitated and smoothed back his thinning hair. The man standing before me looked nothing like the invincible young father I remembered. Back then he'd seemed so tall, his hair so thick with youth. And though he still loomed larger than me, he was smaller now. Less sure of himself, like the world had beaten him. "I know I don't have any right to them," he said, "but I was wondering how you'd feel about bringing the kids here sometime, letting me spend some time with Tucker and Charlotte." His lips curled into a smile, and my stomach soured.

The words slammed into me, and for a moment I just stared at him as my own words lodged in my throat. "They don't even know you," I finally managed to say. For that matter, neither did I.

"You're right." His smile faltered, and he nodded, bringing a fist to his chin. "I feel like I need to try and set some things right. I have a bypass coming up . . . well, it's got me thinking about a lot of things. Actually, Kathy's been a big part of that, helping me get right with the Lord. You'd like her, I think." His eyes looked tired, pulled down by the weight of the years. Looking away, he cleared his throat. "I know it don't seem like there's any excuse for doing y'all the way I did back then."

I tugged at my hair, unconvinced that whatever he was going to say next could erase so many years of disappointment.

"I had a lot of guilt over not being a good enough father to you girls. I should have been there that day at the lake, but I wasn't." Avoiding my gaze, he scuffed his feet against the ground and sniffed. "I was off with another woman. And I left the door open for that monster to take her. It's a shameful thing to admit, but that's about the size of it. And I had to leave because I wasn't worthy of my family anymore."

He looked up at me in a way that made my heart clench, and for a moment the nine-year-old girl inside me wanted to hug him. But I swallowed down the thought and let him feel the uncomfortable silence between us. It was an Oscar-worthy performance, but I wasn't buying it.

"And what about after that?" I pushed back hard. "What about after Mama? You couldn't be bothered to come back for us then?"

"Listen, darlin'. It's like this." He held up a calloused hand to punctuate the words, as if somehow it would make me understand. "Your grandmother is . . . a difficult woman. She never wanted me to marry your mother, and every day afterward she made life hell for me. Now, I know it's not an excuse—"

"You're right. It's not an excuse." My voice was full of steel now.

"I know," he admitted, shaking his head. "It's just that nothing I ever did was right in Marylynn's eyes. She blamed me for Georgia, for ruining your mama's life. She told me to stay away because I was no good for you all. And I guess . . . well, I believed her. After Bev died, I tried to come back, but Marylynn wasn't gonna have it. She made sure I knew that she was the only one who could take care of everyone. Said it would be too confusing for you all if I came back into the picture, that I ought to just let her take over. I was young and confused. I thought . . . well, I guess I thought maybe she was right."

My pulse quickened, adding fuel to my words. "Meemaw is hell to deal with. I get that. But you could have stood up to her. You could have stayed and made her accept it. You could have been our father."

"I wanted to," he said. "I just didn't know how." Shaking his head, he gave a defeated whistle. "Besides, I was such a mess back then in those days, drunk half the time and stupid as hell. I wouldn't have been any good for you girls. I hate to admit it, but"—he looked up at me, squinting one eye as if it hurt to say the words out loud—"Marylynn was right to take you."

I drew myself up to his height, propelled by an anger I hadn't known ran this deep. "See, that's the difference between you and Meemaw. Maybe she was hard on you, but at least she fought for us. You just gave up. She never would have taken no for an answer." And she hadn't. Meemaw had never missed a single school play or Christmas concert for any of us and could always be counted upon to clap the loudest and longest. It had been beyond embarrassing. But somewhere inside me, it also felt like I mattered to someone. I mattered enough to someone so much that she would humiliate herself—and me—just to let everyone else know it.

He fumbled with his pockets, unable to hold his eyes on mine. "I'm sorry. What more can I say?"

Hearing him utter those words to me after all this time did not have the effect I expected it would, and I set my jaw. "Don't you get it? It's not about words. It's about actions. If I'm going to let you back into my life, I need some assurances that this isn't just some phase you're going through. It has to stick this time. I . . . I need to think about it," I said. "I'll talk to Savannah and Sue Ellen. We're staying at Meemaw's."

"Sue Ellen's here?" he asked, perking up.

"Yeah. The three of us are here just for the weekend. Working on a . . . family project of sorts. Actually," I said, letting an idea take hold. I wasn't sure why I hadn't thought to ask him before. Aside from Meemaw, he would have known our mother's friends best. "Did you ever meet Mama's friend Celia? We found her in a few old photos." My voice softened, and I was almost relieved to change the subject.

Something in his demeanor shifted, though I couldn't say what. I sensed I'd said the wrong thing, because he shuffled from one foot to the other and massaged the back of his neck.

"Celia. Sure. I knew her."

"OK," I said, waiting for more. "It seems like she and Mama were close. And then she just left without any explanation. Do you know why?"

"Can't say that I do." He shrugged. A beat of silence passed between us before he added, "But I wouldn't go digging too far into the past, Rayanne. I don't think your mama and Celia ended on the best of terms, if you know what I mean."

"No. I don't."

"It was probably nothing," he said with an easy smile. "You know how girls can be, the kind of nonsense they fight about."

"Right," I said, furrowing my brow. It only made sense he would be a chauvinist, too.

I opened the car door and slid into the seat, my face flushing. "I'll talk to Sue Ellen and Savannah."

"Thank you," he said, bending down and placing a rough hand on my open window. "I know you didn't have to but . . . thanks for coming. It gives me something to hang on to, ya know."

I tugged on my seat belt and secured it, but before I pulled away, he leaned in closer—so close I could smell the alcohol on his breath.

"Listen, I hate to even ask this of you, but I've been out of work for a while with my knee and with this surgery coming up, and things have been a little tight. If you found it in your heart to help me out, I'd be so grateful. It would just be a little something to tide me over until I'm back on my feet."

And there it was. Of course it had been about the money. Ignoring him, I rolled up my window and threw the car in reverse, sending him tumbling backward a few steps. All these years, deep down I'd worried that maybe Meemaw had been too hard on him, that perhaps she hadn't given him a fair shake. But she'd been right.

Now I couldn't help but wonder what else she'd been right about.

CHAPTER 20

Sue Ellen

Saturday Afternoon

Meemaw awoke with a start and stumbled out of her chair. "Where's Rayanne?" she asked, looking around befuddled.

"Out," I said from where I lay prostrate on the couch, scrolling through my phone. I was already knee deep down a rabbit hole I knew I shouldn't have pursued, but I couldn't help myself. Liam never had time or any interest in Instagram, but we shared a mutual friend from college who had posted pictures from a company happy hour at Shanahan's Bar last night—Abby nestled against Liam's chest in a booth, fanning out her fingers to showcase her bejeweled left ring finger. She smiled demurely into the camera as if to say, *Don't you wish you had just gotten engaged to one of NYC's thirty under thirty and moved into his Upper East Side apartment with a twenty-four-hour fitness center?* I studied Liam's face, the severe line of his jaw and strong nose, the way his face had settled into what looked like the start of a frown. Was he truly happy with her?

"Well, where did she go?" Meemaw's voice rustled me from my thoughts, which by now had spiraled into a full-blown existential crisis.

Ignoring her, I scrutinized the slight brow quirk that tended to arise whenever Liam wasn't sure about some minute detail of a case. And I wondered . . . Was there a fragment of him, some small piece of his heart, with my name still written on it?

"Where's Savannah?" Meemaw asked, irritation creeping into her tone.

"Out," I answered again, annoyed and still looking down at my cell. Since the fallout from our conversation, Rayanne had stormed off, followed by Savannah, while I had taken up texting with Gabriela about Liam and the picture I had come across on Instagram. Like the good friend she was, she was doing her best to talk me down, and my phone was blowing up with messages.

It's been four months and you are STILL pining for this loser? You have GOT to get over him! As soon as you're back from Swampland, we are going out and finding a proper rebound.

"Out where?" Meemaw pressed me, crinkling her brow.

"No idea." I sighed, trying to remember if Savannah had mentioned where she was going when she flew away in her truck like a bat out of hell. From across the room, I could feel Meemaw scrutinizing me as I tapped away.

"Well, you might as well make yourself useful while you're here," she said, smoothing the wrinkles out of her shirt. "And I've got a week's worth of vegetables that need canning."

I cringed, realizing that hours of my life were about to be sucked away. One of my earliest memories of Meemaw involved me getting a severe tongue whipping for skipping through the neatly plowed rows of her garden and carelessly trampling over a freshly planted patch of bush beans. Second to us, her garden was the most meaningful and necessary thing in her life. The twelve-by-twelve-foot tract of soft earth flanked by pine trees and bathed in filtered sunlight sat just off to the right of the weathered house. And it was sacred.

Every summer Meemaw coaxed little seedlings from their hardy shells and in just a matter of weeks had nursed them into prolific producers that not only sustained us during the sweltering months but lined the shelves of our pantry all winter long. Somewhere inside the brimming walls of her house lay record-setting awards for Muscadine's sweetest watermelon and biggest beefsteak, which she had accepted with pride at the Muscadine Crawfish Festival multiple years in a row. Summer after summer, each of us had been tasked with a critical assignment on her assembly line as we canned every edible thing she harvested. We washed the jars, scrubbed the cucumbers, chopped the tomatoes, and boiled the brine. For whatever reason, it was the only task that Savannah and I could ever complete together that didn't end in shouting, maybe because we each knew our place in the scheme of things.

So when Meemaw asked me to help in the kitchen, I knew the routine. She pulled out a case of mason jars and a behemoth pot, then filled the entire thing with water. A generous spread awaited us on the worn counter, squash, corn, beans, purple hull peas, tomatoes, and cucumbers stretched out before me. I rinsed them and started slicing the cucumbers into lengthy spears while Meemaw packed the jars tightly, covered them with brine, and screwed the lids on firmly before dropping them into the boiling water.

"You know what separates a good jar of pickles from a bad case of botulism?" she finally asked, rotating the jars gingerly with a pair of tongs.

I sighed. "No. But I have a feeling you're going to tell me."

"Heat. These cucumbers would never keep if we didn't raise their temperature. It changes them. Makes 'em last."

I grabbed a few tomatoes and resumed chopping while silently cursing my sisters, who'd had the foresight to escape another lecture when they'd had the chance. I wondered how long it would take Meemaw to make her point. I loathed these chats, the ones where she tried to casually insert her opinion on whatever sin she believed I'd committed, usually by trying to make some sort of bizarre comparison cloaked in mystery. We'd once spent an entire hour discussing the lengthy ripening process of cantaloupe before I realized she was trying to teach me about sex before marriage. If she'd been aiming for a memorable learning experience, she had achieved it, though I still wasn't certain I'd taken the right lesson away from it. After that I could never stomach melons in any form.

"It gets so hot inside that little jar you think it might burst open. But just when you think it can't get any hotter, that's when the magic happens. See that?" She plunged a pair of metal tongs into the boiling pot, pulled out a steaming jar, and inspected it carefully. "Now that's gonna be a tight seal." She beamed proudly and set the jar on the cloth-lined countertop. "Nothing's getting through that," she said, rapping the top of the tin lid with her chipped fingernails.

"I think I know what you're getting at." I tried to hurry the point along. "What doesn't kill you makes you stronger."

She handed me the tongs and gestured for me to remove the other jars. "No. What doesn't kill you tries again." Her lips twitched into a grin as she watched me clumsily dip the tongs into the pot. "I'm saying that this family has been through hell, and you don't go through something like that and come out the same. You just don't," she said flatly. "Losing them . . . it changed me." Her smile faltered, and I could see how difficult it was for her to keep the tears out of her voice. "Made me harder, more protective of you girls, I guess."

Protective was not exactly the word I would have used to describe some of our grandmother's inexplicable behavior over the years. She'd always meant well, but she loved hard. Too hard, some might say, and from time to time I'd found myself on the receiving end of her ardent brand of loyalty. In the sixth grade, my English teacher had asked if anyone in the class could define the word *bovine*, and of course, I promptly shot my hand into the air. Eugene Seller coughed out the word *fatty* under his breath, and the whole class doubled over. Apparently my ignominy had spread, because after school Savannah told Meemaw what he'd done. Despite all my tears of protest, she'd driven me over to the Sellers' house later that evening to make Eugene apologize, but he denied ever having done it, and his parents had believed him. The next morning, his family awoke to quite the picture, because somehow a person of unknown identity—at least to everyone except us—had managed to empty an entire truckload of cow manure into their front yard. We never owned a truck or any cows, so the question of how our grandmother procured it all remained a mystery.

"*Protective*, huh?" I asked, lifting a skeptical eyebrow. "I think the Sellers would beg to disagree. They'd probably go with *criminal*."

"I will not apologize for that," she protested. "That little bastard had it coming. Pardon my language. Besides, they had the greenest lawn for weeks, thanks to me. Won 'Yard of the Month' that summer, I believe."

"Not sure they'd agree it was worth the smell," I said under my breath. Against my better judgment, I continued pushing her. "And what about Aunt Patty? You pointed a gun at her at my birthday party. Kind of an extreme reaction just because she didn't bring a present, don't you think?" Unfortunately, I had chosen that particular occasion to invite two girls from school whom I'd befriended in poetry club. They weren't allowed to play with me again after Meemaw's theatrics that day. "I'm just saying you didn't always have to turn everything into a battle. Sometimes . . . you drive people away."

Lifting her chin, she waved me off. "You're misremembering. Y'all were too young to understand all the things going on in the family. It wasn't anything for you kids to be concerned about."

Our extended family consisted of Meemaw's two older sons, Uncle Dennis and Uncle Frank. Frank had attempted a string of failed, short-lived marriages that hadn't resulted in any children. Dennis had married Patty, and they'd had Katelyn, who was roughly the same age as Rayanne. I'd always been a little jealous of Katelyn's friendship with Rayanne, because whenever she came to visit, the two of them absconded together, leaving me alone with Savannah, whom I didn't exactly relish being around. Katelyn had been a small-statured child, with long brown hair and doe-like, sad eyes. She was quiet and unassuming, and we all adored her, which was why I had insisted that she come to my party, a small gathering in Meemaw's backyard with a homemade chocolate cake, a blow-up pool, and a donkey piñata.

"OK then. Enlighten me," I said.

She sighed and shook her head. "I know what everyone said about me. 'Crazy Marylynn snapped again. Pulled a gun on her own daughter-in-law at her granddaughter's birthday party.' Well, that part may have been true, but it wasn't because that half-wit forgot a birthday present. And for heaven's sake, it wasn't like it was loaded. At least I don't think so. Anyway, who can remember those sorts of things at my age?" She doused the sweat from her forehead with a tea towel and parked herself down at the table for a rest. "The point is, I could see that she was never gonna be mother material. She was bad for Katelyn, bad for Dennis, bad for the family. And . . . now she's gone." She shrugged and looked at me as if she half expected me to thank her.

I never saw Aunt Patty again after that day and had always held Meemaw responsible for Katelyn's fractured family. Aside from a few postcards and holiday phone calls, Katelyn hadn't had much of a relationship with her mother. Her parents had eventually divorced.

"I tell you all this to show you what I learned the hard way," she continued. "That family is family. There's nothing I wouldn't do for you girls. I just hope you all feel that way about each other. Now, I don't know what Savannah's gone and done, but she's your sister, and you girls have got to forgive her. It can't be easy seeing her big sister go out and conquer the world while she's stuck waitressing and living with a lowlife."

Heat rose in my cheeks, and a familiar indignation swelled within my chest. "That's not my fault. Savannah is responsible for her own choices. She's waitressing because she chose to. She stays with Colton because she wants to. If she's unhappy about her life, she should change it. Why does it always feel like I can't celebrate my successes because I might hurt her feelings?"

"And what good is all that success if you lose the people that are most important, honey? Now I don't care who you are; life don't amount to a hill of beans if you lose that." Meemaw stood and busied herself with wiping down the counters, her face bearing the subtle grin of a woman who knew she had won. I hated that smile.

In my heart, I knew Savannah was never going to let herself be happy until she had closure, something to definitively prove that Georgia was never coming home, so we could all put the past behind us for good. Reluctantly I reached my hand into my pocket and pulled out the folded ticket, then dialed the number into my phone, hoping I was doing the right thing. The line rang twice before he answered.

"Hello?"

"Hey, Derrick. It's Sue Ellen Guidry. Listen, I know it's the weekend, but I was hoping you could help me out with something tomorrow."

He didn't hesitate to answer, and his voice was warm and kind. "Sure. Anything."

CHAPTER 21

Meemaw

April 1987

Cricket slurped the last bit of her soda through a straw, making a rattling sound that sent a shiver of annoyance through Marylynn's nerves. She turned her head to face her friend as if it were connected to a slowly moving hinge.

"Can you stop that, please?" she whispered.

"Why are we whispering?" Matching her volume, Cricket leaned closer to her. "They can't hear us all the way over there." Her friend wasn't wrong. She could have screamed, and not a soul would have heard her from where they sat parked across the street from Muscadine High School in the parking lot of the Sizzler.

Squinting through a pair of binoculars, Marylynn shushed Cricket again. "I don't know," she said, a note of irritation creeping into her tone. "Because I'm trying to concentrate." She supposed this was as good an excuse as any that she could come up with on the fly. She hadn't really thought this through. Trailing Beverly to the prom had seemed a much better idea in theory. But when Cricket had shown up at her house tonight unannounced—as she often did—suggesting they work on a church quilting project for the homeless, she'd been forced to take her with her, covering with the excuse that they would go for Arby's. After they had ordered their burgers, Marylynn parked the Buick just close enough to the night's events to catch sight of every teenager in Muscadine as they fluttered in and out of the gymnasium doors, which had been covered with paper streamers. Most of them came outside to smoke, but a few couples hung about on the porch steps, locked in each other's arms, far away from the watchful eyes of any chaperones.

"You're trying to concentrate on a bunch of teenaged hellions on a Saturday night? Surely we have better things to do with our time." Cricket crossed her arms over her chest and gave a self-righteous shimmy. "Like serving the poor and downtrodden with a new quilt." She drove the point home with a nod of her head.

"Trust me. I'm as downtrodden as they come." The idea of Beverly coming to the dance tonight with Jack had sent her blood pressure through the roof. She had a fairly good idea of what sorts of things happened on prom night. And she was desperate to know exactly what this older boy's intentions were with her naive daughter. She couldn't put her finger on it, but there was something about him that didn't sit right with her. He wasn't good enough for Beverly.

Cricket put her drink in the cup rest and let out an exhausted sigh. "What are we doing here, Marylynn?"

"We are preventing a travesty from occurring," she snapped, as if this should explain everything.

"Well, personally, I don't see what all the fuss is about. The Guidrys are good people. I went to school with his mother, and she was a God-fearing Christian woman. I'm sure Jack's a very nice boy."

Marylynn scoffed, keeping her eagle eyes locked in position. "I'm sure he's nice for someone. But not Beverly." With a wave of her hand, she motioned for Cricket to stop talking. "Shh! I see something."

A slew of teenagers decked out in tuxedos and a rainbow of taffeta trailed from the building. Marylynn scanned their faces, trying to pick out Beverly's black-and-white mermaid dress that she had pieced together herself, but she relaxed her shoulders when she realized her daughter wasn't among this crowd. Just before she tore her eyes away, she noticed the sturdy frame of one of the boys in a tacky powder-blue suit. She took in the thick black mullet, the beady eyes. It was Jack all right. And he had his arm around someone. But it wasn't Beverly. She wasn't sure if she should feel grateful or enraged on her daughter's behalf.

Pressing the binoculars deeper into the soft flesh around her eyes, she gasped. It was Celia. And the poor girl looked scared out of her wits. Marylynn watched him reach around her with his free hand and tug at a loose curl before running a finger down her bony cheek. Marylynn's blood ran hot, and she had half a mind to run them over with her car. Shaking the thought away, she reminded herself that it wasn't Celia's fault. The poor thing was too shy and inexperienced to know what he was up to. He'd probably forced himself on her.

Marylynn felt fit to burst. "That good-for-nothing son of a—"

Cricket snatched the binoculars from her and quickly got up to speed. "This is good, isn't it? We'll just tell Bev that he's flirting with other girls, and she'll break up with him," she said breezily.

"Not just other girls. He's flirting with her best friend."

As if hearing their conversation, Beverly emerged from the gymnasium, and Jack drew back his hand in a hurry, raking it over his stiff hair as if he'd been caught. But Beverly only smiled at the two of them and tugged at his jacket. He scooped her into his arms, leaned down, and planted a kiss on her lips, suddenly entirely uninterested in Celia.

Marylynn stiffened. "No." She shook her head, her eyes still fixed on Jack. "She'll never believe me." At this point Beverly viewed everything Marylynn said with contempt. It would have to come from another source.

"Well, what will you do? Teenage girls are not easily persuaded in matters of the heart."

But even before Cricket had spoken, Marylynn had already begun turning a few possibilities over in her mind. "I'm sure I'll think of something."

~

Tracing the loops in the final word, her fingers trailed along the hot metal exterior. A thin layer of brown paint coated her fingers, and she wiped it onto her jeans, erasing the evidence of what she had done. Drops of afternoon sunlight glinted off the metal file as she tucked it into her back pocket. She glanced from left to right before slipping away unseen into the woods, where she had parked the Buick in a little clearing about a half mile from the mill.

She wasn't proud of herself in this moment, but what else could she have done? Desperation made people do all sorts of unexplainable things. It had been six weeks since Jack had sat on her couch and confessed that he had nothing to offer her daughter, no home or future to speak of. And yet, two days ago, Beverly had come home rosy cheeked and bright as a daisy, showing off her cheaply made engagement ring, which was actually a birthstone of emerald and not a diamond, because Jack said he wanted to be original and do things differently than everyone else. But Marylynn suspected that it had been a convenient excuse to mask the real reason, which was that it was all he had been willing to spend on her, some pawn-store find he had come across when he was perusing for car parts. No matter that emerald was not even the correct birthstone for her daughter, who had been born clear in the middle of March. Little facts like this seemed to be of no importance to Jack—or to Beverly, for that matter. It took everything she had not to push him off her doorstep and forbid him from dating her daughter on threat of death. But she worried it would only send Beverly straight into his arms, and she couldn't risk that no matter how good it would feel.

From a distance, she had watched her daughter slip further and further away until she was only a speck on her horizon, a tiny dot that held her entire world inside it—the last drop of Charlie, the last piece of the life she had loved with him. If she let it slip away, then she would slip away with it. So that evening when Beverly stood in her kitchen as Marylynn cooked up a slab of chicken-fried steak, she did her best to appear as shocked and outraged as her daughter was at the news.

"I mean, who would do this?" Beverly asked, her blue eyes awash in confusion. "He doesn't have enemies."

"It's just awful." Marylynn tsked and feigned concern as best she could. "What did it say, again?"

"It called him a cheater, among other things," she said, shaking her head as if she couldn't possibly fathom those "other things" to be true.

Marylynn dipped a pair of tongs into the grease and turned her steak, revealing a golden brown on one side. "Well, that is upsetting. Do you think"—she paused, hoping to give Beverly a moment to form the thought on her own—"well, do you think there could be any truth behind the rumors? I mean, there aren't any other girls . . . are there?" She raised an eyebrow. "Maybe one of them found out she wasn't the only one. It's not unheard of." She looked up from her work, tilted her head, and waited as the grease crackled between them.

Beverly stared back, her mouth agape.

With an innocent lilt in her voice, Marylynn pushed forward. "I mean, it's just that, why would someone write something like that if it wasn't true?"

"It's not true, Mama." Crossing her arms, Beverly leaned forward as if she were smelling something out. "Wait a minute. Did you . . . no, you wouldn't have. Would you?"

Of course she would. Jack was a thief who had shown up in the middle of the night and taken what he'd wanted without asking her. As far as Marylynn was concerned, this was self-defense, plain and simple. She wished that Celia were here to ease the tension, but it had been weeks since she'd stayed over after school. These days, Bev spent most afternoons with Jack, which made it difficult for Marylynn to curb her smoking and was even worse for her blood pressure.

"I'm not sure I know what you're suggesting, but I can assure you I would never vandalize another person's property. Do you really think so little of me?" She clutched an offended hand to her heart.

Beverly didn't press the matter further and started off to set the table, but she kept one distrustful eye on her mother, as if she weren't fully convinced. So Marylynn approached her next few sentences carefully, suggesting them as casually as if she were commenting on the weather.

"Speaking of Jack, have you thought about where the two of you will live once you're . . . married?" The last word caught in her throat. It still felt unnatural to say it out loud.

Beverly groaned. "Mama, I am so tired of having this conversation. Where I live is not going to be your concern. You don't have to worry about me anymore." She thrust down a plate so hard that the table shook, rattling the silverware.

Try as she may, Marylynn couldn't help herself. "I just don't see how he's gonna care for you with no home and no plans. How will he take care of you if he can't take care of himself?" she demanded.

Rolling her eyes, Beverly let out a sigh. "If it makes you feel any better, we found a little place to rent, and we'll be moving in right after the wedding."

"Well, I suppose that's a relief at least." Marylynn sighed and wiped her hands on her apron. Expertly, she tossed the steak onto a dish of paper towels and dabbed away the grease before returning to the drippings that bubbled in the pan. Sprinkling in a spoonful of flour, she leveled her gaze once more at her daughter, hoping to make some last-ditch argument that would get through to her, something that could turn back the clock and reverse all that had happened over the last few weeks. But all she had left was an ache in her bones and angry quips.

"His back seat isn't big enough for the two of you. Unless he sleeps in the trunk. Come to think of it, that's not the worst idea." She smirked to herself.

"Actually"—Beverly placed her ring-clad hand to her stomach while her lips gave way to a euphoric grin—"I meant to tell you before, but . . . well, I guess now is as good a time as any." Biting her lower lip, she drew in a deep breath, and Marylynn felt her heart go skittering in her chest. "It's gonna be the three of us now."

A whisk fell to the floor and with it a spray of hot grease that sent Marylynn into an obscenity-laced monologue about how bad news should not be sprung so casually upon a person who is not ready to receive it. She crouched on the floor, wiping away the slick spots with a tea towel, her eyes focusing on nothing in particular. Pushing herself into a sitting position, she slouched against the cabinets, the muscles of her face now slack.

"Mama, this is good news. Why do you make it sound so awful?" Beverly nudged her encouragingly, then placed a concerned hand around her waist and helped her stand on shaky legs. But all Marylynn could think as she stumbled into a chair was that she could no longer hold on to anything anymore. Jack Guidry was here to stay.

CHAPTER 22

Savannah

Saturday Night

Selfish. Childish. Stubborn. Reckless. Rayanne's words rang in my ears until I wondered if maybe she'd been right. Maybe I shouldn't have called them home, should have just buried Georgia's memory in the cold earth next to Mama. In just twenty-four hours, they would leave again, and I suspected I'd done more harm to our relationship than good.

The soft evening light disappeared into thick darkness, but the humidity hung in the air and weighed on my damp skin with a heaviness I couldn't shake. I cranked the windows down, let the night breeze whip through my loose spirals, and hoped the wind would carry away the giant stone of regret on my chest. Regret for what, I still wasn't sure. The driving helped, but there wasn't enough blacktop in Muscadine to drive away the hurt. At only eight miles across, a person might not even recognize they'd driven through it. So I doubled back on every street, every open field, every back road until my eyes stopped stinging. I could have driven blindfolded through the entire town if I'd had to.

I texted Tammy, but she'd just been promoted to management at the only motel in town and was working late tonight. So, after a long drive, I figured a bar would be a good place to start. The truck crunched over loose gravel in front of Jasper's as I searched for a parking spot. It was nearly full, which was on par for a Saturday night, but almost immediately I spotted Colton's baby-blue Chevy. I'd told him not to expect me home much this weekend since I would be spending most of my time with Rayanne and Sue Ellen. *So much for that.* Hopefully he'd be happy to see me. I needed to see a familiar face, even if it was his. After doing a quick touch-up of my mascara in the rearview mirror, I pinched my cheeks and headed for the front door.

Passing the pool tables and darts, I searched the crowd for his signature hair but came up short.

"Hey, Jasper." Shaking off the evening, I tried to sound upbeat as I took a seat at the bar.

Jasper had been in Rayanne's grade and had renamed the bar after himself after his father passed away. He jumped a little at the sound of my voice, nearly dropping the glass he was polishing.

"Savannah. Erm . . . didn't expect to see you here tonight."

"Yeah, well . . ." I sighed, blowing a stray curl out of my eyes. "It's been a day. But I think you have the solution to all my problems. Coors Light, please." I forced a smile as he handed me a frosted mug without looking at me. "Hey, have you seen Colton around?"

Jasper's eyes darted sideways, and I could tell that he was nervous about something. I suspected that something had to do with Colton, but I didn't say it and instead watched Jasper fall over his words.

"Look, Savannah," he finally said over the noise of patrons talking and glasses clinking, "he's in the gaming room. I told him it was a bad idea . . ." At my silence, he blew out his cheeks and dragged a hand down the back of his head. "He didn't go in there alone."

It should have come as no surprise. Considering his little rendezvous with Mrs. Henderson last week, another girl would have expected this. But in my heart I had honestly believed it had never gone past a little harmless flirting. He'd never actually cheated on me, which I supposed was what had made it easier to justify staying with him.

"Thank you, Jasper." I downed the rest of my drink and laid down a crumpled wad of cash before carrying myself around the corner to find the back of Colton's long, greasy hair being massaged by the cherry-red fingernails of Mrs. Henderson.

The two of them were so absorbed in their make-out session that neither one noticed my entrance until I spoke. "You should really thank me for that. He was a terrible kisser when I met him."

Mrs. Henderson jolted upright and began smoothing down her updo and tugging at her top while Colton stared back at me open mouthed, his lips so smudged by lipstick that it seemed as if he were having an allergic reaction.

"I'm sure I don't know what you mean," she mumbled as she made a beeline for the exit.

I cut Colton off before he could defend himself. "It's over. I'm finished."

"Come on, Savannah! You don't mean that," he stuttered, throwing out his hands. "She means nothing. She came on to me."

"It's never your fault, is it? Look, I'm not even that broken up about it, all right? It's been a long time coming." As I stopped a tear from trickling down my cheek, it hit me that I wasn't crying over him. And that made it easier to do what I should have done, what I had tried to do so many times before. This time I needed to make it stick. "Just get your trailer off my property."

"You know I can't. My parents aren't gonna let me move back in. My dad's already threatening to fire me. I got nowhere to go."

"That's not my problem anymore. Hey"—I pressed a finger to my chin as if I'd just gotten a novel idea—"maybe Mrs. H. and her husband could adopt you?" I turned and headed for the door, made my way toward the exit as Colton sprinted after me.

"You don't know what you're saying right now. You're angry, and you have every right to be, but we'll work it out, baby. We always do. You need me!" he shouted, jabbing a thumb to his chest.

As I tore out of Jasper's, déjà vu swept over me, and I wondered if he was right. Why did I need him? Why did I keep crawling back to him when I knew that different versions of this same scene would play out over and over again? Come to think of it, maybe I did need a sit-down with Rayanne's therapist. Maybe she would say there was something seriously wrong with me.

With nowhere else to go, I finally headed back to Meemaw's, where I found Sue Ellen waiting for me, looking as if she actually cared where I'd been.

CHAPTER 23

Rayanne

Saturday Night

The drive from Porter's Trailer Park was a blurry one. Tears clouded my vision as I replayed our conversation on a loop in my mind. Tugging down the mirror, I dabbed at my eyes and wiped at the mascara running down my cheeks. I needed to get a handle on myself before I saw Meemaw again. She had always been able to tell when something was bothering me, and I knew she wouldn't rest until she'd sniffed it out.

Barely able to make out the twisting roads through the darkness, I pulled the car into Lavon's empty parking lot and rested my swimming head on the steering wheel. Eyes closed, I wrapped my arms around my shoulders and focused on steadying my breaths until the shaking in my chest slowed. I fumbled in my purse and found the shape of my pill bottle, then popped it open and placed a Xanax on my tongue. Tossing my head back, I swallowed it dry. Contrary to whatever Sue Ellen believed about me, I didn't need the pills to deal with my life now, because I loved my life with Graham and the kids. I needed them to keep myself from reliving the one we had already survived. I'd tried so hard to forget that day, but no matter how deep I shoved the memory down, the guilt never really went away. Where had I been? Why hadn't I been close by to protect Georgia the way a big sister was supposed to, the way Mama had always expected me to? I imagined her standing knee deep there in the water, looking up at me with those cerulean eyes so full of trust. In my dreams I called out to warn her, but my voice was never able to break above a whisper. And then a soft wind rustled the trees, and she was gone.

Shaking the image away, I reached for my phone, wondering if maybe I should call home once more to check on the kids, but I dropped it onto the seat next to me when I remembered that it was dusk, and they had already gone to sleep. Come to think of it, I was tired myself. Suddenly my eyes felt heavy, and I wondered how bad it would be if I took a short nap here. Worrying about the kids from a hundred miles away, worrying about Savannah and Levi—it was all so exhausting. Before I had convinced myself one way or the other, sleep settled over me like a warm blanket, and my limbs felt heavy.

A light rapping on my window startled me awake, and I jerked my head up before smoothing down my hair, pretending I hadn't just been asleep. In a parking lot.

"Rayanne, is that you?" Cricket squinted through the window, cupping her hands around her blue-shadowed eyes.

Oh no. I did not have the mental bandwidth to deal with this woman right now. Cricket was one of the bubbliest people I knew, and normally I would have been able to match her sweetness word for obnoxious word. But not tonight. The only thing I could think about was crawling into bed and counting down the hours until I left this godforsaken town behind.

She motioned for me to come inside the store, and I politely declined with a wave of my hand. "No, thank you," I said loudly through the glass. "I really have to get back now." Blinking away the sleep, I tried to appear alert enough to drive.

"Nonsense. You'll come in the store, and we'll have a drink," she commanded. I had no choice in the matter, so against my will I followed her inside.

~

Sipping a glass of sweet tea as I sat across from Cricket in a booth, I forced a smile.

"You know, Josh and his wife are separated," she said, not realizing that I had stopped paying attention long ago, after her lengthy summary of her mother's bout with shingles. "It's just the most horrible thing." She lowered her voice to a whisper and looked around for prying eyes before continuing. "She's left him for her CrossFit instructor. I didn't want to say anything before, but it's all over town. Which just goes to show that no one's life is perfect. We all have our demons." She shot me a pointed look before taking a dainty sip of tea.

I nodded along, feigning interest, but my head was pounding, and all I could seem to focus on was the thrumming as the blood beat against my skull in steady waves.

As if hearing my thoughts, Cricket asked, "Is everything OK, hon?" She tilted her head intently, doing a poor job of hiding her concern. I couldn't blame her. I supposed I would have been worried, too, if I had just caught her sleeping it off in a parking lot.

"I'm fine," I said, hoping it sounded convincing so I could leave. Cricket was a talker, and if I was going to spend much longer listening to her prattle on about diseases and divorces, I was going to need a softer chair and a stiffer drink.

"I don't say this to be rude," she said, unable to take her eyes off my matted hair, one side of which was now soaked in drool, "it's just that . . . you look . . . tired. And I know how exhausting it can be when you have little ones. No one would blame you if you . . . you know"—she made a discreet drinking gesture with her thumb and pinkie—"every now and then." I covered my eyes and sank lower into my seat, wishing the floor would swallow me up.

"I'm not drunk, Cricket," I whispered, rubbing the bridge of my nose. "It's just . . ." I blew out my cheeks, not sure if I wanted to tell her, but the words came out anyway. "I saw him tonight."

"Saw who?" she asked, straining forward and screwing up her face. Cricket had always been a sponge for gossip, and I knew that whatever I told her would find its way back to Meemaw, but right now it seemed more appealing than talking to anyone else in my family.

"Him," I said again, a little louder. "Our father. Or sperm donor. Whichever is more fitting. Take your pick." I waved a hand.

"I see," she said, settling back into her seat. "And what did he say?"

"Said he wanted to be involved, get to know the kids." I sighed, rubbing my head. "And . . . he needed money." I stewed and flexed my fingers. "Turns out Meemaw was right about him."

"Your grandmother's right about a lot of people, honey," she said flatly. "It's a gift."

"The thing is, I went there tonight, ready to forgive him. And I almost did. But I don't know. I can't let him into my kids' lives if I can't trust him not to disappoint them."

"And disappoint you," she added with a knowing smile.

"I guess so," I admitted. "Maybe. You know what he said to me? He said that Meemaw told him to stay away. Can you believe that? He tried to put it all on her."

Cricket blanched, her rosy cheeks drooping a bit. "Well, he isn't wrong. Marylynn would have done anything to keep you girls with her. Can you blame him for not going toe to toe with her? You know as well as I do she has a way about her." That was the understatement of the century. "She loves you all so much."

"Her love was never in question," I muttered, rubbing at my forehead. "Just her sanity."

"Jack knew he didn't stand a chance against her. I mean, if it were Charlotte and Tucker, wouldn't you have done the same?"

"Yes," I said, absentmindedly stirring my drink. "I guess." My need to protect them was the driving force in my life and had created a growing rift between Graham and me. The source of most of our arguments, in fact. I thought back to the previous week, when I noticed he hadn't tightened the straps on Charlotte's car seat. I'd cried and threatened to ban him from driving the kids anywhere until he watched an alarming video I had seen on social media documenting the injuries that can occur from improper restraint.

I didn't know why it hadn't occurred to me before this moment, but all at once it became impossible to deny. "I'm just like her." The words came out dazed as I heard myself speak them aloud for the first time. "All this time, I've been trying so hard to forget all the ridiculous things she did, but I can't escape her. I'm her." I shook my head in fervent denial, but it didn't make it any less true. I was Meemaw, the new-and-improved version, maybe, but still her. With that same paranoid look in my eyes when someone stared too long at my children or commented on how beautiful they were. Would I ruin Charlotte's prom by spying on her? Scare off all Tucker's dates and make him a pariah at school? Would his friends have a running joke about his stalker mother who tailed the school bus just to make sure it wasn't highjacked by a band of criminals? My breath came hard and fast. Would I meddle in their lives until they pushed me away and left me alone, as we had done to her?

As if sensing my panic, Cricket reached out for my hand. "Is it really so bad if you're like her? Your grandmother loves you girls something fierce. That's nothing to be embarrassed about. I know she can be . . . a lot," she admitted guiltily. "But she had a hard life, losing Charlie so young. Then Georgia. And your mama." Discreetly she wiped a tear from her cheek. "She's just so afraid of losing anyone else. Surely you can understand what that feels like."

I could. I knew what it felt like to abandon all sense of logic when it came to protecting my family. I was so afraid of losing the best parts of my life that I sometimes forgot to enjoy them. Deborah had said on more than one occasion that I suffered from "a compulsive need to control my surroundings." She wasn't wrong. When we finally had Tucker, I knew I would have to be present for all of it, quit my job selling real estate, give him every part of me, and never look away. No one would protect him like his own mother could from sickness or strangers or lakes that could drag him under. I reminded myself that love meant sacrifice. But if I was being honest, I didn't trust anyone else to do things correctly in my place—not even Graham. Sometimes, especially not Graham.

"I guess fear of abandonment isn't the worst thing I could have inherited from her." I laughed once before settling back into the weight of the moment, then chugged down the rest of my tea.

Cricket bit her lip and studied me as if considering whether to continue, but true to her nature, she forged ahead. "Honey, have you ever thought that your inability to trust others has less to do with your grandmother and more to do with your father?"

The words hit me harder than I was prepared for. All that money we had spent on therapy, only for me to be accurately psychoanalyzed by a woman named Cricket between the toilet paper aisle and the Corn Flakes display.

"No. I suppose I hadn't considered that."

CHAPTER 24

SUE ELLEN

Saturday Night

Meemaw agreed to let me borrow her Buick to search for the two of them, but I had only just made it out the front door when I heard the roar of Savannah's truck roll into the drive. As her tiny frame descended from the mammoth vehicle, I homed in on her eyes, which were red and swollen, sending a sharp dose of guilt directly to my gut.

"Where've you been?" I asked, approaching her cautiously.

"Just had to take care of some things." She slammed the door and brushed past me, leaving a trail of palpable hostility in her wake.

"Anything you want to talk about?" I followed after her toward the house.

"No, thank you. Don't need another lecture, Professor."

"Look." I planted myself in front of her, stopping her escape. "We overreacted. And Rayanne was totally out of line."

She looked up at me, stone-faced, without missing a beat. "No big deal. I'm over it." But her words were sharp and obligatory. I didn't believe them.

"Also, I thought you'd want to know that I called Derrick, and he agreed to help me look into Georgia's file tomorrow. I can read police reports and eyewitness statements, see if there's anything they missed." At this, her face seemed to brighten, but I could tell she was trying her best not to let it show. I waited for her to say something, expecting a thank-you at the very least, but she only shrugged. "I mean, I defended you, so I don't know why you're upset with me."

She pushed past me, barely brushing my shoulder with hers. "Of course you don't. How could you?"

Not sure where she was going with this, I drew my eyebrows together, trying to understand what I had missed. "Look, I know things were never great between us, but lately . . . Did I do something to upset you?"

Chuckling to herself, she swiveled around to face me. "You didn't do anything. That's just it. Don't you get it?" She cocked her head to the side, leveling her gaze at me, and I suddenly felt unbalanced. "Does your boyfriend even know you have a younger sister? Because you've done a pretty good job of making me feel like I've been erased from your life."

"What are you talking about? I'm here, aren't I? After you practically begged me to come."

"Yes, you are." Closing her eyes, she shook her head. "And so am I."

An ember burned low beneath my ribs, and I could hear the heat of it escape in my voice. "What is that supposed to mean? I offered to help you leave this place. I sent you brochures for different colleges, looked into jobs for you. You didn't want to leave."

"I *couldn't* leave. Who was gonna take care of Meemaw?"

"Don't do that. Don't use her as an excuse. She has Cricket and Sam. We could have made arrangements for others to look in on her. Be honest. You wanted to stay. So don't try to make me feel guilty for getting out of here." Even as I said the words, I knew I wasn't being fair. Knowing that Savannah had stayed behind made it easier for me to stay away. Not that I didn't have my own problems. The pressure of being the first person in my family to graduate from college, and one of the best in the country at that, had been a heavy weight for me to bear. On top of that, being a recipient of a partial scholarship had made me acutely aware of my need to succeed. Failure had never been an option.

"Forget it," she said, waving me away and heading for the porch steps. "You know what . . . I don't even care anymore."

"If you have something to say to me, just say it," I said, equally confused and offended.

"All right." She turned around to face me squarely. "Why didn't you comment on my graduation? I posted about it. A few months ago. You remember that?" She crossed her arms and waited patiently for me to explain myself. My face flushed so hot I was sure she could see it.

"What?" I laughed, trying unconvincingly to dismiss the accusation. "Are you being serious right now? Come on, Savannah. This is ridiculous. How should I remember what you posted months ago?"

"I don't know. Maybe because it was a pretty huge event for me, considering I finally earned a degree, something you've been on me about doing ever since you left for school. 'An education is the only way out, Savannah. You need a degree to be someone in the world' and all of that holier-than-thou crap about higher education. Ring a bell?"

"So I missed a post. Big deal. You're really going to hold that against me?"

"Of course not." She stared at me, tilting her head as if she were figuring me out, which made me take an instinctive step backward. "But let me ask you a question. Name one thing that's happened to me over the past year—hell, even the past month. Can you name one thing?"

"Yes," I said the word a little too emphatically, which did not add to my credibility. "You work at the Salty Pot. You're dating Colton. There. That's two things about you." I held up my fingers as I counted them off like a proud kindergartner.

"Those are things you could have learned yesterday. Name something specific."

"I can't remember," I lied.

"Ha! You mean to tell me that the same girl who memorized the prologue of *Romeo and Juliet* in the fourth grade cannot remember a single thing I've shared about my life in the past year?"

My eyes darted from the ground to my hands, and that was all it took to confirm what she already knew to be true.

"Tell me the truth. Did you unfollow me?"

"Of course not," I said, stumbling through the words. "I just . . . have a lot of friends, a lot of colleagues and students and . . . there's just a lot of people I have to keep in touch with for work. So maybe I didn't see your stuff."

"Yes, but you only have two sisters." She held up two fingers to drive home the point. "You never thought to see what I was up to? Pick up the phone and send a text? Lord knows, I know all about your dates with Liam, the art shows, the galas, more coffee dates than anyone should be forced to suffer through."

I sucked in a breath, trying to come up with an answer that made sense. "Of course I didn't—"

"You did, didn't you? You unfollowed me," she said, incredulous. "I don't know why I didn't see it before."

My back stiffened, sending a shiver of guilt through me. I opened my mouth to refute the allegation, but no words came out. Not that it would have helped. The truth was written all over my face.

She shook her head, furrowing her brow. "I mean, it is so something you would do, but also just so petty. Even for you." She studied me with disgust, as if she were seeing me for the first time.

"It's not personal, Savannah." I held up my hands to block her exit. "It's not why you think."

"How can it not be personal? It's personal to me. And you don't get to tell me how to feel right now."

My mouth refused to work, and the screen in my head had gone entirely blank. She was right.

"Why?" She stared at me, her jaw set, though her eyes were filled with tears. "What did I ever do to you? Because all that kid crap, the stuff that we used to fight about . . . I mean, most people grow out of that. Why can't you let it go?"

I blew out my cheeks and tried to rebalance myself. "Look, this isn't fair, but . . . it's hard to see you, OK? Like, when I see you, it makes me think of her. And when I think of her, I think of the two of you together. And then I remember how much I hated you both for sucking up all the air in the house, for taking up so much of Mama's energy. For everything that happened after."

She nodded along slowly, as if everything were finally making sense to her, but I saw her blink back fresh tears. "Well, at least you're being honest about it now. You blame me. Well, that makes two of us." She bit her lip, and a flicker of angst crossed her face. "Look, you don't have to explain anymore. I get it. You hate me. You have always hated me." She started to push past me, but I reached for her arm, desperate.

"No, you don't get it." Now I was the one who was crying. "I used to wish you away, the two of you. And then when it happened . . . I don't know. I just felt responsible somehow, you know? Like I was the one who made it all happen. And after that day at the lake, Mama clung even harder to you. I felt . . . invisible." I plopped myself down on the porch steps, my voice thick with emotion I hadn't expected. "I mean, I realize it's ridiculous to think a five-year-old could influence destiny but . . . I did. For a long time. And when I see your face—her face—I just . . . I don't know. I feel all this guilt about everything. It was easier to just . . . cut out the hurt. Does that make sense?"

I held her eyes, willing her to understand, needing her to know that it had nothing to do with her but with me. Of course, now that I was an enlightened, rational adult, I realized that it wasn't Savannah's fault that our mother was distracted, or that she favored her over me. She had been grieving, and I supposed there wasn't any right way to do that. But it still hurt, and if I was being honest, maybe leaving Muscadine had been less about following my dreams and more like a way to prove something about myself to everyone else—to prove that I was worthy, too. And maybe I had been punishing my little sister for too long.

Inching toward me, she nodded, and the tension in the air lulled to a low hum.

"I'm sorry," I finally managed to get out through tears. "It was unforgivable. Of course I care about you. You're my sister. You didn't deserve it." When she didn't respond, I realized I was going to have to dig a little deeper. "If it makes you feel any better, Liam broke up with me. Months ago. And I haven't said anything because"—I heaved a sigh, blowing a stray curl out of my eyes—"because I didn't want you guys to see me failing at yet another relationship." I scoffed. "To top it off, I'm living on my best friend's couch because I'm hoping that maybe he'll take me back. God, how pathetic is that?"

She lowered herself next to me on the steps, cradling her head in her hands. "Oh, I don't know. Not that pathetic." The beginning of a grin tugged at the corners of her lips. "My life is a bit of a mess right now, too. I lost my job today." She rolled her eyes. "And you weren't exactly wrong about Colton." Tears seeped from the corners of her eyes, and she covered her face with her hands. Unsure of what to do, I placed a cautious hand on her shoulder, feeling like a stranger. How had I managed to be such a colossal failure as a sister?

"I'm sorry, Savannah. I should have done a better job of staying in touch. I should have come home for your graduation. Geez, I should have sent a card, at least."

"You should have." She nudged me playfully. It took a few moments before she could get the words out. "I'm sorry, too. It changed all of us." She looked up at the inky night sky and a sea of stars, then closed her eyes tightly, as if she were remembering.

I draped an arm around her shoulder, and she let out a long breath. "There's something I never told you," she said, digging her feet into the dirt. "I did apply to college after high school. Even got into LSU. Hardship scholarship."

My ears perked up and my eyes went wide. "Savannah, that's amazing. Why didn't you tell me? Why didn't you go?"

"It just . . . never felt right. Like I didn't really deserve it. Georgia should have been the one to go. It should have been her. It wouldn't have been fair."

My heart sank, and it took me a long time to say anything. I'd pushed her to get away from this place only because I thought it would broaden her horizons, give her an easy way to escape the weight of the past. It was impossible to drive around this town without feeling that heaviness saturating everything. I'd never thought that the same pain that drove me away from Muscadine was the one thing holding her here. "You can't say that. She's not here, but you are. And she would have wanted you to do what makes you happy."

"Wish I knew what that was."

"And all that time I just kept nagging you about it," I said, feeling sick to my stomach. "I'm sorry. I didn't know you felt that way."

"It's OK. How could you have known?" She smiled at me, but I could tell she was trying to keep from crying. "Plus, it's not your fault I dated a man who never matured past the tenth grade. You were right. He peaked in high school." She chuckled, but there was an air of defeat in her voice. "Whatever. It's over now, so it doesn't matter," she said, massaging tiny circles in her temples.

"You ended things with Colton? How did he take it?" I asked, grateful that there was someone even more terrible than me to discuss.

"He didn't. I told him to move his trailer off my property, and all I want is the land that I bought, but he says he's not going anywhere, and that he'll just wait until I come to my senses."

"Do you think you will? I mean . . . do you want to go back to him?"

She wiped her face with the hem of her tank top. "I don't think so. But I'm scared to death to be on my own. It's like, ever since Georgia left, half of me left with her. And maybe it's stupid, but I hate being alone. It feels . . . wrong. Like it was never supposed to be this way. Guess it was easier to believe that maybe she was still out there. Waiting for me to find her." Wrapping her arms around herself, she scoffed and shook her head. "It was stupid, I know."

I had never been able to put my finger on all the reasons I couldn't be close with Savannah, why we could never seem to break through the wall that kept us from really seeing one another. But now my heart ached, and all at once the only thing I wanted was to make her feel safe.

"You're never going to be on your own. You've got me and Rayanne. And for better or worse, you've always got Meemaw." I nudged her ribs, drawing a stifled laugh. "At the risk of giving you more unsolicited advice, Colton is not a good look on you. I mean, I hate to say it, but Meemaw was right about him. It irritates the hell out of me, but she usually is." I laughed, hoping to coax a smile from her before getting serious again. "You've got to end it with him for good and take back what's yours."

Slowly she nodded her head and dabbed at her mascara with her fingertips. "I know. But I honestly don't know what to do. I don't think he's gonna leave on his own. We've been through this before. So many times. And he always ends up right back on my couch."

The blackness of the night enveloped us while a chorus of katydids serenaded us with their monotonous humming. If I had learned anything from Meemaw, it was that life was too short to wait around on other people to get things right. Maybe our grandmother had done some irrational things in her time, but maybe she'd done them because she knew that time doesn't stand still. Sometimes it was worth risking everything to save the ones you love from heartache, from disappointment, sometimes from themselves. Her heart had always been in the right place, even if her execution had the grace of a cow on roller skates.

"Well . . ." I bit my lip, unsure whether to let the thought take hold. "Maybe you're thinking about this all wrong," I said finally. "Maybe you don't need to ask yourself what to do." I raised an eyebrow and cast a glance over my shoulder toward Meemaw's screen door. "Maybe the question we should be asking ourselves is, 'What would Marylynn Pritchett do?'"

CHAPTER 25

Meemaw

November 1987

The hum of fluorescent lights and the rhythmic whir of machinery lulled her into fitful sleep until a door swept open, carrying a breeze that jolted her awake. Straightening herself against a sticky vinyl chair the color of an avocado, Marylynn tried to gather her druthers.

"Time to try feeding her again," a chipper voice said as a tiny blonde nurse sailed in, carrying a pink bundle to her chest. She nestled the baby against Beverly's breast and tugged down her gown, then brushed the infant's cheek with a finger, gingerly coaxing her to latch.

"It feels so strange," Beverly said, squirming against a pillow as she juggled the child. "Feeding another person from my own body. Knowing that she's depending on me for everything now."

"Yes, I know the feeling well." Marylynn leaned in and reached out a hand to cup the baby's fuzzy blonde head. "It never stops, you know," she said, catching Beverly's eye. "The sacrifice. The needing. Things are gonna be different now."

"Mama, why do you have to take a happy moment and ruin it? My life is going to be different—yes, I understand." Brushing away tears, she spoke the words to the child in her arms. "But can't you just be happy for me this once? For us?"

"It's not that I'm not happy for you. I just want to know what's going to happen when you leave here. What will the next eighteen years of this child's life be like? Hell, let's start with the next twenty-four hours. How is he gonna take care of you both? Does he even want to?"

"I told you. We'll manage," Beverly said through a tight grimace.

"For God's sake, Bev, he's not even here." Throwing out her hands, Marylynn jerked herself up and began pacing. "Now, it was all fine and dandy playing house before you had another person to think about, but things have changed. It's not about him anymore. Or you. It's about her." She pointed a finger at the child, who was blissfully nursing away. For a moment Marylynn was lost again in the beauty of her grandchild, the softness of her skin, the way her tiny body struggled against the tightness of the blanket, and the way those little noises she made sent a stab of motherly ache through her chest. Her voice softened. "Why don't you come on home with me? Your room's there waiting for you just as you left it. You could take classes in the evenings, and I'll watch the baby."

"For the millionth time, I don't want to take classes. And I'm not going home with you. Jack will be here." She shifted herself abruptly, jostling the baby, which sent her wailing. "He's busy trying to get things ready for us is all," she said over the crying.

Marylynn sat down at the edge of the bed and pressed a hand to her forehead. Realizing she was out of patience and time, she spoke softer. "Baby was born yesterday, Bev. If he ain't here by now, he's not coming."

"He'll come," she said firmly. But Marylynn could see the uncertainty in her eyes, the way she drew the baby a little closer and shushed her as if she were trying to convince her, too.

The door creaked open again. For a moment Marylynn wondered if perhaps she would be proved wrong, but Celia's birdlike frame crept into the room, her arms stretched out for the baby before she'd even reached Beverly's bed.

"Let me see her," she crooned.

Beverly beamed up at her friend, looking prouder than Marylynn could remember.

"She's beautiful," Celia said, tucking the baby into her arms. "You're a mother now." She shook her head, and her eyes filled with tears. "I can hardly believe it." With a wistful smile, she seemed mesmerized by the child, and it made Marylynn's throat grow thick with emotion.

"I'm here now," Celia said, resting a hand on Beverly's arm. "Whatever you need, I'm here for you."

Marylynn's heart leaped a little at the thought of Celia being there for her daughter, knowing she had someone besides Jack to count on.

"Thank you." Beverly placed a hand over her heart and let out a contented sigh, then dropped her head back onto the pillow.

Celia looked from Marylynn to her friend and back again before asking, "Where's Jack?"

Steepling her fingers together, Marylynn hung her head as if in prayer. Even worse than hating Jack was the realization that perhaps he didn't love her daughter back with the same fierceness Beverly gave to him. Marylynn had watched her offer him her whole self, body and soul, and what had she gotten in return? It was so much easier when and all she needed was a Band-Aid to fix a skinned knee and a kiss to heal the hurt away. But now that she was grown, a woman in her own right with a child of her own, what was a mother to do? Adrift in a sea of uncertainty, she was completely helpless to the whims of one unremarkable man who couldn't make up his mind. Pulling herself up, Marylynn reached for her purse and headed for the door.

∼

The windows of the old Buick were open, sending her curls whipping back and forth as she drove across town, flicking sparks of cigarette butts along the highway like bursts of hot flint against steel. The car weaved furiously through traffic, until she was caught behind a semitruck. Laying on the horn, she swerved around it onto the shoulder and barreled her way toward the mill. It loomed ahead in the distance off the next exit, its puffy clouds of smoke and sulfur rising into the air like whirlwinds of gray.

She parked the car in the busy lot and sauntered to the door, passing dump trucks and stacks of lumber and giant trailer beds laden with heavy cylinders. With a determined gait, she searched for Jack's beat-up car that bore her handiwork but saw only a handful of dusty trucks in the lot next to a bright-red Thunderbird. She eyed it suspiciously and barreled toward the entrance.

Ignoring the incensed shouts of men in yellow hard hats, she pushed her way toward the giant metal door of the mill and pounded a fist. A befuddled young man with a ponytail in a yellow vest pried it open a smidge, eyeing her distrustfully. Though he tried to tell her no visitors were allowed inside, she sensed correctly he wasn't willing to put hands on a woman. She pushed past him easily and shouted as she paced the halls.

"Jack! Jack Guidry!" Inspecting each room for signs of life, she moved along until she reached a giant chamber with a conveyor belt and men lined up along its sides, feeding the logs into it with metal rakes.

Jack turned to face her at the sound of his name, his face so pale and somber that Marylynn sensed he might have wet himself from the shock of seeing her there. Fumbling to put away his tools, he excused himself from a few confused coworkers and crept toward her cautiously.

"I see you're working, so at least there's that," she said, inspecting her surroundings as if for the first time.

"Can I"—he looked around as if to make sure no one was watching the two of them, but it seemed the other few men were all locked in on their conversation—"help you with something?"

"Well, now, I don't know. Can you help me?" She placed a finger to her chin and pursed her lips. "Maybe try showing up at the birth of your child. Maybe try to be a husband and father instead of telling tall tales to my daughter about how you're gonna make something of yourself."

"Listen, I don't know what she told you. She knew I couldn't get out of work this weekend. I'm doing the best I can, Marylynn, but I told her I ain't got the money yet for the house she wants. I'm weeks away from first month's rent and deposit. She got it in her head that it's all gonna happen right now, and I just . . . can't." He shrugged, not meeting her eyes.

"You can't?" She mulled it over. "Or you won't? Wouldn't have anything to do with that shiny new car in the lot, would it? Now correct me if I'm wrong, but here you are with a new car, slap outa money and intelligence, and you got the nerve to impregnate my daughter while you ain't got a pot to piss in? Now I don't know how a person manages with that kind of manure for brains, going around making the kind of senseless decisions you been making around here, but I know one thing for sure." She jabbed a finger into his chest, sending him back a step. "My daughter and my grandbaby will not be living in the back of that car. I don't care if it does have leather seats! And since my child seems to have temporarily lost her senses, I'm gonna make sure that doesn't happen."

Sighing, she reached into her handbag and pulled out her checkbook, then hastily scrawled in the blanks and signed a messy signature. Was this what Charlie had meant when he said that she would have to trust their children? Maybe signing away what was left of his meager life insurance would finally make Bev happy. How else was she supposed to hold her world together, even if it meant including this sorry excuse for a son-in-law?

She held the check up and pushed it into his chest. "This should cover rent for the first few months. After that, it's up to you," she said. "All I ask"—her voice cracked, and she had to look away from him while she said the next part—"is that you make her happy." Lord knew she had tried and failed.

"I don't know if I can. I . . . I don't know if I'm ready to be a father," he stammered, eyeing the check as if it were a grenade.

Leveling her gaze at him, she gritted her teeth and placed a firm hand on his shoulder. "I got news for you, Jack. It don't matter if you're ready. My daughter is lying in a hospital bed, recovering from the birth of your offspring. The decision has been made, and whether I like it or not, we are all stuck with you. Now"—she brushed off his shoulders and straightened her spine—"first you're gonna get yourself down to that hospital, and then you're gonna go to that landlord and see about that house."

He reached for the check reluctantly, but she held it back just out of his reach. "But if I find out that you squandered this on some hare-brained scheme, so help me, Jack Guidry, I will call the bank faster than your slow country ass can string two sentences together and claim it's a forgery."

Lowering his eyes, he gave a single nod, and she loosened her grip, finally letting him take the money. Composing herself, she plastered on a smile and headed for the door. Before she walked into the sunlight, she turned to face him once more, her cold exterior giving way to something softer.

"She's beautiful, by the way. Your daughter. In case you cared to know. Rayanne is beautiful."

CHAPTER 26

SAVANNAH

Saturday Night

"Come in, Black Widow. Are you in position? Over." I extended the heart antenna on a pink Barbie walkie-talkie. When I was ten, they had been among my most prized possessions, a Christmas present from Meemaw, who rarely got me what I asked for, much less anything that wasn't "gently used." In her house, buying something with original tags was the equivalent of blasphemy. I hadn't considered the fact that you needed two people to make them work, and Sue Ellen hadn't the slightest interest in playing detective with me. For once, it appeared that Meemaw's hoarding had paid off. A few weeks ago, as I was searching for a box of my summer clothes, I had found the walkie-talkies perfectly preserved in a giant Tupperware container of our old things in the carport. Somehow I'd convinced Sue Ellen that if we were going on a mission tonight, we had to use them. It had been easier than I thought, since she felt especially guilty about cutting me out of her life and all.

"Seriously, Savannah? Can we please not do the code name thing? Just use my real name. Isn't it embarrassing enough that we have to use these?"

"Fine." I rolled my eyes. "Are you in position? Over."

"Yes. And you don't have to keep saying 'over.' From here on out, just assume I can hear you every time you press the red button."

"Why do you have to take the fun out of everything? You were always the one who insisted on being Carmen Sandiego every time. I never got to be Carmen. When do I get to be Carmen, huh? When?"

"Fine. Whatever. Black Widow to Carmen Sandiego. Over. Now listen up. You need to back up about two more feet," she whispered.

I put down the radio, shifted my Chevy into reverse, and slowly inched my way backward.

"A little more," Sue Ellen said, trying to keep her voice low. "Keep coming. Almost. That's good!" She held up both hands in front of her, but judging from the sound of things, I hadn't been able to stop the truck fast enough. "I said that's good!" she shouted before covering her mouth with her hands. It was too late. The truck had smashed into the rusted-out camper and left a dent the size of a watermelon. Sue Ellen made a quick dash to finish latching the chain onto the ball hook of the trailer and jumped into the passenger seat at lightning speed. "Go! Go! Go!"

I shifted the truck into drive, and we began to cruise forward before stalling out in the mud under the weight of the load. The wheels spun furiously in place, kicking up a spray of brown sludge. "We're stuck!" I wasn't sure why it had taken until this moment for me to realize what a monumentally stupid plan this had been.

"Way to state the obvious. Do something!"

"What do you think I'm doing?" I shot her a look as I threw the car into reverse again. "I don't know what I was thinking. Why did I go along with this?"

"Because you wanted to get that loser's piece of crap off your property and build a real home for yourself. One that can't get parking tickets!" Sue Ellen shouted. "And I'd like to point out that you were much more amenable to the idea a couple of hours ago."

I tried to keep calm and continued trying to work the wheels out of the rut. "Yeah, that's because I was an emotional train wreck. I would have said yes to running naked through town." I had done that only once on a dare and only after a few too many shots with Colton after I lost the job at Dillard's. Without warning, the truck lurched forward with the trailer in tow, and we took off into an adjacent field, headed for the blacktop. As we pulled onto the road, the trailer bounded along behind us like an out-of-control water-skier, occasionally slamming into the tailgate before weaving from side to side. At the sight of the empty lanes stretching out before us, I breathed a sigh of relief that there were no other cars in sight.

"Uh, Savannah. I thought you said Colton wasn't home tonight." The color had drained from Sue Ellen's face, accentuating her freckles as she peered into her side-view mirror.

"I told you. His car wasn't there, so he must still be at Jasper's."

"Then do you want to explain to me why there's an angry, half-dressed man hanging out of the bathroom window?"

I whipped my head around to see for myself, and sure enough, there was Colton, topless and sporting a towel around his waist, his hair dripping wet. Through the window above the tow hitch, I could now make out the profile of a thin woman with frazzled red hair in a bathrobe, frantically speaking into her cell phone.

"Cheryl Henderson! Should have known she'd be there. Even after I humiliated the both of them, he had the gall to invite her into our home." I rolled down my window and leaned over so that they could see me clearly as I stuck up my middle finger. "Home-wrecker! You deserve each other!"

"Get back in here!" She tugged at my tank top, and the truck swerved a little as I repositioned myself in the driver's seat. "You want to tell me what we're supposed to do now that we've added kidnapping to our list of felonies?"

"I don't know. This was your idea," I shot back, trying to keep my hands steady on the wheel.

"Yes, but you said he would definitely not be home. Those were your words, not mine. I don't know about you, but it sure looks like he's home to me! What do we do? She's probably already called the police."

"I don't know. I can't think." I tried blinking myself out of what I was sure was a bad dream. "But I know we can't stop."

Keeping my foot firmly pressed on the accelerator, I hoped that something would come to me. But before anything enlightening sprang to mind, blue and red lights flashed in the distance behind us, inching steadily closer.

"We're going to jail." Sue Ellen had doubled over in her seat and was clutching her chest as if she couldn't breathe.

I was able to hold myself together a little better than she was. "It's OK. Just stay calm. I'm not going back there. Follow my lead."

"Back where? Are you telling me you've been to jail already?" Her tone was bordering on hysterical now.

"Let's just say the 'running naked through town' part was not a complete fabrication," I said, before shaking away the memory.

Sue Ellen gaped at me, her expression a mixture of disgust and disbelief.

"I didn't make the best decisions when I was with Colton, OK?" I flashed her an are-you-happy-now look before checking behind us again. "Besides, now is not the time to be discussing my past. Don't worry. Just let me do the talking," I said, though I had absolutely no idea how I was going to spin this. What was I going to say? "Sorry, Officer. My family is prone to temporary bouts of insanity, and I suppose it's finally caught up with me." Slowing the truck to a stop, I tapped out a nervous rhythm on the steering wheel. I couldn't see the officer's face at first, only the blinding brightness of his flashlight as he pointed it through my window.

"Evening, ladies. Everything all right?"

My shoulders relaxed when I saw Derrick's kind eyes staring back at us. "Oh, hey there, Derrick . . . I mean Officer Cunningham. We're doing fine. How about yourself?" I said with all the cheerfulness I could muster, as if my vehicle were not attached to a piece of tin that contained two very-pissed-off people. He peered into the truck and threw a curt nod to Sue Ellen, who looked as if she had just eaten a vat of bad sushi.

"Well, it's been quite the night for my partner and me." He gestured to Officer Turnsplenty, who had appeared on his left.

His hat in his hands, he gave us a curt nod and grimaced. "Hello there, girls. Good to see you again."

I smiled weakly and cringed. The Muscadine grapevine was a short path from Cricket's husband to Meemaw. She would be hearing about this in no time.

"We received some pretty disturbing phone calls from a man who says his house is being stolen right out from under him," Derrick continued. "You ladies wouldn't happen to know anything about that, would you?" He flashed his light toward the trailer before zeroing in on me again.

"Oh, really?" I feigned ignorance, then cleared my throat. "You see, the thing is . . . ," I began but was soon interrupted by Colton, who was directing a string of obscenities toward us as he approached the driver's side of the truck. He'd exchanged the towel for a pair of jeans and looked none too thrilled about having his shower cut short.

"What in the hell is wrong with you? Have you lost your mind? You realize we could have been killed? You're insane! Her whole damn family's crazy! Officer, they stole my house! My house! Arrest them!"

A shirtless and fuming Colton continued his tirade, arms flailing, but I couldn't process everything he was saying. Visions of orange jumpsuits flashed through my mind as I doubted that Meemaw could front the bail money we'd likely be needing in a few hours. We would have to ask Rayanne, and she would lecture us on how irresponsible we had been and educate us on the many ways we might have been killed.

By this time, Colton had noticed the substantial dent in the front of his home and appeared genuinely distraught, as if he might break down right there and cry. "Oh, would you look at that. Do you see what you've done? This is vintage! They don't make this siding anymore. It's irreplaceable."

I couldn't resist laughing through the window. "Ha! Oh, it's vintage, all right. You forget I was there when you stole it from the junkyard? That thing's a garbage can on wheels. We practically did you a favor!" I shouted.

Officer Turnsplenty, a stout little man pushing seventy and sprouting a gray mustache, tried to calm Colton down. "Clearly you've been wronged here, sir, so if you want to press charges, you're free to do so. I'll go ahead and start a report right now."

"Yeah, you do that." He spat at the ground and glared at me, but I pretended as if I couldn't see him, and Sue Ellen shrank down in the passenger seat.

"Of course," Derrick reassured him. "We'll just need to make a proper investigation, maybe have a look around the camper, see if anything was damaged on the inside. It could take some time, since we'll have to be as thorough as possible. Why don't you folks wait out here with my partner while I have a look around?" He grabbed his notepad and headed for the door of the trailer.

The color drained from Colton's face, and suddenly he had the look of someone who might throw up. "That's OK, Officer. You don't need to file a report." He stuffed his hands inside the pockets of his tattered jeans and fixed his eyes on the ground. "Savannah's my," he stammered, "my girlfriend. We can work this out on our own. I wouldn't want to get her in any trouble."

Derrick stopped in his tracks and turned around slowly. "Are you sure? If a crime has been committed here, I have a responsibility to report it."

"Yes, I know, Officer. But this is just a misunderstanding is all. A private matter. We don't need to get the police involved." Deflated, he ambled over to Mrs. Henderson, who appeared baffled by his behavior as he tried to explain himself to her.

Derrick returned to the truck to find me and Sue Ellen, who was furiously biting her thumbnail and doing a stellar job of avoiding eye contact with him. "I don't think he'll be pressing charges."

I was sure I'd heard him incorrectly, but Sue Ellen perked up in her seat, so maybe I had heard him right after all. "Really? What did you say to him?" I asked.

"As you probably know, we've picked up Colton a couple times before on possession. I just took a wild guess that he probably wouldn't feel too comfortable with me poking around in his things." He flashed his light at Sue Ellen, who began spouting a hurried apology.

"Derrick, I'm so embarrassed. Really, you have to know, I never do this sort of thing."

Smiling, he shook his head, his expression softening. "To be honest, I'm surprised your grandmother didn't have anything to do with this. You know this is the second time in one day I've had to pull a Guidry sister over. If I didn't know any better, I'd say you were looking for excuses to see me." His tone was playful, and it set my stomach at ease. "I *am* going to have to write you a ticket for driving without that hitch properly attached. It's a miracle it didn't come loose, and then you'd have had a real problem." He pulled out a pen and began scribbling something onto his citation book, then ripped it out and handed it to me through the window.

Relieved, I took the ticket from him. "Of course. We'll fix it right now. I promise no more moving violations for us." Placing a hand over my heart, I glanced at Sue Ellen, who was nodding emphatically.

"See you tomorrow, Sue Ellen." With a half grin, he ducked and held up a hand in her direction, then turned to face Colton and Cheryl, who were arguing with each other in animated whispers. "Well, folks. This here looks like a domestic dispute to me, so I'll leave you all to work it out. Maybe start by finding a place to park this thing." He gestured toward the heap of rusted metal behind them. "There's a campground about a mile south of here and a junkyard two miles east, if that helps at all."

"Yes, sir. Thank you, sir." Colton groveled, and I couldn't help but wonder exactly what he had stashed away in that piece of junk.

CHAPTER 27

Rayanne

Saturday Night

I pulled up to find Sue Ellen and Savannah on the porch steps, their faces illuminated in the soft glow of the porch light. Their guarded smiles told me something had shifted between them, but their puffy eyes made me hold off on asking them what it was. Passing her truck, I lifted an eyebrow at the sight of a futon resting in the bed of it, surrounded by disheveled boxes.

"I'm sorry," Sue Ellen said, drawing herself up as I closed in on them. "I said horrible things to you." She winced, and I felt my heart squeeze.

"It's fine." I cleared my throat and brightened my tone. "I needed to take care of some things anyway. We're good," I said, and I meant it. Since confronting our father, I'd almost forgotten about our epic fight, but seeing the two of them now brought everything into focus again.

"Are we, though?" She drew back, studying me. I could tell she had her doubts.

I nodded, trying to decide how much to share with them, then drew in a deep breath. "I went to see him tonight."

Sue Ellen made a face that told me she knew exactly who I meant, and that she did not approve. "Why? We don't owe him anything."

"Honestly, I don't know." I shook my head. "But I'm letting you off the hook for now. Tonight I'm blaming everything on the fact that he screwed us all up long ago." I was going to let myself off the hook, too. After all, I hadn't asked to be an adult when he left us, and I shouldn't have felt the weight of protecting a family that was never mine to raise.

Sue Ellen must have sensed I was holding something back, because she tilted her head and asked, "Are you sure you're OK? I feel really bad about what I said. And you weren't wrong, because I can be a—"

"Forget it. I'm through tearing this family apart, so let's just . . . start over." My chest collapsed with a heavy sigh. If I couldn't count on our father, I needed my sisters. They were the only ones who had both survived the chaos of Meemaw's house and knew the crushing disappointment of being Jack Guidry's daughters. "Savannah"—I turned to face her and felt my heart contract—"I'm sorry for losing my mind tonight. It wasn't about you."

"I know," she said softly.

"But you have to know that whatever Levi said . . . you can't trust it. You can't keep living like this, wondering if she's out there somewhere, putting your life on hold. Waiting. Because it's passing you by."

"I know," she said again, stealing a guilty glance at Sue Ellen, who smiled back at her.

I reached out my hand and cupped her cheek, needing her to hear the next part. "And just so we're clear, I didn't forget her. I can never forget her." I gave her a pained smile. "She's a part of my heart. And so are you." Brushing a stray tear from my cheek, I struggled to keep myself from breaking down all over again. "Forgive me?"

With watery eyes, she smiled back at me and reached for my hand. "Already forgiven."

~

I found Meemaw puttering around the kitchen with Bessie underfoot. Crouching down to pet her, I ran a hand over her prickly fur.

"Everything OK?" Meemaw asked, arching a suspicious eyebrow.

"Fine," I said. "Just needed to clear my head."

"Your sisters have had quite the night." She tutted as she shuffled to the refrigerator and started pulling out ingredients, setting them on the counter. "How's Graham? Because we're oh for two on men around here."

"Yeah, he's fine," I said, thinking that I would have to ask them about it later. I cleared my throat, unsure if I could say what I needed to get out. I took a breath, then stopped myself before I could start.

"You sure you're OK?" she asked, putting the back of her hand to my forehead.

"Yeah." I nodded. "It's just that . . . I'm sorry about before. At lunch." I hesitated. "And I'm sorry for not bringing the kids here this weekend."

Diverting her eyes, she turned her attention to a pot on the stove and began stirring. "Well, I don't know how much longer I'll be able to make that drive to your place with my cataracts. I can't tell a possum from a dog after dark."

"I know," I said, slipping my arms around myself. "I was thinking that . . . maybe they could come for your birthday next month?" I tried to gauge her response but couldn't see her face.

"I suppose that would be all right," she said softly, without turning around. "Only if you want them here, of course," she added over her shoulder. "I certainly don't want you to feel . . . afraid for their safety." My words came back at me, landing with painful accuracy.

The truth was it wasn't just Meemaw's house that terrified me. I was always afraid, incessantly worried that something or someone would take my children away from me. But with Meemaw, it was more than that. I hated coming here because it always brought me right back to the most awful part of myself. The part I'd never wanted to admit to anyone, much less her.

"Meemaw, do you remember that day they almost took us away?"

Though I still couldn't see her face, I could see the way her shoulders flinched, as if someone had punched her in the gut.

"I remember," she said softly, still stirring but slowing her pace. "How could I forget?"

My insides burned at the memory of my hands shaking as I scoured the phone book, found the listing for Child Protective Services, and pecked the number out. As I spoke to the woman on the other end, my voice had been so small, so raw with anger and confusion from Meemaw yelling at me after I had worked so hard to make things nice. To make things normal. And though I hadn't actually believed it would happen, they came. I don't remember what they said to her, but I remember the way she looked at me as if she no longer recognized me. Like she knew it was me. They didn't take us away, but they came back a few more times to see to it that we were being cared for. And each time they did, it stole a piece of her pride.

Taking in a shaky breath, I tugged at my collar, bristling at the memory of how a woman in a gray pantsuit had taken me aside and asked if our grandmother ever hit us. It had made me angry on her behalf. "No, she'd never hit us," I'd pushed back loudly. I'd never wanted anything bad to happen to her, only wanted them to take away her things, and just maybe take me along with them.

"Did you know it was me?" I asked.

Still turned away from me, she wrung a tea towel between her hands before answering softly, "I knew."

The hum of the air conditioner flitted between us until I asked, "Did you hate me? I mean, I wouldn't blame you if you did. I would have."

"Is that what you thought?" she asked, whipping around to face me. Her eyes wrinkled at the corners. "I could never hate you. You were only a child. If your child had done something like that to you, would you forgive them?" She turned away again, gripping the counter for support.

"Yes," I admitted, struggling to keep the emotion out of my voice. "I don't know why I did it. It was the worst thing I ever did. I don't have any excuse for it," I said, relieved that she was turned away, because I couldn't bear to face her. "And then . . . when Graham and I . . . when we got pregnant so young . . . you were just so . . . disappointed in me." Tears pricked at the corners of my eyes as I replayed the moment she learned I was dropping out of college to get married. I'd felt like such a failure, repeating the same mistakes our mother had made even with the advantage of knowing how her story had ended. I'd been stupid and irresponsible. And even though she had every right to be angry with me, I had shut her out. And she had pushed even harder until I couldn't bear to come home anymore. She'd never made it easy to love her.

"Oh no, honey. That's where you're wrong. I was never disappointed in you." She spoke the words so firmly I almost believed her. "I just wanted all the best things for you. That's all. I wanted you to have . . . all the things she never got to have." Her voice wavered, and I could tell how hard it was for her to talk about Mama.

A tenderness rippled through my chest, melting away everything else. "I just want you to know . . . I'm sorry," I managed to say. "You did the best you could for us. And it couldn't have been easy on your own."

Her shoulders shuddered, and I sensed she was crying.

"It wasn't enough, though," she said, her voice thick with tears. "Not for Georgia." Her voice cracked on the last word.

"It was enough for me," I said, touching her shoulder.

She reached back a hand and clasped it over mine. I felt the weight of it as it rested there, the familiar wrinkles and knobby knuckles that had always been hers. And something loosened inside me—that knot in my stomach that had always kept me from letting myself miss them. The hardness and anger, but most of all the guilt, ebbed out of me, dissipating like a fine dust as it hit the air.

"Well, now." She sniffled and dabbed at her eyes before dusting out her apron and turning to face me. "I think that's quite enough of all that. You look washed out." Running a hand over the side of my cheek, she inspected my features. "Nothing a good meal can't fix."

CHAPTER 28

Sue Ellen

Sunday Morning

If looks could kill, I might have died when I told Meemaw I would not be joining her for Sunday services. It wasn't just that I deemed organized religion a tool of the patriarchy to oppress half the population. I had plans with Derrick. So I waved goodbye to the three of them as they headed out the door, deftly avoiding the disappointment in Meemaw's scowl.

"An idle morning is the devil's playground," she said, turning back and raising an accusing eyebrow.

"I won't be idle. I have plans. Besides, I told you I don't want to go to church." Unlike Rayanne, it had been years since I'd stepped inside a building of worship—unless you counted SoulCycle—and I didn't have any plans to break my streak.

"No one wants to go to church!" she shot back. "But we don't do it for ourselves. It's for the Lord."

"I'm pretty sure the Lord would prefer I hang back today. I don't think He's forgiven me yet for the Easter-pageant debacle." I had once suggested that the resurrected Jesus be portrayed by a woman, an idea that did not go over well with the sister running the show. Undeterred, I'd taken matters into my own hands, astonishing the audience with a surprise appearance. And instead of just the one Jesus, there were two trying to elbow one another off the stage.

At this, Meemaw breathed out a relenting sigh. "I'll pray for you." She jabbed a finger at my chest. "But the Lord only saves those who want to save themselves."

"Noted," I said through a tight smile, hoping that it would be enough to get her out the door.

After they finally left, I made quick work of getting ready, throwing on a pair of high-waisted jeans and a loose-knit top. At eleven on the dot, a white Camry purred into the drive. Derrick emerged, then sauntered up the steps of the porch and knocked out a confident rhythm. Wearing gray slacks and a checkered button-up shirt, he looked so different from the last two times I'd seen him that I had to do a double take when he appeared in Meemaw's doorway. I slipped out the screen door and pulled it shut, hoping he hadn't caught sight of the boxes towering behind me.

"You look . . . almost normal," I said, sizing him up before following him toward his car. "No cruiser today?"

"Nope. Didn't want you to get too comfortable in it, if you know what I mean." He smirked, then guided me to the passenger side of the Camry and opened my door.

I snapped my fingers. "Dang it! And I was hoping we could turn on the sirens. So? Where to? There are literally like five establishments in Muscadine that qualify as restaurants." As soon as I said it, my gut sank, and I wondered if maybe he had planned to take me to Taco Bell or Wendy's. When Derrick had suggested we discuss Georgia's case file over brunch, I had assumed he meant in a restaurant, but maybe he'd been planning to shell out only for fast food. I still wasn't sure if this was a date, but the fact that he had invited only me led me to believe that maybe it was. In any case, I would definitely offer to pay my way so he didn't think I'd assumed anything. Still, being alone with him now outside of our established cop–robber relationship made my skin prickle with heat.

"Oh, we're not eating anywhere here unless you're in the mood for a Big Mac." He winked at me as he pulled away from Meemaw's. "Buckle up, S.E. We're going for a drive."

"I like the way you think," I said, blushing at the nickname he'd just given me, as if we were old friends. It felt both intimate and insanely sweet.

We drove along the interstate, passing fields of wildflowers dotted with lofty pines and oaks. Finally I broke the silence. "So what's your story? How'd you end up working for the police force?"

He furrowed an eyebrow. "You mean, how did I get stuck in Muscadine?"

"No, I just meant . . . well, yeah," I admitted sheepishly. "I thought you wanted to go to LSU and study—what was it again?"

"Entomology," he said. "Yeah, I had an unhealthy fascination with bugs back then. But a few years after our dad passed, our mother got sick, and one of us had to stay and take care of her. Aliyah was the one with the scholarship. So"—he shrugged—"I stayed. Got married. Enrolled in the academy. And here I am."

"Wait. Back up. You got married?" I squinted my eyes in search of his high school girlfriend's name. "Sasha Monroe?" I asked.

"Yep."

"I'm guessing it didn't work out, or you wouldn't be here with me."

"You're very perceptive. Turns out the human brain isn't fully developed until age twenty-five, so we had no business getting married at nineteen. Wish someone would have told me that back then. It didn't last long. She left for Ohio, got a job up there selling real estate. I think she always knew her dreams were too big for this town." Tearing his eyes from the road for just a moment, he flashed me a half smile. "Like you."

The way he was looking at me made me feel exposed, and I fiddled with my hair. "What do you mean?"

"Nothing. It's just that I always knew you'd leave here and do something amazing."

My cheeks burned, and I shifted in my seat. I hadn't thought he knew me well enough to have formed an opinion about my future. "I don't know that I'd call teaching amazing, but I'm happy. And just so you know, I think what you did is really admirable—putting your life on hold for your mother."

"Oh, it's not on hold. My family is my life. Mama and Aliyah and her kids—they mean everything. Doesn't really feel like a sacrifice. Besides, I love this place."

A fresh wave of shame took up residence in my gut, and I bit my lip. Why did I always seem to choose the worst words? Even I could hear how pretentious that must have sounded.

Maybe he sensed my embarrassment, because he let out a heavy sigh and added, "Plus, I think my obsession with bugs was just a phase. It was probably a good thing Aliyah broke my ant farm." He chuckled. "Besides, what could I have done with that degree besides work in some dusty museum, pinning dead butterflies inside of frames?" Giving me a once-over, he added, "No, my job is much more fun. Get to meet all kinds of interesting people."

"Like people who steal trailers?" I winced but graciously accepted his olive branch.

"*Occupied* trailers," he clarified. "Don't sell yourself short, S.E." He shot me a mischievous grin, and I couldn't help but laugh. "What about you? What's it like living on the East Coast?"

"Well, at first, it was practically another planet. I got lost in the city every day, which is completely unexplainable since it's on a grid. But now I don't know. I love getting to meet so many different kinds of people and being able to order Chinese food any time of night." I shrugged. "It has its perks."

"Chinese food, huh? I guess that's one for NYC and zero for Muscadine." He brought his thumb and index finger together.

"No, it's not like that. I like it here, too. It's . . . familiar. Plus, I get to have lunch with a folksy police officer, so I guess you could say they're even." My cheeks flushed hot, and I diverted my gaze out the window, trying to stifle a smile.

"You ever think about moving back?"

"Not really." Though I cringed to admit it, a part of me knew my self-confidence would be off the charts in Muscadine if I ever chose to move back. Being a big fish in a little pond did have its appeal—not enough to prompt my relocation to a town that once earned the distinction of being named the most pungent town west of the Mississippi. But still. I thought about it sometimes, what my life would have been like had I stayed and gone to community college or taken a waitressing job like so many of my classmates had. Shaking the thought away, I cleared my throat. "Besides, it's not like Muscadine has any openings for an associate English professor."

He shrugged. "Maybe not, but UL would, LSU, Loyola. Just something to think about."

I wondered if he'd made the suggestion in light of my family situation or because he wanted to see me again. His next question cleared up any confusion I may have had.

"So what's the deal? You got a boyfriend there?"

I tried not to react to this, but a stubborn smile threatened to give me away.

"No," I replied, as the photo of Liam and Abby danced across the screen in my head. My smile died at the edges, and I shook away the image. "Not anymore."

"Sorry, I shouldn't have asked. Don't feel like you have to explain."

"It's OK. I don't mind." I shrugged. "Turns out I'm not marriage material, so he found someone who was." I could feel him wincing on my behalf and immediately regretted saying this aloud. It made me

211

sound pathetic, and for some reason I had the unexplainable need for Derrick to approve of me, especially considering how we'd met the last two times.

"I take it he's not very bright then?"

I laughed him off, but his words had me flustered. "Thanks, but you don't have to make me feel better. I'm not hung up on him or anything," I lied. "Besides, it was probably all for the best. We weren't . . . I wasn't . . . the right kind of girl for him, you know what I mean?"

Diverting his eyes from the road, he cocked an eyebrow at me. "I find that hard to believe."

"It's hard to explain, but . . . he had a different childhood than me. Like totally different. His family is wealthy. Tons of connections. Appearances are really important to them, and I'm not sure I ever really fit the mold of what his parents wanted for him," I admitted.

"Oh, you mean he's a jerk," he said with an almost imperceptible grin.

"No"—I chuckled, waving him off—"we were just . . . different. I never even worked up the courage to introduce him to my family. I mean, can you imagine how that would have gone?" I said, envisioning how an environmental lawyer would have reacted to Meemaw's theories about global warming.

"No, but I would have paid good money to see it."

"Yeah, well, let's just say I'm pretty sure my grandmother's musings on Area 51 would have proven too much for him."

"Area 51." Shaking his head, he spewed out a sigh. "That's some shady stuff, man."

I fixed my gaze on him. "Don't tell me you've got a tinfoil hat at home, too."

"Hey, I was an eighties baby raised on *Goosebumps* and *Unsolved Mysteries*. The truth is out there."

"Remind me to never leave you and my grandmother alone in a room together." I shot him a pointed look, while curiosity pricked at the edges of my mind. "Hey, what did you mean the other day when you said that my grandmother was a legend?"

"Oh, that." He grinned, deepening those perfect dimples. "Just something that happened when we were kids."

Oh no. Had she tried to run him over with her car? Because it would not have been the first time. "What was it?" I asked, trying not to sound too interested.

He pressed his lips together and squinted an eye. "You remember Eugene Seller?"

My gut soured at the name, but I tried to play it cool. "Yeah, I knew him. I mean, I didn't *know* him know him, per se." I bit my lip, trying to stem the tide of words that was sure to follow. "We were . . . acquainted. We had computer science together in the sixth grade," I clarified.

"Well, then you'll remember what a mean little shit he was. Pardon my language, but it was the truth. Made my life miserable every day, teased me about those bugs I carried to and from school. Everyone always wondered who covered their yard in manure, but I had the good sense never to tell what really went down." He looked over at me and arched an eyebrow. "I was there that night. I'd snuck out late to meet a friend over at the ditch behind his house. And I saw her."

The words reverberated in my head as if they were coming from a loudspeaker I couldn't quiet. He *saw* her. He saw *her*. My grandmother. Derrick saw *my* grandmother spreading cow manure onto someone's lawn in the middle of the night. The humiliation of this fact should have been enough for me to jump out of the car and roll to my death. For one dark moment, I considered it. Then he said, "It was that neighbor of hers that helped her do it. Sam. I think that man would do anything for your granny. It was"—his eyes glazed over as if he were replaying the sight in his mind—"epic."

A wave of heat made the car feel as if it were spinning out of control. "I can't imagine what you must think of her," I said finally, because there really wasn't anything else to say.

With a satisfied smirk, he winked at me in a way that made me feel only slightly better. "Like I said. Legend."

~

When the car rolled to a stop in front of a Panera, I could have kissed him right there, but I thought that might set an awkward tone for our meeting.

"Will this work?" he asked.

"This is manna in the desert. I feel like I owe you my firstborn child or something. Do you know how long it's been since I've seen fresh microgreens? Lavon's stops at water chestnuts, and when I asked the clerk if they had any arugula, he thought it was some kind of foot cream."

He circled around to open my door, then led me into the cool, air-conditioned restaurant, where we ordered and settled across from one another at an empty table.

As we waited for our food to arrive, Derrick produced a thick manila folder stamped with a pelican seal and began thumbing through the contents.

"I took the liberty of reviewing the basics, the list of witnesses and their statements, items recovered at the scene, which wasn't much. It's all here if you want to read it."

"Perfect." I reached for a few loose papers he had extended to me and promptly began poring over them. My eyes followed my finger as it slid down a list of witnesses, then went wide at the name printed in neat black ink. "Celia." I looked up at him, unable to hide my excitement. "This is the woman we've been looking for. The one who was there that day." My eyes scanned the text hungrily.

Ms. Peters reports seeing the two girls swimming in the water, but says she left before the child in

question vanished. She has no idea who may have
wanted to take the girl. It is my opinion that she
was being truthful.

At the bottom of the last page, it was signed by Sheriff Humphries.
"That's it?" The words had ended abruptly, and I felt certain there should
be more, but Derrick only pursed his lips and shrugged.

"Look, Sue Ellen." He set his jaw, and his voice took on a softer
tone now, jostling my concentration. "There's something else you should
know. I did some more digging and asked around at the department.
A few days ago, there was a development, some news out of Memphis
PD." Derrick reached out a hand and gently placed it atop mine, such
an intimate gesture that at first it confused me. "Morrison is willing to
talk. Says there were others, and he can tell them where the rest of the
bodies are buried. He wouldn't give names, but he said there were at least
two other victims in addition to Marissa and Georgia. I guess something
or someone must have gotten through to him. Memphis says something
happened last week that set him off, got him thinking about . . . forgiveness, you know?" The way he said it made it sound like he felt sorry
for me. Lowering his eyes, he shook his head. "If you ask me, it isn't so
much about forgiveness as it is about his upcoming execution. Tends to
have an effect on folks, if you know what I mean."

I did. And a week ago, I would have welcomed this development,
but now a numbness radiated from my chest and throughout my limbs.
Levi Morrison was finally going to start telling the truth. But now I
wasn't sure I wanted to hear it.

CHAPTER 29

MEEMAW

July 1994

The beach was busier than usual that afternoon, and Marylynn had to squint against the blazing sun to pick her daughter's petite frame out of the crowd of bustling bodies. Shading a hand over her temple, she caught sight of Beverly sitting in a foldout chair, red faced and flustered, doing her best to blow air into tiny arm floats as she wrangled the twins out of the water with her free arm. Beads of sweat cropped up along Marylynn's hairline as she made her way to shore, where she unfolded a beach chair and plopped herself down beside Beverly in the wet dirt.

The older girls had already found a spot for diving off the dock and were busying themselves with cannonballs and flips. Rayanne was a decent swimmer, and at just a year younger, Sue Ellen was quite the little fish herself. It was the twins who sent Beverly into daily—sometimes hourly—fits of panic. Twins could threaten to undo any mother, but Savannah and Georgia were the most mischievous little four-year-olds one could imagine. They couldn't swim for beans, though Savannah was perfectly content to strut out into the deep water without floaties on, with Georgia trailing behind her just as she always did. If they'd had it their way, they would have sunk to the bottom of the lake like stones long ago. Even before they could talk, it was as if the two of them had developed a secret language and could alert the other to whatever naughty activity she had cooked up. It always ended with Beverly running toward them in a panic, hoisting them up and scolding them for coloring the walls or cutting each other's hair or locking one another in cabinets.

Having grown accustomed to the daily phone calls pleading for help, Marylynn had come straight from her shift at the nursing home to save Beverly's sanity. Scooping up an impatient Savannah wearing her purple swimsuit, Marylynn did her best to restrain four flailing limbs as her granddaughter wiggled to free herself.

"I want to swim now!" she shouted, doing her best to squirm out of Marylynn's grasp.

"You'll wait until your floaties are on." Her tone was firm, and Savannah stopped her writhing even as she poked out her lower lip in silent protest.

When the twins were ready to go with pink-and-blue mermaid floaties, Beverly sent them on their way, but not before raising a finger of caution. "Stay where I can see you. No swimming out to the dock, girls. I mean it," she warned. With that, they darted in and splashed about in the warm water, the two of them laughing and chattering, their tiny voices woven together while Marylynn scanned the horizon in search of their older sisters. She spotted them quickly among a group of children out on the dock, the lot of them holding hands and counting to three before they plummeted into the water all together in a frenzy of giggles. Marylynn smiled, so content that for a moment she almost forgot about the matter she had planned to discuss with Beverly, the thing she knew would ruin the rare calm that had settled over the two of them.

A single cloud sailed across the blistering sun, providing a blessed moment of reprieve from its relentless rays. Beverly rummaged around in a beach bag and produced a camera. She waded through the water until it was ankle deep, positioning herself so that she faced the beach, then snapped a candid of the girls as they played. As she pulled away from behind the lens, a smile of adoration tugged at her lips. The look of pure joy on her face sparked a fire of pride in Marylynn's chest. Beverly had turned out to be a good mother—the kind of mother other children wished for. Even so, most days, Marylynn could sense her overwhelming stress—the weight of caring for four small beings who sometimes seemed bound and determined to destroy themselves and each other. And though she did her best to hide behind a show of hugs and kisses and impromptu playdates at the park, the tiredness radiated from her in the deep circles that rimmed her eyes, in the way her step had slowed from that of a carefree young mother to that of a weather-beaten woman who knew the struggle of never having enough—enough money, enough time in the day, enough of a husband who was becoming increasingly unavailable to his wife and children. Though she knew she was treading in forbidden territory, Marylynn couldn't stop herself, and the words tumbled out unprovoked.

"He's cheating on you, Bev," she finally said. "How can you not see it? Cricket's done told me she saw him down at some sleezy hotel in the city—the kind that charges by the *hour*." She raised her eyebrows, hoping she understood the implication of the word. It wasn't right for a married man to be out running around on his wife in broad daylight with some floozy, spending money they didn't have, while Bev worked at that horrible excuse for a gas station and never bought herself so much as a trip to the salon. Marylynn thought of the money that she had given him once, of the promise he had made. How foolish she had been to entrust her daughter's happiness to a man she wouldn't have trusted to feed her dog.

"Mama, I don't want to discuss this with you right now." Beverly squeezed the bridge of her nose, closing her eyes. "What happens in our marriage is not your concern."

"Honey, I've checked, and there ain't a construction job out there that requires him to be out all hours of the night." When Jack was out "working late" and Bev was working the register, Marylynn had been the one to sleep over and watch the girls. And she wouldn't have minded if she'd actually believed he had been providing for his family instead of providing for his own disgraceful self.

"Mama, I said leave it alone," Beverly snapped, though Marylynn suspected she knew the truth, too, because there were tears in her eyes. Making a show of it, Bev picked herself up and stormed off down the dock, where the older girls played. Muttering to herself, Marylynn continued listing off all the things that Bev didn't want to hear. *Maybe if you hadn't married a lowlife in the first place and then proceeded to have not one, not two, not three, but FOUR of his children, you wouldn't be in this position.* To his credit, Jack had never tried to disguise the fact that he was a worthless idiot and was only behaving in the way she always knew he would. She crossed her arms and watched Beverly fade from her sight as she had always done, completely uninterested in hearing the truth when it concerned her.

After stewing for a bit, Marylynn shielded her eyes and scanned the rippling water for the twins. The hairs on her arms prickled when it hit her that she hadn't really been watching them during her unproductive conversation with Beverly. Her heart quieted a little when she spotted Savannah shoveling water into a bucket, but it picked up a sudden and furious speed when she realized she was playing alone.

Where was Georgia?

Dread settled in the bottom of her stomach. How long had it been since she'd last seen her face? Two minutes? Five? How could a single minute suddenly amount to the longest stretch of time in the history of a person's life?

She fought her way into the water and snatched up Savannah, then called out Georgia's name, but her throat had tightened and felt coated in sand so that she could hardly get out the word. "Georgia!" Whipping from side to side, she pleaded with anyone who could hear. "I'm missing a child! She looks exactly like this one except she has a little red mark on her shoulder just there." Flustered and rasping for breath, she pointed to Savannah's shoulder as if the act would somehow produce the child's missing half. With tears flooding her eyes, she barreled down the dock to where Bev stood, her broken expression giving away that something was horribly wrong.

"Is Georgia with you?" she panted, nearly folding over. Beverly reached for Savannah and propped her on her hip, her eyes wide and searching.

"No, I haven't seen her since I was with you." Marylynn's anxiety was contagious, and Beverly's face was now twisted with worry, too. Her voice quavered as she spoke. "You're scaring me, Mama. Where is she?"

"I don't see her anywhere." The two of them looked out across the lake toward the beach where they had been sitting just moments ago, Marylynn fighting off a growing nausea.

"You don't think she took her floaties off, do you? Or that she tried to swim out to the older girls?" Beverly implored, appearing desperate that she would say no, but Marylynn only shook her head, her features all wrong, arranged in a strange shape she couldn't recognize. Scrambling down the dock, they shouted while other families looked on, confused. When they realized a child had been lost, nearly all of them joined the search, calling out her name, tugging off shirts and diving under the water, fanning out in groups along the shoreline. Marylynn's neighbor Sam jumped in his little pirogue and paddled out past the buoys, but he couldn't spot anything in the water except lily pads and a few pieces of driftwood.

With every unbearable second that passed, Marylynn thought this had to be the most terrifying moment in her entire life, scouring the bottom of the lake to see if her grandchild was lying somewhere down there, helpless and dying. Maybe already gone.

After what felt like ages of searching, two police officers arrived and brought in a pair of hounds. Every moment they didn't find her little lifeless body gave Marylynn a short-lived sense of relief. But when the sun began to descend below the pines and the cicadas began to chirp with still no sign of Georgia, she was overcome by a different kind of fear, the kind that ate a person up from the inside out with a thousand "what-ifs." What if they never found her? What if the lake just swallowed her up and they never saw her again?

Once, she thought she'd spotted her but quickly realized that it was only Savannah, and her heart skipped a beat in her chest before it sank to her stomach. Two police officers turned into four, until eventually a swarm of uniforms dotted the scene like ants descending on an abandoned picnic.

After the evening light faded to darkness, Sheriff Humphries arrived and took charge of the situation. He'd graduated in Dennis's class and couldn't have been older than thirty. Looking at him now, Marylynn could hardly believe that someone so young and inexperienced should be charged with the task of mending her whole world. A short, balding, and slightly doughy man, he told everyone to go home and promised that they would continue searching through the night. Unwilling to leave, Marylynn proceeded to call him and his officers a bunch of damned fools and wanted to know if they had ever worked a case in their lives, because it seemed to her that they didn't know their asses from their elbows. She threatened to call their supervisors, call the governor, the FBI, and the National Guard while she was at it. "Find my grandchild!" she shouted through tears.

Beverly clung to Savannah, her wet eyes sticking to her daughter's soft yellow curls. Her hollow voice sounded small and far away, her face gray and empty. "Mama, how can I just leave without all my babies? How can I go home when a piece of my heart is lost?" A howl emanated from within her, piercing Marylynn's insides so deeply that she wondered if it had actually come from her. How could she have been so careless to misplace a child?

Clutching her stomach, she figured this must be what drowning felt like. Except she didn't die. But something died within her. And no matter what happened to Georgia, she knew one thing for certain.

She would never forgive herself for this.

CHAPTER 30

RAYANNE

Sunday Evening

Before sunset, I drove Sue Ellen to the airport, and this time we had plenty to talk about.

After I recounted my conversation with our father, she stared at me open mouthed. "So he just came right out and asked you for it?"

"Pretty much," I said.

"Wow." She seemed to turn the idea over in her mind. "But . . . it doesn't mean he wasn't telling the truth about wanting to see Charlotte and Tucker." She was trying her best to find a silver lining, and I loved her for that.

"Maybe. But his timing sure was convenient. Something tells me we'll only be hearing from him when he's short on cash"—I tipped my sunglasses in her direction—"or needs a kidney." Resignation settled over me, and I shook my head. "No, the more I think about it, the more I think Meemaw was right about him."

Sue Ellen groaned. "I hate when that happens."

"You and me both."

"So are you going to give it to him? It's not like it would be a hardship or anything. He must know the Penningtons are loaded."

Straightening in my seat, I said, "Well, technically I may be a Pennington, but biologically I'm Marylynn Pritchett's granddaughter, and right now I have no intention of letting him off the hook that easy. If he wants the money, he'll have to put in some effort first."

"And what about the other part? Are you going to let him meet the kids?"

I squinted an eye and pursed my lips. "I haven't decided yet. What about you?"

"I have an easy out. Don't live here, remember?" A smile tugged at her lips. "But I'm glad I came. I don't think I realized how much I missed this place. And you," she added, looking out the window.

"So does that mean you don't think I'm—what was it you called me before—a medicated mom from white suburbia?"

She cringed and sucked in a breath through her teeth. "Yeah, sorry about that. I wasn't at my best this weekend."

"It's fine. Besides, you weren't wrong."

"I was one hundred percent wrong," she said, her tone more serious now. "I should never have said that about you. The part about giving up."

I tried to swallow the growing lump in my throat and forced a smile. "I knew you didn't mean it. So?" Aiming for a change of subject, I shot her a quizzical look. "Will Liam meet you at the airport?"

She blew out her cheeks, letting her chest deflate until she finally said, "Yeah . . . about that. I should have told you before. We broke up months ago."

I mined my brain, trying to understand how I'd missed it. "Why didn't you say anything?"

"I don't know. I think I was still trying to earn your approval or something. But I think it's time I stop trying to be someone I'm not."

"What do you mean?"

She sighed. "When I first moved to the city after college, it was like another planet I'd only seen in magazines. It took a while for me to navigate the subway, even just feel comfortable enough to order dinner without sounding ridiculous. I had the fashion sense of . . . well, you saw the way I dressed in high school." She flashed me a guarded smile. "And when I met Liam, it was like, I didn't have to work so hard anymore because he knew all the secrets. He knew how much to tip to get the best seat, how to schmooze his way into a sold-out show. He even told me where I should shop for clothes for work. It was easier, you know? Being with him made me feel bigger. But somehow smaller, too?" She shook her head. "That probably makes no sense."

"It makes perfect sense," I said. "You stopped trusting yourself. And I have no idea why, because you are literally the smartest person I know in real life."

"Really?" She looked at me, and for the first time it occurred to me that maybe I hadn't ever told her this. I'd always assumed she knew how proud I was that she had made it out of Muscadine and followed her dreams.

"Really. I'm glad you left. You would have suffocated here."

Catching my gaze, she gave a little shrug. "Guess I didn't have much of a choice. I couldn't exactly stay here, not with all the history. Sometimes," she said, almost to herself, "it's too hard coming home, you know—facing all the crap we had to go through with . . ." She didn't finish her sentence, but I knew exactly what she meant. I hadn't wanted to stay, either. "It's easier to pretend it happened to someone else."

Seizing the silence, I cleared my throat. "Speaking of our father, there was something else," I said, second-guessing whether I should say it. "Something weird about the way he reacted when I mentioned Celia. I didn't want to say anything about it to Savannah. But he made it sound like she and Mama fought about something. Something big."

"You think that's the reason Celia left?"

"Maybe." I shrugged. "It's hard to know what to think anymore." I supposed it was all just as well. After my conversation with our father, I had my suspicions about him and Celia but didn't have it in me to pursue it. As much as I hated to agree with him, maybe he was right. Some things were meant to stay in the past.

"Doesn't matter anyway," Sue Ellen said, her shoulders drooping ever so slightly. "Derrick seems pretty convinced that we're going to have some closure in Georgia's case soon."

A stillness settled between the two of us, and while I couldn't be sure, I had a feeling she was thinking of Savannah, too. Even though I'd never wanted to come on this trip, it broke my heart to leave things the way we had, with our little sister alone again in her grief.

After parking the car in the departures terminal, I circled around to the trunk and helped Sue Ellen with her luggage. "Hey, maybe don't stay away so long next time," I said, pushing a bag toward her. "It wasn't the worst thing in the world to see you."

"Maybe." She nudged my shoulder. "It wasn't horrible to see you, either."

I pulled her into a hug and held her there a beat too long before letting her go.

CHAPTER 31

SUE ELLEN

Two Weeks Later

Boxes of clothing and stacks of cherished books rested on the IKEA bed I'd purchased yesterday when I'd finally moved my things from Gabriela's place into the basement of a charming little brownstone in Midtown. It wasn't ideal, but at least I had my own space to figure out who I was without Liam. It had taken two Allen wrenches, YouTube, and a kind neighbor who'd heard me cursing all the way from the stairway to put the thing together. Studying it now, I couldn't decide if it represented a pathetic failure or a new beginning. I made a mental note to rustle up a futon or a chair at least so visitors would have somewhere to sit besides the tiny kitchen counter. Then I realized I wasn't sure who those visitors would be, since I hadn't made much of an effort to form my own friendships outside of Liam's. It made me feel as if I were starting all over again. At least I still had Gabriela. I suspected she had scheduled a reminder on her phone to check in on me every hour.

Leafing through the contents of the boxes, I thought of Savannah. Derrick hadn't called yet with any news about Levi or the case, but the authorities seemed all but certain that very soon our worst fears about Georgia would be confirmed. Even if we never discovered the truth, I'd seen the resignation in Savannah's smile the last time we'd said goodbye. It would take some time, but ultimately this would be a good thing for her. She'd finally begun to accept what the rest of us had known all along and would eventually come to terms with it in her own way.

My phone chimed with a notification, and I fished it out from beneath a mountain of unfolded laundry atop the bed. Checking the screen, I smiled. Ever since my date/meeting with Derrick, he'd fallen into the habit of sending me ridiculous conspiracy theories he stumbled across. Yesterday he'd texted a photo of the cover of the *National Enquirer* at Lavon's with the bold caption "Rat Boy Escapes Lab, Terrorizes Residents." Beneath it, he wrote, Have suspected this all along. No other way to explain all the missing food from my kitchen.

Today he had sent a link to an article from a website called NewsNMore that claimed the government was releasing mind-controlling fumes into NYC subways. The article was vague on specifics, but apparently Russia was also somehow involved in this ruse. Beneath the link he wrote, Saw this and thought of you. Be safe out there.

Suppressing a grin, I texted back, Thanks, but I'm pretty sure the fumes are just BO . . . And gas. At least that was the case for the guy who sat next to me this morning.

Was he wearing a trench coat?

Yeeees . . .

A badge?

So what if he was?

That's a dead giveaway. Total government plant. Man, you are so lucky to have me looking out for you.

My chest swelled, and I bit my lip, trying to think of something flirty without coming off as too eager. It was stupid to pursue a guy who lived a thousand miles away in a town I knew I could never live in again, but I couldn't ignore the way my stomach flipped whenever I saw those trailing dots attached to his name.

Is that what you're doing? Looking out for me?

Maybe . . . I think it's what your grandmother would want. Don't you?

Why do you care what my grandmother wants?

Maybe because I want her to like me . . .

My stomach contracted, and my heart ticked up speed as I debated whether to ask what I was really thinking, then settled on, And why is that?

Holding my breath, I tried to keep my feelings in check, simultaneously dreading and dying to hear my phone chime again. I wasn't sure I had the emotional bandwidth to engage in a long-distance relationship, but I also didn't want these daily check-ins to end. A trail of dots blinked back at me, then disappeared before returning again, followed by the words, Because I'd rather not get a yard full of manure?

Squeezing my eyes shut, I cringed, but even so, a bark of laughter escaped my throat. Holding the phone to my chest, I sifted through a few possible responses, but nothing clever came to mind. Evidently, my prolonged silence concerned him, because he sent four more texts in quick succession.

Too soon?

Just kidding!

That was a joke.

Oh no. It's too late. The fumes have already affected your ability to recognize how incredibly funny I am.

Satisfied he had suffered enough, I shook away my embarrassment, my fingers eagerly typing out a response.

Hilarious. Don't mind me. Just going to wear a bag over my head and suffocate of humiliation. Can we please never speak of 'the incident' ever again?

For sure. Putting it in the vault.

I placed my phone atop the laundry and continued unpacking, but just as I lifted another box and headed for the closet, it chimed again with a link to a gas mask and another message: Just in case. You can never be too safe.

This guy. It had surprised me how easy it was to joke about my upbringing with Derrick when I had always done my best to avoid any mention of my family like the plague when I was with Liam. I hadn't ever lied to my ex. Not exactly. Only left out the parts that made me look like a poor country hick when I told him I lived in your run-of-the-mill suburban neighborhood in a quaint Louisiana town instead of clear out in the middle of nowhere in what can be described only as "the sticks." But with Derrick, the learning curve was less steep. I didn't have to exhaust myself trying to fit into a box. It was easier. Safer. If also completely unsustainable.

My phone rang, jarring me out of my thoughts, and I answered to hear Gabriela's brisk voice already midsentence. "I'll be there in ten to pick you up. And wear the red halter top, the one that's open in the back. So help me, you'd better not be in a power suit when I get there. We're trying to pick up guys, not get them to vote for you."

"Noted." Still holding the phone in one hand, I tugged open the closet door and rifled through the hangers. "Can I at least wear clogs? I can't dance in stilettos."

"Absolutely not," she protested. "Tonight is not about being practical. It's about getting over Liam, which is much more likely to happen if you don't dress like a retired schoolteacher." She had a point, though it surprised me just how little I had thought of Liam since coming back here. Annoyingly, Derrick's face was the one materializing in my head when things got too quiet. "Besides, you're not allowed to dance. It will only hurt the cause."

"Harsh," I said, feigning hurt. "Stilettos it is." Balancing the phone between my ear and shoulder, I dug the shoes from the back of the shelf, but as my fingers fumbled to grasp them, the phone slipped to the ground with an ominous thud. Cursing myself, I bent down to retrieve it and discovered that the screen was unharmed, but the call had dropped.

It rang again, and I sighed, preparing to get another earful from Gabriela, but the number was one I didn't recognize—a Louisiana area code. Cautiously, I slid my finger across to answer.

"Hello?"

"Sue Ellen?" I recognized Cricket's soprano voice on the other end and puzzled over why she would be calling me, of all people. "Is that you, hon?"

"Cricket?" I sat down on my bed and adjusted the volume before speaking again. "Cricket, is that you?"

"Hello, dear."

My stomach churned as I noted the sadness in her voice, and I found myself afraid to ask her the next question. "Is something wrong?"

"I'm afraid so. I didn't want to be the one to tell you this, but Savannah was just too upset to make the call. It's about your grandmother."

CHAPTER 32

Savannah

August 2022

"I have to leave early today." I pulled off my name tag and reached for my denim jacket. After gathering up the rest of my things, I circled around the welcome desk to face Tammy. "I'm going to visit Meemaw. Send soap and towels to room 204 when you get a chance."

"That's the fourth time in two days they've requested refills," Tammy said. "What exactly are they bathing up there?" She gave me a sad smile, the same one a lot of people had been giving me lately, and I felt my heart contract. "Give Meemaw a hug for me," she said, softening her tone. Her face was scrunched up in that pathetic way people do when they feel sorry for you. "How's she doing, by the way?"

My face fell, but I kept my voice light. "Not so great. But I'm dealing with it." Trying to sound casual, I did my best to keep my chin steady. "She's indebted to you for getting me this job. Only mentioned it about a thousand times." I rolled my eyes. "So thank you for not letting me turn into a—what was it she called it?—unemployed freeloader." Moving back in with Meemaw had come at the steep price of suffering through her unfiltered opinions.

"Of course." She smirked at me, raising one eyebrow. "What good is being promoted to management if you can't hire your best friend?"

I shot her a look. "You know that's nepotism."

"Is not," she said, putting a hand to her hip. "I hired you for your amazing interpersonal skills."

"You must not have heard about this morning."

"What happened this morning?"

I cringed, wondering how I could spin the fact that I had gotten into a shouting match with Mr. and Mrs. Rutherford when they had complained about a horrible smell in their room. It wasn't my fault if I'd had to be the one to tell them the odor was coming from them, and now they were threatening to leave a negative review on Yelp.

"Nothing." I diverted my eyes and headed for the glass doors. "Just avoid room 302, and if they mention anything about a funny smell, act natural." I was outside and in my truck before she could pry for more details.

When I reached the hospital, I made my way to the lobby, where Cricket sat thumbing through a copy of *Good Housekeeping*. At my arrival, she popped up and captured me between her thick arms. An invisible cloud of her Elizabeth Taylor perfume enveloped me, and I coughed.

"You made it." She reared back to inspect me before shaking her head regretfully. "She's not in the best of moods today."

"Shocker," I said flatly, pulling away from her. "You can leave now, Cricket. I'll take the next shift."

"Oh, come on now, hon. When are you going to forgive me?" She must have picked up on the coldness in my tone, because her eyes filmed over with tears. "I begged her to tell you all. Honestly, I assumed that's why Rayanne and Sue Ellen came home last month." She placed a contrite hand over her heart.

How many times had I visited Cricket, brought her lunch, shared gossip about family, and the whole time she'd neglected to tell me that my own grandmother was dying? I stewed with my arms crossed, unwilling to look at her, but Cricket prattled on anyway.

"She swore me to secrecy. Threatened me! Now, I'm a grown woman, and I hate to admit this, but your grandmother can be downright scary at times."

"Yes, I know," I admitted, the edge in my voice giving way to a softer tone. "I'm not angry at you." Cricket had happened upon Meemaw's diagnosis when she'd had to drive her home from a biopsy and pried it out of her as only Cricket could do. And I had learned of it only when I arrived at Meemaw's place to drop off some groceries and found her lying on the linoleum, her face slack and her hands sweaty. "I appreciate you looking out for her over the past few months. I just wish I'd known sooner. Maybe I could have . . ." The words escaped me. Even if I'd known, there was nothing I could have done. Stage four lung cancer was a formidable enemy, even for someone who had Meemaw's cantankerous disposition. Guilt tugged at my conscience, and I felt my insides loosen. "Thank you, Cricket."

"You're welcome," she said, blinking back tears. "Well, I'll leave you to it. Call me if you need anything." She gave my shoulders a final squeeze, and I watched her walk away, steeling myself to see Meemaw again. It was unnerving to see her so vulnerable, so weak, and out of breath—though she was still combative enough to keep the nurses on their toes, stubbornly demanding her cigarettes, which were understandably not allowed in hospital rooms. I took a slow breath and closed my eyes. When I opened them, Rayanne was barreling toward me past the nurses' station, leading Tucker by the hand and carting Charlotte on her hip. Her eyes were red, and it looked as if she hadn't slept in days.

"How is she?"

"Same as yesterday," I said through a smile for the sake of the kids. "Mad as hell." I reached out for Charlotte and nestled her chubby body against my chest. I'd seen the kids more in the last few weeks than I had in the last few years and found myself looking forward to their visits. Charlotte babbled at me and planted a sloppy kiss on my cheek, and my heart melted.

Rayanne shot me a look. "Language, please."

"Sorry." I covered Charlotte's ears a beat too late. The four of us padded down the hall, then crept quietly into Meemaw's room, which smelled of stale cafeteria food and mothballs. A lunch tray rested untouched on a rollaway table, and the television softly played an episode of *M*A*S*H* in the corner of the room. Tucker wriggled out of Rayanne's grasp and climbed up onto the bed near Meemaw's feet.

"Tucker, get down from there! We have to be gentle."

Meemaw cracked one eye open and wriggled a hand free from underneath the thin coverlet to reach for him. "Oh, let him come. I'm not dead yet."

A flicker of pride crossed his freckled face, and he crawled up next to her. Gingerly, Rayanne fluffed a pillow behind her head and propped her up. "How are you feeling today?"

She wheezed before sputtering out a phlegm-filled cough. "Like I could use a smoke."

"Absolutely not," Rayanne said firmly. "Those things are the reason you're here. And I'm not going to get in trouble with Dr. Weaver."

"Dr. Weaver is an infant." She gave a weak flick of her wrist, dismissing the name. "What can a person know of life and death when he's only thirty-five? When I was that age, I didn't know a turnip from a sugar beet."

"I'm sure your intuition is less accurate than his. The man only holds three degrees. Which reminds me—Sue Ellen's on her way. She'll be here tomorrow."

Meemaw furrowed an eyebrow, staring at her down her nose. "I really must be in bad shape."

"Don't talk that way," I said, hoping that my words didn't sound worried. "She just wanted to see you is all."

Tucker nestled himself into the crook of her elbow, and she pulled his head into her chest. With one hand stroking his fine, blond curls, she closed her eyes and let her head fall back onto the pillow. I looked over at Rayanne and caught her staring at the two of them, her head tilted with a wistful expression on her face. The whir and beep of machines was punctuated only by the rise and fall of their chests, breathing in tandem as Tucker's eyes flickered shut and he settled. I lowered myself into an adjacent love seat, pulled Charlotte close, and breathed in the baby-fresh scent of her—shampoo and milk and something sweet that smelled like cookies.

Unable to tear my eyes away from Meemaw, I replayed Dr. Weaver's words in my mind. "Not much longer," he had said with a sullen look about his face. "You'll need to make arrangements with your family soon." I was certain I could arrange a funeral, but I was less certain about how to arrange my life once she was gone. It was hard to imagine a world without her in it, and once she left, my sisters would be gone again, and I'd be alone. Again.

"Did you find her?" Meemaw's reedy voice broke into my thoughts, and Rayanne and I shared a worried look.

I strained forward, not sure if she was lucid. Yesterday she had held an entire conversation with Charlie and berated him about a broken toilet. Apparently he'd had the audacity to die before he got around to fixing it. "Find who?"

"Celia," she breathed. "Did you ever find her?"

"No," I answered, swallowing a lump in my throat. I didn't have the heart to tell her the truth.

With her eyes still closed, she took a deep breath and released it slowly before saying, "You will." A weak smile tugged at her lips, and she drifted into a peaceful sleep.

CHAPTER 33

MEEMAW

July 1996

The early-morning sun had barely emerged from beyond the pines when she settled herself behind the wheel and steered the old Buick down the familiar roads that led to the little redbrick home where Beverly still lay sleeping. By now the girls would be awake, Rayanne burning the french toast while Sue Ellen and Savannah ran amok.

Since Jack had taken up driving an eighteen-wheeler across three states, there were no other adults around to see to it that the laundry was tended or that the dishes were washed. Though in Marylynn's opinion, he hardly counted as an adult. She steeled herself for the task of pulling them all into another day before she had to head to the nursing home for a shift. But this one would be harder. *Two years.* How had everyone else managed to keep time when their world had stopped spinning?

Everyone kept telling her that the only cure for grief was motion, losing yourself in the mundaneness of the everyday. Try as she did to throw herself into the work of her garden and keeping her family clothed and fed, it hadn't been enough to stem the steady drip of agony. Losing Georgia had ripped open her chest once more, exposing the hole that still gaped there as fresh and raw as when she had held Charlie's hand for the last time. The pain of losing him had never really left her, but she'd been able to live with the ache because of all the pieces of himself he'd left behind. Though she regretted Beverly's hasty marriage, she never regretted her granddaughters. Each time Beverly had announced that another was on the way, she would curse Jack and dive into a monologue on the blessed benefits of birth control. But once they arrived, she saw that each was a light she hadn't known she needed, filling up the darkness with their smiles and laughter and endless questions, running all over the yard and her heart, carrying Charlie's and Bev's features in their tiny faces. Whenever she held them close, a warmth spread inside her chest that kneaded her insides like a stiff dough softening at their touch.

And then it happened, the few seconds that altered everything. No matter how often she replayed the events over and over again, rewinding and fast-forwarding in slow motion, she could not recall the precise moment Georgia was whisked away into thin air, plucked up by some unseen hand, perhaps a bird or a ghost. She'd always been so careful where her family was concerned, so attentive to every detail of their comings and goings. She'd never missed a school performance or a sick visit to the doctor and checked the girls out of school if Beverly couldn't get out of work when they needed her. But she had failed them all when it mattered most. It crushed her to see the way Beverly had given up entirely, the way she had let the grief consume her until she had to be reminded to bathe, to feed herself, and to get the girls to the school bus on time.

The car puttered to a stop in the driveway, but she couldn't pull herself out of it right away. Instead, she sat in the silence, closing her eyes and savoring the last few seconds alone, when she could pretend that everything was as it should be. In her mind's eye, all four girls would run out to greet her, and Beverly would trail behind them, her hair pulled back and her face fresh, basking in their excitement. Marylynn would make some unwelcome remark about Jack's absence and the lack of shoes on the girls' feet. She would demand to know their sizes and promise to pick up a few pairs at an estate sale this weekend, and Bev would smile and say that they were fine and that she should stop worrying herself so much. Nothing remarkable. It was the ordinary days she missed.

Shaking free of the image, she reached for her handbag and fished out a palm-size birchwood carving of a horse the color of burned honey. Struggling to decide on how she should mark the day, she had spotted it last weekend at a lawn sale, perched between a set of antique lamps. It had spoken to her, reminding her of all those mornings Beverly had spent describing the mares and colts on the track, their vibrant coats and swift strides. Clutching it to her chest, she pushed her way out of the car and up the drive, passing the overgrown yard and abandoned flower beds full of decaying stems.

"Meemaw!" Savannah swung open the door and barreled into her waist, wrapping her in a tight hug. The television blared in the background, some show about talking dinosaurs who wore clothes and went to work. It amazed her that Beverly could sleep through it all.

"Well, good morning to you, too." Marylynn gave her a squeeze and patted the top of her sun-kissed curls. Seeing Savannah was perhaps the most difficult part of coming here each morning. If she studied her too carefully, she might lose herself in a fit of tears. Everything about her was a living, breathing reminder of what Georgia would be like. What she *should* be like. *If only.*

Giving each of them a thorough once-over, she concluded that none had seen the likes of a brush since she was there yesterday morning.

"Where's your mama?"

"Still sleeping." Rayanne's voice emerged from the kitchen, where she clumsily poured a bowl of cereal at the counter, then drenched it in so much milk that flakes went spilling over the sides.

"Here. Let me help." Marylynn busied herself with cleaning up the mess, then pulled out a skillet and rummaged around in the fridge. "Now"—she clasped her hands together—"who would like some eggs? Sue Ellen? What about you?"

Sue Ellen scrunched up her nose from the kitchen table, where she sat reading a book an inch thick, a feat for anyone but especially a seven-year-old. "Do you *know* what eggs are, Meemaw?"

"Well, yes. I believe I do. They're delicious and healthy and, most importantly, versatile. Would you like yours scrambled or over easy?"

"They come from their you-know-whats. And that's after they've pooped all over each other because there isn't enough room for them to run around."

"What's a you-know-what?" Savannah asked.

"Well." Marylynn bristled. "When you put it like that." She pushed the eggs away and dug out a canister of flour from the pantry. "How about pancakes?"

"Me, me!" Savannah jumped up and down.

"Still has eggs in it," Sue Ellen muttered from behind her book.

Swooping around the kitchen, Marylynn whisked and poured and flipped until there was a tidy little stack of buttered disks. After preparing each plate and cutting Savannah's pancakes into bite-size triangles, she removed her apron and sneaked down the hall. Gingerly, she pushed open the bedroom door and poked her head inside.

A groan surfaced from somewhere underneath a pile of blankets. Marylynn slipped inside and crept to the bed, then softly eased herself down on the mattress beside her.

Stretching her limbs, Beverly peeked out a puffy eye and yawned. "Morning, Mama."

Hoping to start the day off on the right foot, Marylynn produced the tiny little horse and balanced him atop the quilt near Beverly's head. "Thought of you when I saw him. He looks just like that little filly you and your daddy bet on. Remember?"

A tired smile tugged at Beverly's lips but disappeared before she let it take hold. "Thank you," she said, accepting it with heavy fingers. She set him atop the nightstand before plopping herself back down.

"So." Marylynn did her best to muster a nonchalant tone. "When does Jack get back this time?"

"Are you asking because you really care to know or to prove a point," Beverly said, her barely open eyes still struggling to adjust to the light.

"Just curious is all. I didn't say anything."

"Of course not. That would be so unlike you."

Marylynn ignored the venom in her tone and pushed forward. "Honey, you aren't taking care of yourself. You need help around here. If I didn't have to be at work today, I'd stay," she said, drawing her eyebrows together as she checked her watch. "Isn't there anyone we could call?" She thought of Celia. It had been almost two years since she'd left, headed out west to see about a job. Sometimes she wondered how different Beverly's life might have turned out if she'd spent more time with her best friend than with that low-down filthy cuss she'd gone on to marry. But she always came to the swift realization that if things had happened differently, she never would have had Rayanne, or Sue Ellen, or Savannah. Or Georgia.

At this point, Marylynn was willing to call Christine Dupree or her insufferable mother if she thought Beverly would allow it. Anyone who might shake her child back into reality.

"We're fine, Mama." After peeling away the covers, she shuffled to the toilet.

"You all can't keep going on like this," Marylynn shouted above the sound of Beverly relieving herself. "The girls need stability. They need to be able to count on you."

"Thank you for reminding me what a failure I am." Beverly flushed, then stopped to poke at her complexion in front of the mirror. The fresh wrinkles in her brow gave Marylynn the impression she was cracking in more ways than one.

"I didn't say that. It's just that all I ever wanted is for you to be happy. It's killing me to see you do this to yourself."

"As sorry as I am to have disappointed you again, could you please stop pinning all your happiness on me? It's exhausting." The words landed hard in Marylynn's gut.

"Now, that is not true," she said, knitting her hands together in her lap.

"It absolutely is." Beverly narrowed her eyes at her mother. "Dennis and Frank could leave. They could go off and do whatever the hell it is they're doing, but no, not me. Never me. Face it, Mama. If I weren't here for you to fix, you'd fall apart."

Again with that kernel of truth that cut Marylynn as deeply as if she'd been slashed by a knife.

"Well, now you're just being spiteful. I did not raise my daughter to speak to me this way."

Stumbling back to the bed, Beverly lowered herself into the mattress, bracing herself with her hands. She was out of breath.

Steadying her with both arms, Marylynn placed an ear to her back and strained to hear.

"What's all this? How long has this business been going on?"

"Don't know. Few weeks, maybe, but it comes and goes. It's worse today, though." She coughed through labored breaths. "Like I can't"—she clasped a hand to her heart—"like I can't fill my lungs all the way."

"Well, has it crossed your mind that maybe that's not normal?" Marylynn chided. This would never have gone on this long if Beverly had just come home with the girls, where she could see to them all the time.

Her eyes unforgiving, Beverly snapped her head around. "I seem to remember someone telling me that normal is relative. What's normal now anyway, Mama? You tell me how much pain is the right amount. How should I feel?"

Guilt swept over Marylynn like a tidal wave, and her features cracked for just a moment before she jutted out her chin. "Well, I'm calling Dr. Heiden. You shouldn't be so tired all the time. Shouldn't be falling all over yourself when you go to the bathroom."

At that, she hurried down the hall and dug out the phone book, trying to swallow back the worry that had gathered in her throat.

Please, Lord. Not again.

CHAPTER 34

Rayanne

September 2022

Atop an easel rested a framed photo of her—a fiftysomething-year-old version of herself scowled into the camera with hard eyes, as if it had just verbally assaulted her, while the three of us hovered about her waist like hitchhiker seeds. My tiny face held the beginning of a smile, but my shoulders hunched inward. I seemed so small and timid, so fearful of a world that could take so much from me before I'd even hit puberty. Behind the photo, an array of pink tulips and white roses adorned the podium, and the heavy chords of "Amazing Grace" drifted from the organ. I closed my eyes, letting the hymn seep through me like a fine mist. In my imagination, I conjured an image of her, bone tired and still grieving as she dragged herself over to help us bury our treasure.

That saved a soul like me. The words washed over me like a prayer. She had saved me. All of us. I hadn't been able to see it at the time. And maybe it hadn't been in the way I had wished for. But still. She'd been there after everyone else left. She made space for us even when I couldn't make space for her and all her things.

Near the end, I'd had to divide my time between home and Muscadine to tend her, hauling the kids with me back and forth between the hospital and Cricket's place. All at once I was frightened at the thought they would never know Meemaw, that they would never get to help her harvest tomatoes from the garden or listen to any of her embarrassing stories about us. My childhood memories were all wrapped up in her, and when she died, they would die with her. Over the past few days, I had found myself thinking about the last weekend we'd spent with her. It hadn't been enough, but I was grateful for the time I had to make things right.

Catching sight of Savannah and Sue Ellen down the pew, my eyesight went fuzzy with tears. On my other side, Graham slipped his hand into mine as he balanced Charlotte atop his lap with the other. Since we had found out about Meemaw's illness, he'd been nothing short of amazing, offering to pay for a hospice nurse and covering the cost of her funeral. She would have hated it, but it only made me love him all the more.

The pastor's voice broke through my thoughts. "And now Marylynn's granddaughters will favor us with her favorite hymn."

Sue Ellen nudged my side, and I jolted upright. They were waiting for us. To sing. And I did not sing. The three of us shuffled onto the stage, where Katelyn joined us at the podium, and lacing our elbows together, we pieced together the words as best we could manage. *When the shadows of this life have gone, I'll fly away.* The words lodged in my throat as I looked out into the pews to find a collection of familiar faces: Cricket, Uncle Dennis, and Uncle Frank. Our father. I hadn't seen him before the service, so he must have slipped in after it began. His presence here made me want to cry, which only made me angrier. The man always knew how to make an entrance. Perfect timing, as Meemaw had already done the difficult work of raising us. I closed my eyes and refocused on getting the words out. Derrick was there, too, though I suspected it had less to do with Meemaw and more to do with Sue Ellen, who couldn't seem to stop fidgeting with her hair anytime he looked her way. In the back row, Sam Beaufort sat like a sullen statue with a tragic look about his face. Had he been in love with her? It occurred to me there was so much I still didn't know about my grandmother, and I wished that I had asked her. In the row ahead of Sam sat Christine Dupree. I hadn't noticed her before, not until I was face-to-face with the sparsely dotted pews as we sang. Her face was sharper now with a few fine lines, and her chestnut hair had the benefit of a fabulous colorist and was swept into a bun. When our eyes locked in on one another, her smile faltered, and she cut her gaze to the side, then shuffled out of her pew toward the exit.

After the service, we greeted Meemaw's friends with hugs and well-wishes, remembering her life through tearful smiles. I deftly managed to avoid our father and toted both kids toward the back of the chapel doors, while Graham was locked in a conversation with Uncle Dennis. As soon as we entered the lobby, Tucker let go of my hand and raced ahead of me, swishing past an array of floral arrangements and bumping into a woman who was heading in the direction from which we'd just come. He fell down against her legs, and with a warm smile, she bent down to offer him her hand.

"You all right there, honey?" Christine asked, tugging him up. My heart caught in my throat when I realized it was her. Wearing a black sheath dress, pearls, and dainty heels, she was one of the most put-together women at the service.

"I'm so sorry," I said, my cheeks aflame. "I hope he didn't hurt you."

"Oh no, dear," she said, meeting my gaze with a sympathetic tilt of her head. "I'm fine. I remember when my kids used to run around like little bottle rockets." She managed to hold a smile, but her lower lip quivered, as if her expression might give way at any moment. "You all turned out so beautifully," she breathed, bringing a fist to her lips as if she were seeing me for the first time. Fresh tears shimmered in her eyes, and she dabbed at them with a crumpled wad of tissue. "Seeing you up there together, I know your mother would have been proud."

Trying to keep myself from crying, too, I smiled weakly. "Thank you. That's very kind of you to say."

"Beverly was one of the purest souls I knew. And I wasn't always the best friend to her." She lowered her gaze. "I'm not proud of the way I treated her at times. But she was a good person. A wonderful mother. After you came along . . . well, we lost touch. She was so in love with you, and no one else could compare. I guess I didn't understand that kind of love until my son was born."

"That's good to hear," I said, unprepared for the emotion in my voice. "Honestly, I wasn't sure if she had any friends," I admitted. "I can't remember much about her."

"Oh, we stayed friends after high school. We weren't as close as . . ." She stopped herself, freezing her smile in place. I could tell she was holding something back. "Listen to me just carrying on like a lark," she said brightly, "when I'm sure you all must have so much to do. I hope you'll let me know if you need anything at all." She reached out a hand to brush my cheek, then blinked herself out of a daze.

As she moved to leave, I couldn't help myself from calling out after her. "Why did Celia leave?"

"Pardon me?" She swiveled around to face me, appearing confused, but I could tell I had struck a nerve from the way her shoulders bristled. "I'm not sure I understand."

"They were friends, and then all of the sudden, they weren't. And I'm just curious to know why. Something happened between them. And I don't know what it was, but I think that maybe you do."

"I'm not sure it's my place to tell. Besides"—doubt crept into the whites of her eyes, and her voice wavered—"they were only rumors. I was never sure what to believe."

"What rumors?" I asked.

She looked around again as if to search for prying eyes before continuing discreetly. "Like I said, I'm not sure it's my place to say anything."

"Celia's dead," I said flatly, hoping to convince her. "There's no more reason to keep secrets. Besides, I think our mother would want us to know the truth. Don't you?"

That got her attention, because her mouth went slack, and she wrinkled her forehead with a worried crease. "I didn't know that. It's a shame," she said softly. Bringing a nervous fingertip to her mouth, she cleared her throat and smoothed her dress before finally saying, "Celia betrayed your mother. She did something that was unforgivable, but I can't say for sure what happened."

"It was our father, wasn't it?" I said, remembering the way he couldn't look me in the eye when I mentioned Celia's name. "He had an affair with her, didn't he?"

Shock rippled across her face, and her eyes went wide. "It wasn't public knowledge," she said through a shaky smile, as if she hoped that would be enough to end this uncomfortable conversation. "A lot of women in this town knew your father . . . intimately." The muscles in her neck tensed, and I couldn't help but wonder if she had been one of those women herself.

"And?" I waited for more. My gaze traveled behind her, and I caught Sue Ellen staring at the two of us from across the room with a curious expression on her face, no doubt wondering what we were discussing. We locked eyes for a second or two before I turned to Christine again at the sound of her voice.

"And Celia was temping as a secretary for the trucking company he worked for." She offered this information timidly, as if Celia herself might show up behind her at any moment. "The two of them struck something up, and Beverly found out about it. After that their friendship was ruined. And she left."

All at once Meemaw's words found their way into my head and out of my mouth. "Jackass ain't worth a sack of potatoes," I heard myself mumble.

"What was that, dear?"

"Nothing." I shook the thought away and mustered a grateful smile. "Thank you, Christine. And please know that you didn't do anything wrong by telling me this." I reached for Tucker's hand and readjusted Charlotte on my hip.

"You're welcome," she said, though she seemed disappointed in herself. I detected a note of regret in her gaze as she gave my shoulders a gentle squeeze before walking away. She'd made it only a few feet before she slowed to a stop and heaved a sigh. Turning on her heel, she dropped her shoulders and pinched the bridge of her nose. "There's one more thing. Lord, forgive me," she said to the ceiling, as if against her will. "I'm not sure I should tell you this, but I don't want it on my conscience in case there's anything to it."

I steeled myself for whatever was coming, certain that nothing else could shake me at this point. With our mother and Georgia long since gone, Meemaw almost in the ground, and our father a confirmed adulterer, I felt I'd lived enough heartache for three lifetimes.

"Before she left, Celia came to me, asked me to help her with some bus fare. She was in a bad way, didn't have any friends left in the world. Her mother was an addict, and I knew she and Beverly had a falling-out with one another. I could tell that something was . . . different about her. And I suppose I've always wondered what happened after she left."

The hairs on my arms stood on end, and I braced myself. "What was different about her?" I asked, unable to hide my curiosity.

Christine's perfume overwhelmed my senses as she drew closer and whispered into my ear, looking almost ashamed of herself for speaking the words aloud. "I think Celia might have been pregnant."

CHAPTER 35

SUE ELLEN

September 2022

After we had executed the funeral to Meemaw's oddly specific instructions, including a very questionable performance from the three of us, Derrick caught up with me as I exited the pew.

"It's good to see you again, S.E. I wish it were under different circumstances," he said, plunging his hands into the pockets of his khakis, his voice tinged with regret.

I nodded, drawing a hand to my hair, and forced a smile. "Yeah, me too." Matching his steps, I shuffled alongside him toward the back of the chapel. "Of course Meemaw is having the last laugh."

"How's that?"

"She finally got me to set foot inside a church."

He gave a gentle laugh, and for just a moment my heart lifted.

"How you holding up?" he asked softly, drawing his shoulders together. The warmth of his body brushing against me sent an electric jolt through my veins, but I did my best not to let it show on my face.

"Physically? Fine. Emotionally?" I pursed my lips and squinted. "Racked with soul-crushing guilt."

Tilting his head to the side, he gave me a probing look. "I can't imagine why."

I grimaced, struggling to hold back tears. "Let's just say I'm not winning any awards for granddaughter of the year."

Slowing his pace, he furrowed a brow and shot me a healthy dose of side-eye. "Really? How's that? The Sue Ellen I remember always had to be the best at everything."

Something sharp twisted in my chest as I counted all the Christmases and birthdays I had missed over the years. All the times she'd begged me to find a job closer to her and away from a city that—according to her—was filled with criminals and naked people. "I avoided her," I admitted through a sigh. "And this place. I mean, I left as soon as I graduated high school and never looked back. I didn't even feel bad about it. I left . . . everyone."

"I'm sure she understood why. She must have known you never would have survived here teaching English at Muscadine High." It was sweet the way he was trying to soften the reality of what I'd done, but it didn't make it hurt any less. "She was proud of you, Sue Ellen." With his shoulder, he gave mine a little nudge. "Did she ever go visit you? I mean, the idea of Marylynn Pritchett on the East Coast is kind of amazing." He let out a little whistle and shook his head.

By now we had made it into the foyer, where I glanced over to see Rayanne locked in a serious conversation with someone who looked incredibly familiar. After a few moments of staring her down, I realized it was Christine Dupree and wondered what they were talking about. Tearing my gaze from them, I tried to remember Derrick's question.

"Once." I cleared my throat, debating how much to say. "She came for my undergrad ceremony at Yale. Let's just say that once was enough for the both of us." Inwardly I cringed at the memory of her trip, which had been an utter disaster. Having never flown before, Meemaw did not appreciate being wanded by a security guard who promptly confiscated a jar of homemade blackberry jam from her purse. I remembered this incident as if I had been there myself, because she had grumbled about it the entirety of the three days she'd spent with me in New Haven.

"Didn't even eat it. Just threw it in the trash. Made me take off my shoes and treated me like I was the criminal when he was the one who stole it right out of my purse," she'd said over and over again to me, to our cab driver, and to any unsuspecting stranger who'd had the misfortune of being seated near her at the ceremony. The fact that I'd bought her three different flavors of Smucker's had done nothing to abate her irritation.

Shaking away the memory, I wrapped my arms around myself. "It's just that . . . she always had a way of making me feel guilty about never coming home. She used to say we would miss her when she passed and tell me she'd be dead soon and I'd regret it. God, it really irritates me that she was right." Tears pricked at the corners of my eyes, and I blinked them back.

"Hey." He stopped short and with a gentle hand brushed my cheek. Instinctively I looked up at him, and our faces were inches apart. My breath caught when my eyes locked in on his, so rich and entirely sincere. I'd forgotten how easy it was to get lost in them. "You can't carry around all that regret. She wouldn't want you to," he said firmly, as if he needed me to believe him.

His hand was warm and safe, and it felt so right against my face. Closing my eyes, I let myself imagine what it would be like to have him hold me like this all the time. But as soon as I did, I realized that I could never be happy in this place, even if it meant being closer to Derrick. Living in Muscadine was a nonstarter, which meant that whatever feelings were building between us were already dead in the water. "I know. I just . . . wish I'd done things differently," I said, pulling away from him as I dabbed at my mascara. "Called home more. Checked in on her instead of depending on my sisters to do it. To think I missed out on the last years of her life because I was, what . . . embarrassed? What kind of person does that?"

"But you did come home. And that's the memory she had with her when she went. That's all that matters."

"Yeah, maybe." I heaved a sigh and drew in a shaky breath. "You're probably right."

His gaze flickered between me and his shoes. "Listen, I know things are going to be tough for you for a while. If you ever need to talk to someone, about your grandmother, about Georgia's case, I'm here." He looked at me now with a pained expression on his face, and I winced. Thousands of men in the city, and not one of them had ever looked at me that way. Not even Liam. Why did he have to be so nice? It only made it harder to tell the truth about the reality of our situation. "Derrick, I appreciate your friendship. Really, I do. But I think you need to know up front that I'm not built for long-distance relationships. And there is a zero percent chance of me ever moving back here. I don't want to lead you on." Had I assumed too much? Maybe he was just being friendly, but I'd been so certain there was a flirtatious undercurrent in those daily texts.

He stared back at me, unmoved. "Are you finished?"

I nodded, my cheeks practically on fire.

He opened his mouth to speak, then closed it before starting again. "I'm going to say something that might make me seem pathetic, but I'm going to say it anyway because I don't want to kick myself in another fifteen years for never saying it when I had the chance." He took a deep breath, and I felt my stomach clench. "When I was in high school, I got a huge crush on my big sister's friend. And I knew I could never tell her how I felt about her because she would never date Aliyah's kid brother—and more importantly because Aliyah would kill me." At this, my lips twitched into the start of a smile. "When she moved away, I jumped headfirst into a relationship with a girl I knew I didn't love. Got married. Got divorced. Grew up. And then one day, that girl walked back into my life—actually she was speeding, doing ninety in a seventy-five. And I'll be damned if I don't feel the same way about her.

Now you say you can't be in a long-distance relationship and that you can't move back. But those aren't the only two options here, S.E. And I think a woman as smart as you knows that. Even if she doesn't want to admit it."

I bit my lower lip, letting his words seep inside me. I didn't know if he was right or whether I could trust the way my body reacted whenever he was around. After Liam, my heart had become such a confusing place, and I was never sure what was real. The only thing I knew for certain was that for once in my life, I didn't have all the answers.

~

"Maybe we should hire a service." I heaved a black garbage bag and thrust it into the donate pile, nearly throwing out my back. "There are people we could pay to do this." I had to get back to my classes after the weekend, and so far we'd made it through only the living room. It could take months to get the house ready to sell, and even if we did, I couldn't imagine what poor soul would want to buy it. We suspected a crack in the foundation, the roof was in dire straits, and the cosmetic updates alone would make it a Realtor's nightmare.

Savannah ripped open another mystery bag, and clothing spilled out onto the floor. "No. She was very clear at the end about the three of us doing it together. She didn't want strangers going through her things."

"I remember a time when she didn't want us going through them, either," Rayanne mumbled, ripping a piece of duct tape with her teeth before smoothing it down along the seam of a box. "But now it's suddenly convenient."

I busied myself with filling in the holes in the wall where Meemaw's pictures had hung, while Tucker and Charlotte cornered a panicked Bessie underneath the kitchen table.

"What am I even supposed to feed a pig?" Rayanne asked, eyeing them as she rifled through a box of random kitchenware.

"Never mind that," I said. "I'm still trying to come around to the idea of you walking a pig in *your* neighborhood."

"It's just temporary," she said. "Until we can find a proper home for her. This may come as a surprise to you, but there aren't many pig rescues out there. Besides, I looked up the stats, and pig bites are far less common than dog bites."

But as I looked over at the kids stroking her ears, I could see that Bessie was already a part of their family, and I smiled. Finally I let myself ask the question I'd been holding back since the funeral. "So are we going to talk about it?"

"Talk about what?" she asked casually.

"What to do about him?" With Meemaw out of the picture, if we were going to attempt a relationship with our father, it seemed as good a time as any.

"I'm not sure I know who you're referring to," she said, ripping off another piece of tape.

"What did you decide? About letting Jack meet the kids?"

She stopped moving for a beat before pasting on a fake smile. "I've decided that there's no reason to mess with a good thing. We've been fine on our own without him all this time."

Savannah's ears perked up, and she tilted her head to the side. "I think he's sincere. He did come to the funeral, after all. Maybe he's changed. People can do that."

"He can't."

"You don't know that."

"Trust me," she scoffed. "I do."

"But what if he—"

"I'm not discussing it anymore." Rayanne held up a hand to shut her down. "He left us. He didn't care enough to come back for us back then. He doesn't care now. If y'all want to have a relationship with him,

I won't stand in the way, but I can't." Tears gathered in the corners of her eyes. "I just . . . can't."

Thinking back on the funeral, I couldn't get the image of Rayanne and Christine out of my head. I'd seen the vacant look on my sister's face as the two of them discussed something. I hadn't wanted to bring it up before, but I had a niggling feeling that she was holding out on us. "What did you talk to Christine about? At the funeral. I saw the two of you, and it seemed like whatever she said rattled you."

Her smile faltered for the smallest moment before she shrugged me off. "Nothing. It was just . . . memories of Mama. That kind of thing."

"It was more than that," I said, still not convinced. The look on her face had reminded me of our mother's when she had learned that Georgia was missing—sadness and outrage and confusion all wrapped up together. She looked broken. "Was he cheating on her with Christine? Tell us. Whatever it is, we deserve to know just as much as you do."

Finally she pursed her lips and inhaled long and deep through her nose. "It was . . . about him. About his affairs. But it wasn't Christine," she added.

"So Meemaw was right about him," Savannah said, shaking her head. "Can't say I'm surprised."

Rayanne gave a sarcastic laugh. "She sure was."

"OK, now you *have* to tell us," I said, not willing to let her table this for a second longer. I nestled myself in the chair across from her and waited.

She let out a sigh before beginning. "He didn't have an affair with just anyone. It was with her best friend." As the words left her mouth, I couldn't be certain I was hearing them correctly. A white-hot rage gathered in my chest, and I suddenly understood why my sister had been so out of sorts since the funeral.

"Celia," I nearly whispered. "I can't believe it." If I thought our mother's life had been tragic before, now it seemed entirely unjust. Cruel even.

"That's not the worst part." Her shoulders shook as she collected her breath. "She thought . . . she suspected . . . Celia was pregnant."

Unable to process this information, I stared back at her blankly, the words echoing around inside my skull. I wasn't sure how a person was supposed to respond to the news that they may have another biological sibling wandering around the planet, but I had no words to offer.

"Did she keep the baby?" Savannah's voice broke through my thoughts, and an unspoken sadness settled between the three of us. For some reason, my thoughts cut to Georgia—what she would have looked like, how her voice might have sounded, what kind of life our baby sister might have lived if she'd had the chance. I suspected that was where Savannah's mind had gone, too, because her eyes had filmed over with fresh tears.

Rayanne only wrapped her arms around herself and blew out her cheeks. "I don't know. Hard to know much of anything when everyone is dead."

Something in Savannah's expression shifted. I could tell that she was practically brimming with plans about what to do with this information. "This is amazing," she breathed through tears.

Rayanne stiffened. "No. It's not."

Ignoring her, Savannah crinkled her brow and pressed on, conversing with herself. "We need to find out what happened to him. Or her." She looked up at me. "Do you still have the obituary?"

I thought back to the death announcement, the image of the girls sitting in Celia's lap and how Savannah had mentioned how they looked like me. For the first time, I wondered if they could be my nieces, and my stomach flipped.

Rayanne answered her before I had time to form a coherent response. "We're not actually going to do anything about this," she said, leveling her gaze at Savannah.

"Why not? It's exciting. To know that there's someone out there who might look like us. Another sibling?"

Rayanne stood and turned her back to us, then struggled to lift a box atop another one. "No."

"But maybe she needs to know her health history or . . . she needs an organ donor."

"It's the twenty-first century." Rayanne waved a dismissive hand. "They're growing livers in labs these days. Trust me, she'll be fine."

Savannah's eyes went wide. "How can you say that? This is family we're talking about."

"It's not family," Rayanne said, almost shouting the words. A swath of pink crept up her neck and spilled onto her cheeks. "DNA does not change things here." She stole a glance at her children and lowered her voice. "This is the product of our father's raging infidelity. I mean, who's to say this child wasn't just one of dozens? Who knows how many others he fathered?"

"Which is exactly why we need to talk to him," Savannah said, her voice rising an octave. "You're married, but I'm still on the market, and this is a small town. What if I unintentionally date my brother?! We need answers, and he's the only person who can give them."

"I'm not going to see him again." Setting her jaw, Rayanne pinched the bridge of her nose. "Besides, it's not like he would tell us the truth anyway."

"Aren't you the least bit curious?" I asked, surprised to find myself agreeing with Savannah.

"Honestly?" She fixed her eyes on me before diving back into her task without missing a beat. "No. I don't want to know. And I don't need a living reminder of his mistakes."

"And you think you'll be happier not knowing?" Savannah asked. "Not knowing what happened to Georgia"—her voice wavered before she collected herself again—"wondering if she's out there somewhere— it's so much worse than not having proof. But we can actually do something about this."

Rayanne's hands went still, and she directed a fiery gaze at the two of us. "And what exactly are you proposing we do?"

"We try," Savannah said, giving me a probing look, as if I could cast the deciding vote in her favor.

Picking up on her cue, I gave a reluctant shrug. The heat in my chest had cooled into something else, something hopeful and full of possibility. Meemaw's words floated into my thoughts, and my heart tightened at the realization of what she would say if she were here. I could almost feel her smiling as I heard myself say the words she had said so many times before. "Family is family."

CHAPTER 36

MEEMAW

February 1997

The last dregs of winter hung on an icy breeze as it tousled her pinned-back hair, sending a few silver-tinged curls fluttering against her wet cheeks. The air was crisp and sharp, but the sun shone stubbornly, which only irritated Marylynn all the more. A dreary day would have been appropriate, would have matched the foggy canvas on her soul, but a cloudless blue sky seemed irreverent—an infuriating reminder of everything her daughter would never be able to enjoy.

How had she allowed it to happen again? Another empty chair around her dinner table. Would they disappear one by one until eventually she would be left alone?

Six Mary Jane–clad feet dangled in a neat little row on all sides of her. Six red-rimmed eyes followed the cream, tulip-lined casket as it sank steadily into the earth. Her pastor was conducting the service since Beverly hadn't claimed membership in any church. Apparently she had told the children some nonsense about the Lord being everywhere, so there was no need to go to some stuffy building one day a week if you carried Him in your heart on all seven of them. When Sue Ellen had apprised Marylynn of their enlightened belief system, Marylynn had taken a long drag from her cigarette before shouting that she wouldn't be raising a bunch of new-age pagans and that if a person expected the Lord to feel welcome in her home, she ought to go and visit Him in His at least once in a while. From here on out, there was no question about whether they would be attending church.

Yea, though I walk through the valley of the shadow of death, I will fear no evil. The pastor's words settled over her uneasily, reminding her that no matter how hard she had prayed for strength, these days she was always afraid. It seemed that anything was possible now—every illness and evil lurked in broad daylight, threatening to upend everything she loved most. Reaching an arm around Savannah and sidling her into a bear hug, she sifted her memories, trying to understand how she had missed it—the weight loss, the bone-tired weariness that shone through her glassed-over eyes. It had been so easy to chalk it up to the loss of Georgia. But looking back now, she seethed at herself for not recognizing the signs sooner. A mother always knows. *She* should have known.

Dennis and Frank joined the pallbearers, and she stood as a string of mourners dawdled past her, embracing the girls and offering tearful condolences. She searched their faces for Celia, but there had been no sign of her today. *She was too young. So sorry for your loss. She was lucky to have you. What a tragedy.* One by one, they came, and though she knew the messages were sincere, she wasn't ready to let go of the anger.

"Mrs. Pritchett?"

Recognizing the voice, Marylynn lifted her head to find Christine Dupree standing in front of her. A dizzying sense of déjà vu pricked at her heart. But unlike her own mother all those years ago, Christine's face appeared genuinely distraught, with mascara messed about her face and cheeks that had been rubbed raw. Her red hair was swept into a bun, and her face was sharper, less round than when she was in high school, but Marylynn recognized her instantly.

"I want you to know how sorry I am. And that I should have been a better friend to her." Her voice cracked with emotion. "You know how it is once you have kids," she said, wrapping an arm around the little boy at her side, who looked to be about the same age as Savannah. "It's easy to forget each other." Fumbling to wipe her tears, she gave a rueful smile. "I put some money away for the girls. For whatever they need. It's not much, but my husband and I wanted to do it. For Beverly." She gave a tiny nod before reaching a hand into her fitted trench coat and producing a slim white envelope, then clasped Marylynn's fingers around it inside her own.

Touched by the gesture, Marylynn pulled her into her chest and whispered a thank-you in her ear. "That's very thoughtful, Christine. I appreciate that."

Rayanne's face screwed up in a tearful pout while Sue Ellen and Savannah both clung to Marylynn's skirt on either side, their noses raw and their eyes puffy. As the mourners continued to drift toward her, she focused on keeping her legs from giving out beneath her. *Stay in motion,* she told herself. *Drive home. Put a casserole in the oven. Get them into a bath. Breathe.*

Cricket appeared before her, wrapping her into a tight embrace. "I'm so sorry. We prayed so hard. What can I do, Marylynn? What do you need?"

"Can you take the girls to the car for me?" She feigned a smile, fighting back the tears. "There's something I need to take care of."

Cricket nodded and reached for their little hands, shuttling them off like a mother hen. She looked back once more and offered a nod of encouragement to Marylynn, who tucked away her loose curls and began the long walk in the other direction.

With every step, Marylynn's heels sank into the soft earth as she approached him, lingering at the back of the service behind the final row of metal chairs. Creeping around sullenly near the tree line, he had the look of a trespasser rather than a grieving husband.

"Don't worry about paying me back," she said, fumbling to light a cigarette. "She wasn't your responsibility after all."

She had to admit he looked as if he had at least tried to make an effort today with a clean button-up shirt and striped tie. She couldn't remember the last time the man had donned a pair of slacks. His hair was freshly trimmed and slicked back, his face shaved. Beverly's diagnosis hadn't slowed Jack down when it came to his job. In fact, Marylynn suspected he stayed away for longer stretches because it was easier than seeing his wife slowly fall apart. But the last week of Beverly's life, Marylynn had reached out to the trucking company to track him down, desperate. Beside herself with worry and afraid of being alone, she was willing to share in Beverly's final moments. And he had been there at the end—an unwelcome but necessary body alongside her to bear witness to the most precious life she'd ever known.

He rubbed at the back of his neck. "No. I'll pay for half. Just let me move a few things around, and I'll get you the money."

"It's not about the money." She breathed out a puff of smoke slowly, watching it unfurl into a stream before it dissipated on the wind. "It's about the girls. We both know what needs to happen here. I'll take 'em. They belong with me."

"Now hold on a second there. No one's deciding anything right now." He ran a hand through his gelled hair, his eyes darting nervously to the Buick, where the girls sat waiting. "She never said . . . at the end . . . she never said she wanted you to do it."

"That's only because she wasn't lucid. She would have. If she'd had her druthers, she would have said it. Admit it, Jack. You don't want them. Nothing hinders a man on the prowl like three kids."

"It's not like that, Marylynn. I want them," he said, his voice harder. Stuffing his hands into his pockets, he shifted from one foot to the other. "But being on the road all the time . . . it means I can't be there for them the way they need me to be." At her silence, he pleaded with more urgency: "What do you want me to do? Choose between my job and my kids? I'm doing the best I can here, but you're not making it easy."

She fought back the urge to slap him. "I'm so sorry things aren't easy for you, Jack. I'm sorry that you might have to actually put some effort into this family." She scoffed. "She wasn't going to be able to carry you forever." Flicking the end of her cigarette, she blew out another puff of smoke, then dabbed at her eyes with a lace-trimmed handkerchief. "Truthfully, I don't know what she ever saw in you. Why she couldn't see you for what you are."

"And what is that?" he said, tilting an ear, his jaw tightening into a rigid line.

"A sorry excuse for a man," she said without hesitation. "The kind of person who turns tail the moment things get difficult. You've always been weak. But she thought she could fix you." She flicked the end of her cigarette.

"You know what?" He shook his head and plastered on a tight smile. "You're right. Maybe I am. You know what's best, right? Always have. It's your way or no way—is that how it's gonna be?"

"Now you're getting it. Hallelujah! He has a brain." She lifted her hands to heaven. "You didn't want them. And you've never really been there for them. Not in the way a father should be. Why start now?" she said, grinding out her cigarette. Dusting herself off, she turned on her heel, but he called back after her, his tone more forceful this time. It struck her that it was the first time he'd ever raised his voice at her.

"She hated you," he said loudly enough for the stragglers still in attendance to hear. "Always said you ruined her life, tried to take every good thing she had away from her."

Straightening herself, she whipped around to face him. "Well, now, I think you've gotten the two of us confused. I am not the one who ruined her life." Giving an angry laugh, she drew herself up to him, though he still towered a solid foot above her. "You were the one who left her pregnant and alone, always sneaking around with other women, couldn't stay home longer than a hot minute." Tilting her head, she zeroed in on him, making sure he understood. "Who do you think she called when you were gone? Who do you think has been there this entire time raising your children? Show a little more gratitude." She turned again and headed for the street and the Buick, where Cricket sat consoling the girls.

"Then where were you?" he called out. "When we lost Georgia. What were *you* doing? You like to lay the blame all on me, and that's fair. I should have been there that day, and I have to live with that. But don't forget that you failed her, too."

She didn't flinch, didn't allow the words to turn her head, but kept walking toward the car, where the girls sat squished together in the back seat, waiting for her. They needed her. No one else would protect them as she would. *Don't look back.* Her pace quickened to match her racing heart. And with every step, the soft parts of her turned solid, hardening into cold, gray stone.

He wasn't wrong. She hadn't kept Georgia safe, hadn't been able to breathe life back into her daughter. But it would never happen again. Not if she had anything to say about it.

CHAPTER 37

RAYANNE

September 2022

Tucked inside a booth at Lavon's with my fingers wrapped around a steaming mug of coffee, I scanned the front door every few seconds. Outside, a leaden sky hung overhead, and a bitter storm wind beat against the windows of the shop, rattling the bird feeders and wind chimes with a furious persistence. Impatience bubbled up inside me as I checked my watch again, then blew a stray wisp of hair out of my eyes. "He's not coming. Can we go now?"

"He's five minutes late." Directly across from me, Savannah picked at her french fries. "Give the man some grace." She popped one into her mouth nonchalantly as if she didn't care whether he showed, but I could see the way her gaze flitted to the door, too, every so often.

"I've done that for twenty-five years. So I'm sorry if I'm all out of grace today." I stood and collected my purse when I heard the chime of the bell, and our father's wilted shoulders appeared like a shrunken oak tree in the doorframe. His green eyes smiled at me so deeply they almost winked in the way I remembered he used to do when I was small, though now they were framed by crow's-feet and two bushy tufts of gray hair. He wore a pair of jeans that had faded at the knees and a blue flannel shirt that flayed open, revealing a too-tight white ribbed shirt beneath. He limped to the back of the store and met us with an effervescent smile, shaking his head as if he couldn't believe the three of us were here. I almost couldn't believe it, either, but Savannah had a way of making the impossible happen.

"I never expected to see all my girls together again."

My stomach clenched at the way he used the phrase, as if he still had a right to claim us after all this time.

His face faltered as his gaze fell on Savannah and lingered there a moment too long, making her shift in her seat. I thought he might cry, but he cleared his throat and motioned to sit. I cleared a space beside me, and he settled in across from Sue Ellen with a groan and a creaky stretch of his leg. "I can't believe how grown-up you girls are," he said, taking us in.

My heart gave an angry quiver, but I forced myself to skip over all the things I wanted to tell him and dived straight into the reason we had come here. It was best to be as diplomatic as possible about the whole thing. "Thought it might be best to meet in a public place." Meemaw's house was still a disaster, and I had no interest in returning to Porter's Trailer Park. "We need to ask you a few questions."

Still smiling, he looked from me to each of my sisters with a confused wrinkle in his brow. "OK." He dragged out the word, making it sound like a question. "Sounds serious."

"When I came to visit you before, you didn't tell me everything."

At this, the muscles in his neck tensed, and he frowned at his restless, weather-beaten hands. "I'm not sure what you mean," he said into his chest.

"We know you had an affair with Mama's best friend."

He let out a long puff of air and shook his head as if to clear the words. "I'm not sure what your grandmother told you, some deathbed confession, but—"

"She didn't tell us anything," Sue Ellen said in a steady voice that was as firm as it was determined. For the first time, I could picture her as an esteemed professor standing in front of a classroom full of selfie-obsessed Gen Zers. She'd always been able to hold her own. "We figured it out. And now we want to hear it from you. Was Celia pregnant?"

Hearing a tiny gasp, I whipped my head around and caught sight of Cricket, who was pretending to busy herself with restocking the cereal boxes behind us. She stiffened her back as she reached for another box, but I had seen the surprise in her horrified face.

Screwing his eyes shut, he rubbed the bridge of his nose and gave a defeated sigh before finally responding, "She was."

My pulse ticked up steadily until it seemed my heart was thrumming in my chest in double time. Disgust soured in my gut as bits and pieces of my childhood flashed on the screen in my mind—Daddy heaving me up onto his shoulders at the fair, swinging me around the living room by my arms, teaching me how to bait a hook and how to hold a fish in the perfect space on its belly so it wouldn't fin me. I couldn't seem to square my scattered childhood memories of him with the man who was sitting in front of me now. A man who could so easily throw away his family.

"So you just let her leave?" Savannah asked, her eyebrows furrowed together in a V shape. "You abandoned the woman who was carrying your child?"

"He abandoned us," Sue Ellen answered for him, setting him squarely in her sights. She crossed her arms and settled back against her seat, looking unimpressed. "So I suppose we can't accuse him of favoritism. I'm assuming he didn't pay a dime in child support to Celia, either," she said to me, as if the person she was talking about were not sitting across from her.

"Celia never asked me for a thing." Leaning forward, he rested an elbow on the table and raked a hand through his disheveled curls. "I sent her a few checks over the years, but she never cashed them. Said she didn't want to take away from what I owed you all." His shoulders sank even lower. "It nearly broke her . . . what we did." He cleared his throat and rubbed a thumb against his nose. "For what it's worth, I sent Marylynn some money for you all, too."

I studied him, trying to gauge if I believed him. Knowing how much Meemaw had struggled over the years, taking on so many extra shifts at the nursing home to feed us, I doubted that was true. "And you never told Mama?"

"There was never a good time. Not after"—he raised his eyes to meet Savannah's before lowering them again—"not after losing your sister like that. And I couldn't let Marylynn know about it. Not after everything she already believed about me."

"You mean because she was accurate in her assessment of you?" Sue Ellen cocked a sassy eyebrow, and he blanched.

"Look, I'm not perfect. I've made mistakes. I wish . . ." He worked his hands together, rubbing at his dirty fingernails, then started again. "I'm a work in progress. And I'm not the same man I was all those years ago. Trust me, you girls wouldn't have wanted me around."

Though that was probably true, I wasn't about to let him off on a technicality and dug in even deeper. "Did you know Celia passed away?" Maintaining my composure, I unfolded the obituary and slid it over to him, then tapped a finger on Celia's face.

There was a subtle crack in his features, and he tugged at his scruffy chin with his thumb and forefinger. Staring down at the black-and-white photo of Celia and the little girls resting on her lap, he answered softly. "I didn't know that."

"Well, you wouldn't, would you?" Sue Ellen said with a deadpan delivery.

Gripping the table, Savannah leaned forward. "We want to meet our sister. And just so we're clear, you don't have any other offspring wandering around out there, do you?"

He grimaced, then arched an eyebrow as if he were considering the possibility. "Well, not that I'm aware of. No."

Savannah let out a relieved sigh. "And you didn't write to Celia? You didn't feel any obligation to ask after the child you fathered?"

"She sent me a few pictures that first year. A few mementos and a letter. I wrote back, but after a while we just kind of . . . fell out of touch. I couldn't bring myself to go looking for her. Not after losing Georgia. It was like . . . like the universe was trying to replace one daughter with another, like Georgia was just a cog in a machine that could be switched out." He blinked back tears, and the sight of it left me fending off my own. For the first time, I considered the guilt he must have carried at not being there to protect Georgia or Mama. I wished he could have found the strength inside him to try to protect us. "It felt wrong to be a father again. I didn't think I deserved a second chance with Evangeline. Hell, I probably didn't deserve the first."

Evangeline. My ears perked up at the mention of her name, and I exchanged a cautious glance with my sisters. Hearing him say it aloud made her real now. And it changed everything.

CHAPTER 38

EVANGELINE

November 2022

Dear Savannah, Sue Ellen, and Rayanne,
I must admit, I was surprised to receive your message. I'd like to be able to say I didn't know about the three of you, but that isn't quite the truth. As a child, I begged my mother to tell me about my father, but whenever I brought it up, she outright refused. It has been a struggle to go through life not knowing where you came from or why you were born.
And then she got sick—non-Hodgkin's lymphoma. At the end of her life, I could sense that she wanted to tell me the truth, but I didn't push her, worried that maybe it would break her soul if she did. Whatever she was holding back, I knew it was bad.
After she died, she left a letter with her estate, and I learned who my father was. Of course, I researched the three of you right away, but as I'm sure you'll understand, it didn't seem appropriate to

make contact. I could hardly imagine you wanting to connect with the love child of your father's mistress, especially after all you'd been through. And I never wanted to feel like a shameful secret that walked into your lives unannounced.

I can't begin to understand how my mother could do what she did, but her letter helped me find some answers. I hope it will do the same for you all. I look forward to hearing from you again, if you feel comfortable reaching out, of course. I'll leave that up to you.

Sincerely,

Evangeline Peters Wright

P.S. I was an only child, so the idea of having three sisters is amazing!

~

Dear Evangeline,

The only thing that makes this letter bearable to write is knowing I'll be dead when you read it. All these years, the shame alone has been enough to nearly suffocate me. You have always wanted to know where you came from, and I suppose every child deserves at least that much. So here goes. Your father is a man named Jack Guidry. You have three half sisters who I wish you could have met, but for reasons you will soon come to understand, this would never have been possible.

I've heard it said that a person is better than the worst thing she's ever done. I hope that's true, because the worst thing I ever did was break my best friend's heart, and after that, I became someone else entirely. Someone I didn't recognize; whether good or bad is for only God Himself to decide.

I never meant for things to go as far as they did. But some mistakes can't be unmade. And the moment I decided to have an affair with my best friend's husband, I knew there would be no going back. I was temping as a secretary at the construction company he worked for, and one day he looked at me. He looked at me the way he used to look at her, and for the first time since I was a misfit teenager praying he would notice me, I wondered what it would be like to kiss him. After all, I had seen him first, had wanted him first.

I'd only meant for it to be a little harmless flirting, but somewhere along the way, I fell for him. I don't know who I was kidding, because I'd already fallen for him long ago, the night he saw us stranded on the side of the road and offered to drive us home. But it wasn't me he held at the end of that night. It wasn't me he wanted. Even now, in my heart, I knew he would always choose Beverly, that I was just a fun distraction for him to escape when things became too serious at home with their children that seemed to keep coming. Still, I hadn't prepared myself for how much it would hurt when he ended it.

Beverly's mother was ever the detective and had begun to suspect that he was seeing someone else. She never would have believed it was me. I had thought we were so careful, had taken so many pains to cover our tracks. But one day Beverly came to work to drop off his lunch, and she caught sight of me laughing at something he said, trailing a hand down the curve of my neck. I tried my best to shake it off, to act natural and pretend that nothing was amiss. But I could see it in her eyes.

She knew it was me.

After that, I tried to work up the courage to apologize, to tell her that I never meant to hurt her. But I was a coward. Once, I came close—at the lake I watched her, surrounded by her children, laughing and playing with them all, and I knew that I would never be able to make up for what I had taken from her. I couldn't tell her. And after that day, I knew I never could. She suffered an unimaginable loss, and it would have broken her to know about you.

I didn't have anything left in Muscadine. My own mother was too caught up in her own demons to offer much support. And so I left with you growing in my belly and with what little dignity I had left. I may have been a terrible friend, but I'd like to think that I've at least been a good mother. I hope you will agree with me.

You are my heart, Evangeline. Forgive me. All my love,
Your mother

CHAPTER 39

MEEMAW

June 1999

Sheriff Humphries took the brunt of Marylynn's constant pestering. Each passing summer with no new leads in the case seemed to take more of his hair, along with his pride, until patchy wisps of gray had steadily receded to the nape of his neck. The jowls of his chin sagged even lower under the weight of the investigation, giving him a permanent frown. Every Monday morning, Marylynn called the station, demanding updates and reassurances that the case was still open, and every Tuesday afternoon he would ring her back and offer the same tired phrases of comfort. *We're doing everything we can. These things take time. Must have patience.* She got little out of these exchanges, but she kept them up, mostly to make sure that Georgia hadn't been forgotten, that they hadn't stashed her file away in a dusty corner or locked it down in the basement under a pile of expired parking tickets and old receipts.

On a sweltering Wednesday afternoon, Marylynn dragged all three girls down to the station and planted herself on a vinyl chair in the wood-paneled lobby. Perhaps she shouldn't have brought them, but Rayanne was just eleven, not old enough to mind the other two, and

Marylynn wasn't ready to leave them unsupervised. Not yet. Maybe not ever. He hadn't called her back, and he always called her back. Something had changed. She was certain he had news, maybe a flicker of something good that he wasn't ready to share because he didn't want to get her hopes up. Whatever it was, she would pry it out of him.

Having just returned from a lunch break, Sheriff Humphries appeared to be in no mood for visitors when he barreled through the entrance of the station, his eagle eyes focused on his office door just off to the right. Brandishing a thirty-two-ounce soda and half of a sandwich, he stiffened at the sight of Marylynn and the three little girls blocking his escape. Though she could sense his reluctance, he invited her into a tiny room that smelled of mothballs and offered her a drink, which she refused. Holding her eyes on his, she lowered herself into a tattered leather love seat and nestled Savannah onto her lap while Rayanne and Sue Ellen settled on either side, their faces a mix of curiosity and uncertainty as they examined the bare walls of his office.

"I'm sorry I haven't called yet," he said, leaning his weight against the desk in front of her. Placing a meaty hand on her shoulder, he said, "Maybe you'd rather the girls sit in the lobby with Nancy while we talk." He motioned to the clerk, who hurried over at his urging. "This isn't going to be something you want them to hear."

"They're fine right here." Marylynn pulled away from him and waved Nancy away before straightening in her seat. "Whatever you have to say to me, you can say in front of them," she said, jutting out her chin. She wasn't sure she believed this but hoped that somehow their presence would be able to thwart whatever bad news was coming. She knew it was selfish of her, but she had hoped for all their sakes that it would make them impervious to whatever he had been holding back from her.

His shoulders deflated with a bearlike sigh. "We got a tip. From a local who saw Levi Morrison's truck a half mile down the water on the day Georgia went missing."

Marylynn recognized the name. It had been all over the news the past few weeks. He had murdered someone, somewhere in Tennessee, perhaps? A young girl, though not as young as her Georgia. Her stomach heaved at the thought that her granddaughter could be among his victims. *Murdered.* The unspoken word echoed in her skull so loudly she drew a hand to her head to silence it.

"The Tennessee case is rock solid against him," he continued, his voice tender and his eyes warm. "I can promise you he will never see the outside world again. I realize this is difficult to hear, but at least now you can start to move forward."

Marylynn clutched Savannah a little tighter. *Move forward? Move where? Move how?* At the moment she couldn't even breathe properly. After Beverly died, finding Georgia had been the only thing she could hold in her mind, the only path forward that made any sense. If she found her, maybe she could make all of them a little more whole, a little less damaged, a little more capable of facing the next day. And the next. It wouldn't have all been for nothing. Beverly's death wouldn't have been in vain. Yet here she sat, face-to-face with a reality that she could not bring herself to accept.

"Where's the evidence?" Her voice was laced with anger but quavered so shakily that she feared it might give out. "You've never found her, so she could still be out there. She's waiting on you to do your job!"

Once more, his gaze fell on the girls, and he flinched. Leaning in close, he spoke so that the heat in his breath brushed her ear. "Marylynn, he confessed. Last night."

Through tears, she looked up at him as if he had slapped her. A pang pierced her insides so sharply she had to steady herself against her granddaughter's tiny frame. After so much loss, so much heartbreak, was this really how it ended?

He stole one last sorrowful glance at Savannah, who was hiding her face in Marylynn's chest, before leveling a sympathetic gaze at her again. "I know it's difficult to see it now, but this means you can move on with your life. Now take some solace in that, and take care of these girls you've still got."

~

It had taken an entire three hours to blow up the pool because in all Charlie's tools, he had failed to leave behind an air pump. Her lips had gone numb halfway through, and she'd had to enlist Rayanne and Sue Ellen to finish it in shifts. Sue Ellen had insisted that the party was going to be outside. In June. In Muscadine. A pool was a necessity, even if it might be carried away by a gust of wind. A donkey piñata stuffed to the seams swayed from the giant oak out front, and a chocolate ice-cream cake sat cooling in her freezer. A picnic table draped in a sheet of checkered plastic held a tray of hot dogs and a cooler of juice boxes waiting for little hands to pluck them up.

The afternoon heat pressed down on her, but she'd been so busy fluttering about the yard that she hadn't noticed the sweat stains forming in the armpits of her floral sundress. Sue Ellen hadn't wanted to mark the day at all, would have rather hidden underneath her bed with a thick book and a pile of sugary snacks, but Marylynn had insisted. After all, double digits were a milestone. Besides, these days she needed something to celebrate, especially after Sheriff Humphries's news. Dennis was driving down for the weekend from Kansas, and he was bringing Katelyn, whom she hadn't seen in months. The girls were going to be over the moon when their cousin arrived, and she was desperate to see them smile again. Checking her watch, she made one more trip inside the house to retrieve the cake, then set it out proudly on the table. Almost everyone was here.

A flurry of bare feet flitted past her. She smiled as they piled in the pool and fell over one another, their giggles intertwined in a nearly perfect melody that made her heart ache. An engine hummed steadily louder in the distance until Dennis's pickup rolled into the drive, honking out a welcome. Katelyn clambered out of the car before it came to a full stop and pummeled into her, nearly bowling her over.

"Meemaw! I missed you," she said into her dress, clinging to her like a koala.

"I've missed you, too," Marylynn crooned, giving her a firm squeeze and tousling her hair. She tried to run her fingers through it, but it was a mess of tangles, and she had to tug hard to pry them loose. "Let me look at you," she said, stepping back and sizing her up. She was too small, not nearly as filled out as Rayanne, and they were the same age. Her clothes were smeared with stains, at least a size too small, and her knobby toes peeked out over the edges of her dirty sandals. But even that had not been what set her off.

When Katelyn lifted her shirt over her shoulders, revealing a two-piece swimsuit, Marylynn scrutinized a string of purple and brown blotches along her arm, trailing her fingers along the jagged pattern. Her breath caught in her chest, and her pulse ticked up a few notches, threatening to unhinge her.

"Go on and play now, honey." Regaining her composure, she patted Katelyn gingerly on the back and watched her scamper off to join the others.

Catching sight of Dennis and Patty ambling toward them, Marylynn breathed out a silent prayer for strength, mostly the strength to resist giving Patty a dose of her own medicine. Her daughter-in-law's eyes were rimmed with dark circles, and her already-skinny frame had taken on a childlike frailness. How many times had Marylynn told him not to marry her, that she was weak? Too weak to be a mother. Pulling Dennis into a hug, she spoke softly into his ear. "It's been too long, son." Stepping back to look him over, she gave a curt nod to the wisp of a woman at his side. "I see you're doing well, Patty." Though anyone could see that she looked even worse than she had the last time she'd been here a few months ago. They had already been through this last year with the "accident" that had sent Katelyn to the hospital with a third-degree burn. Apparently it had not been enough to make her change, and it hadn't been enough to make Dennis leave her.

"Dennis, can I speak to you inside?" Marylynn said, attempting to hold a smile, though her face hurt with the effort.

"Mama, whatever you got to say, you can say in front of Patty." He wrapped an arm around his wife and pulled her a little closer. How had Marylynn managed to raise such a fool?

Taking in a deep breath, she tried again, this time abandoning all subtlety. "I don't think Patty will like what I have to say." She crossed her arms and stared her down, but Patty only matched her body language. This wasn't the first time Marylynn had confronted the two of them about Patty's abysmal parenting skills, though usually she waited until everyone had had a drink or two.

"I'm sure I won't," Patty said, glaring over at Dennis in a way that made Marylynn's face flush even hotter.

"Fine, then." Marylynn pushed ahead. "That's an abused and neglected child if I've ever seen one." She jabbed a finger at Katelyn, who was thankfully splashing away with her cousins and the other children, blissfully ignorant of the argument taking place on her behalf.

"She's lost it now," Patty said, tossing her head back in an irritated laugh. "I told you we shouldn't have come."

"I didn't say that," Marylynn shot back, dispelling the idea with her hands. "Katelyn can stay. But you're right. *You* shouldn't have come."

"Dennis, are you gonna let her talk to me like that? Say something." Patty gaped at him.

"Mama, this is my wife." Dennis wedged himself between the two of them and held up a hand. "You can't speak to her like this."

"Well, I am your mother, and this is my house, and I'll say whatever the hell I think needs saying."

He dragged a hand down the side of his face and back up again. "Mama, I don't want to do this again. If you don't want Patty here, then you don't want me here, either. Now let's just drop it and put on a good face for the kids. Today's about Sue Ellen, after all."

She couldn't disagree with that. But the way Katelyn had looked up at her and clung to her as if she were her salvation set her insides on fire. She had to do something.

"That woman has no business being a parent. And if you can't see that, neither do you."

Tossing up his hands, he shook his head. "Fine, Mama. Have it your way. Katelyn, let's go!" He hollered above the girls' laughter, drawing a blank stare from his daughter.

Marylynn drew herself up to her full height, which was still a good foot shorter than her oldest son. "Katelyn stays with me."

"Like hell she will." Patty planted her hands on her hips.

Dennis waved Katelyn over, sending all the girls into a tizzy of confusion.

"Why does she have to go?" Rayanne asked, nearly in tears. "She just got here."

"She isn't going anywhere," Marylynn tried to reassure them over their crying, but Patty had already put hands on Katelyn and was dragging her toward the truck as she tried to free herself.

Marylynn couldn't explain what she did next, and it would make her the talk of the town for years to come. But as soon as she caught sight of Katelyn struggling to free herself from Patty's bony grasp, the only thing she could see was Georgia's face, so helpless and small, so dependent on Marylynn to protect her. Something inside her snapped, sending her scurrying into the house. She emerged a few moments later brandishing an iron will and Charlie's Colt .45, just as the family of three were about to make their escape.

"Katelyn stays with me," she said again, this time pointing the gun squarely between Patty's wide eyes. She never intended to shoot the woman, but the act had been convincing enough to send the pair of them hightailing it to the police station. When four officers and the sheriff arrived, sirens blazing, she calmly explained to Sheriff Humphries how she had been doing only what he had asked her to do when he'd said to take care of her girls.

"It was self-defense, plain and simple," she told him, fanning herself in the afternoon sun.

"Damn it, Marylynn. You know that's not what I meant. Now you can't go around terrorizing folks and claiming I told you to do it."

"Fine. But what would you have had me do? What would you do if it were your grandchild in harm's way?" Crossing her arms, she hoped the weight of her gaze made him uncomfortable. "I won't lose another one."

Perhaps still feeling sorry for her, he lumbered back to his cruiser before declaring the whole scene a domestic disturbance and sending everyone home.

As she watched him drive away, she didn't regret having done it. She would die before she ever let anyone else be taken from her.

She just didn't count on them leaving on their own.

CHAPTER 40

Sᴜᴇ Eʟʟᴇɴ

July 2023

Humidity hung in the afternoon air as the faint smell of liquor and fish wafted in the cool breeze. The moisture here wasn't any less brutal than it was in Muscadine, but the diversity was refreshing, and I breathed it in, closed my eyes, and reveled in the uniqueness of it all. As a professor at the University of New Orleans, my days were still filled with lectures on style and grading remedial essays on the classics, but somehow I felt as if I were finally living in my own skin again.

I'd long since tired of buying shoes I couldn't afford to wear to parties I had no interest in attending. Somewhere along the way I realized that I'd traded my family in for strangers and in the process had lost an essential part of myself, the part that tethered me to home and to the memories of the ones I loved most. Since making the move here six months earlier, I'd begun to catch glimpses of the girl who used to run wild with her sisters, like a feral pack of wolves, unafraid to explore every inch of the land and the muddy water. Though the air was thick and heavy, for the first time in years, it felt as if I could finally breathe deeply again.

Walking briskly past the manicured grounds of the campus dotted by palms, I plunged my hand into my purse and fished out my keys, which held the familiar shape of my pepper spray. Luckily I'd never had to use it, but it reminded me of Meemaw, and I smiled. I cranked the engine of my newest purchase, a sleek red hybrid that had a sunroof I always kept open even though it ruined my hair. With the radio on full blast, I headed along the winding road bordered by Lake Pontchartrain to the north and caught sight of the pontoons and fishing boats drifting aimlessly on the sparkling water. It seemed they had nowhere in particular to be, no destination outside of their directionless floating. The slower pace of living here had left me lighter, and I knew that I would never regret the decision to leave the pricey real estate of Manhattan for the friendly streets of New Orleans.

As I parked the car in front of the pink, refurbished two-bedroom shotgun house I was renting, I beamed at the sight of my humble abode, the brightest house on the entire street, dwarfing all the others in their understated tones. Meemaw would be proud. A few months ago, I had flown down to find the perfect place, inspecting each one personally to ensure a top-notch HVAC system, since that was really the most important thing when it came to surviving this part of the world.

My phone chimed with a message from Derrick, and I smiled as I read the words on my screen.

When do you get in? Your sister is harassing me for your ETA.

She's scary.

Excitement fluttered in my chest as I thought about the romantic dinner he had planned for this weekend. The closer proximity to Muscadine made it easier to date him, but he wasn't the only reason I was going home.

Savannah's face lit up my cell, and I slid my finger across the screen to accept the call. She was already midsentence by the time her face materialized. "You're on your way, right?"

"Yes! And texting me a thousand emojis of your current mental state did not help me leave work any faster."

"Well, hurry up and get your cute butt back here! We're already behind schedule."

"On it. Just packing a bag and I'm on my way. See you soon."

Since Evangeline had come into our lives, things between Savannah and me had shifted. I supposed there wasn't any time for rivalry anymore because all of us had thrown ourselves into the task of teaching Evangeline the history of our family—Meemaw and Mama and Daddy and a million other things she had missed.

After everything, I couldn't say what exactly had made the difference between all of us, but I knew one thing for sure: now that I had them all, I wasn't ever going to let go of them again.

CHAPTER 41

RAYANNE

July 2023

In the low light of our bedroom, Graham pulled me into his chest and nestled his nose against my hair.

"Did you just smell me?" I pulled back and cocked an accusing eyebrow.

He looked guilty but didn't try to hide it. "So what if I did? You smell good." He sniffed me again, then pressed his lips against mine and held them there as if he were afraid I might disappear. Finally he pulled away, leaving me dizzy with the raw kind of excitement we'd had for one another as newlyweds. "I'm going to miss you," he said with puppy-dog eyes.

"You sure you'll be OK this weekend without us?"

"I'll be fine," he said with a sad sigh. "Besides, this is good for you. I'm glad you're finally getting to spend some time with all your sisters."

All my sisters. It was still surreal to think that Evangeline was my sister, too. Not in the way Savannah and Sue Ellen were. Or Georgia. My heart clenched at the memory of her. But still. Evangeline was someone I wanted to know better, and I couldn't help myself from feeling a bit excited at the idea of her coming along this weekend. Even if it also made my eyes well up with tears for everything that had been lost.

"Yeah, it will be great. Evangeline's bringing her girls along, and Charlotte and Tucker are already smitten with them."

"I'll miss date night, though," he added.

"Me too."

Lately we'd decided to make some changes together. Nothing major, just baby steps that would help me relinquish control in a few areas of our lives. Date night was a priority now—and on a normal weekend, nonnegotiable. I had also enrolled the kids in the church's Mother's Day Out program and had an entire ten hours away from them every week. It wasn't much, but it would give me some space to work on myself. Maybe I would start a blog or go back to work part-time. We agreed that Graham would drive the kids there on Tuesdays and Thursdays on his way to work, and that I would not call him afterward to make sure he hadn't forgotten them in the back seat of his car. He didn't have to know that I still called the school just in case, because leaving one's children in the car was incredibly dangerous and surprisingly easy to do if you weren't used to carting your kids around like Graham wasn't. Baby steps.

He grinned and tugged me closer. Just as he leaned in to kiss me again, Charlotte's faint cry pierced the silence on the baby monitor, and I groaned at the thought of climbing the stairs again. "She's cutting a molar."

"I'll get her this time," he said, fending me off with one arm as I moved for the door.

Ignoring him, I pushed past him and headed for the medicine cabinet in the bathroom. "She just needs a little—"

"Baby Motrin," he said. "Two and a half milliliters. I know."

He stole the words right out of my mouth, and I stared back at him, mesmerized.

"What? Are you surprised that I actually know a few things about how to parent our kids?"

"I never thought you didn't," I said, feeling my heart sink. For the first time I realized how pathetic all my micromanaging must have made him feel. "You're kind of amazing." I nuzzled my head into his chest and held on to him firmly before letting him go to her.

It took me some time to realize that everything that happened to us wasn't my fault. That sometimes all it took for a father to leave his family was a poorly thought-out affair and a bad case of self-doubt. That sometimes all it took for a child to be abducted was for a criminal to have access. These were things I could not have controlled. And my carefully constructed world was not going to implode if everything in it was not orchestrated to my own specifications. Maybe if I stepped back to let others in, they just might surprise me.

I invited our father to come to Tucker's fifth birthday party this year. I wasn't sure I'd call it forgiveness. Maybe just a step in a new direction. He may have left us behind, but at least he left me with something—the best thing. He gave me my sisters. And for that I will always be grateful.

After everything that happened, I think this was what I'd taken from it. We could never keep every bad thing from happening. All we could do was cherish the good when we had it for however long it was ours.

EPILOGUE

SAVANNAH

July 2023

As the date of Levi's execution inched closer, the hope that we would ever find Georgia grew bleaker. In spite of it, I felt lighter somehow, like maybe I didn't need to know after all, like maybe finding Sue Ellen and Rayanne and Evangeline had been enough for now. Then one spring morning Levi suddenly recalled the events of that day—the day my life was divided into two sections. I liked to think it was my visit that finally convinced him to tell the truth, but it was more likely the realization that he wasn't long for this world.

Two months ago, in exchange for a life sentence, he led police to a wooded creek bed along the Texas-Louisiana border. And we learned—for the second time—that Georgia was dead. She'd been one of at least four girls taken for no other reason than she'd been in the wrong place at the wrong time—easy prey for someone who took advantage of a bustling scene and a distracted adult. When the news finally came that they had found her, I went to pieces. I hadn't known my heart was strong enough to break twice. If Sue Ellen and Rayanne hadn't been there with me, I'm not sure I would have been able to keep standing.

But together they held on to me, and as much as I tried, I couldn't seem to get rid of them after that.

Losing Georgia is a permanent kind of heartbreak, an earthquake that shifted every birthday, every Christmas, every graduation I had to sit through alone. It left behind a crack that runs straight through the center of me. But it's only a crack. It didn't stop my breath, and for better or worse, I'm still here. I've finally decided it's for the better. My sister is buried in the grassy patch of earth that sits between Mama and Meemaw in the cemetery behind the library. And there is some relief in knowing where she is. Even so, she isn't there. Not really.

A neon sunset hovers across the lake's horizon, shimmering its pink-and-orange reflection off the muddy water as it slips away. Carefully, I finish the final strokes on the wooden sign that will hang above the door, outlining each letter with a cerulean blue that makes me think of Georgia's eyes. I lay it out to dry on the picnic table and wipe my hands on my apron. When I first bought this land, I never thought it would be anything more than a shrine to her memory, a way I could keep her with me always. But when I received my share of the money from Meemaw's house, Sue Ellen pushed me to go big or go home, and for the first time in my life, I listened to her. On the patch of weeds where Colton's trailer once sat, I built this bed-and-breakfast to remind myself that Georgia never really left me.

I sit myself down on my front steps and watch the muddy water lap itself up onto the grassy banks in rhythmic patterns. Closing my eyes, I try to remember the sound of her laughter, our tiny voices woven together, indistinguishable from one another. And I feel her here with me—Mama and Meemaw, too. I feel them in the wind as it rustles through the lofty cypress and pines that surround this lake. I feel them in the sunset each evening as it stretches across the sky, lighting the tops of the trees on fire, and in the swamp canaries that call out their songs overhead as they return to these parts every spring.

Through the pines, I spot two cars trailing around the dirt path that borders the lake. They roll to a stop, and Tucker darts out of the Lexus. He launches into me, wrapping his arms around my neck before I have time to brace myself. We tumble back into a patch of weeds, and I tickle him under the arms until he squeals for me to stop. Catching sight of Rayanne and Sue Ellen, I dust myself off, reach for his hand, and head over to meet them.

"The armadillos?" Rayanne says, lowering her sunglasses at my decor that lines the front-porch railing.

"They add character," I say, flashing a proud smile. "Besides, she'd love it." My heart contracts at the memory of her. Though we'd sold most of Meemaw's things in the most epic garage sale Muscadine had ever seen, I held on to a few things to furnish my new business.

"Well, if you decide you need a pig, just let me know." Bessie trails behind them, rolling happily about in a patch of dirt. "This one is spoiled rotten."

I smile and pull her into a hug with more force than I intended.

Sue Ellen holds a sleeping Charlotte in her arms, rubbing her back gingerly as she takes in the cabin. "It looks amazing," she says. I'd gone for a traditional look with wide cedar beams, a scrap-metal roof, and a wraparound porch with hand-painted rockers. Around the back, I'd added a raised deck for bird-watching and a few feeders to attract the rare ones.

"Thanks." A flicker of pride burns low beneath my heart. "Just adding a few finishing touches." I gesture to the sign, the freshly painted words shimmering in the evening sun. Sue Ellen had been the one to suggest the name, and I had to agree it was perfect. My Sister's House already had a bustling page on Vrbo and Airbnb. But its opening weekend had been reserved for the four of us.

"It's perfect," she says.

Two little girls with green eyes and brown curls spill out of the silver SUV that has parked behind Rayanne's car, and Evangeline follows after them, offering us a tentative wave. She is still cautious around us, still unsure if she fits into this family, though we have reassured her over and over again that she is right where she belongs. We can't punish her for anyone else's mistakes, and though it's not been easy, we are coming to know one another, and the kids have all taken to each other without any help from us.

The sunlight catches the auburn highlights in her dark hair, and I am reminded again that she looks a lot like Sue Ellen. I smile back at her, and a puzzle piece settles into place inside my heart. Evangeline is not Georgia, and she can never be her. But she is my sister. And we have things to learn about each other, a whole life lived that I'm only just beginning to know about.

I think of the time capsule, how I had wanted to bury it for Georgia, hoping she would be there with us when we dug it up. I'd never let myself be all the things I wanted, because somehow it felt wrong to let myself have it. But now it feels like the best parts of my life are at my fingertips, and I don't want to live a half life anymore. I don't think she would want me to. Instead, I've decided to start living enough for the both of us.

I watch the kids running and playing, chasing each other through the dandelions and the cattails that line the lake, and it occurs to me that maybe that tug I felt from Georgia wasn't her telling me to find her. Maybe it was her telling me to find myself.

ACKNOWLEDGMENTS

When I set out to write this novel, I assumed I would be doing it alone. I had no idea how many hands it would pass through and how many people along the way would help it succeed.

I am so grateful for thoughtful beta readers who gifted their time to read this manuscript in its many forms. Some of them were total strangers on the internet, and some are near and dear to my heart. Thank you to my sisters and my mom, who read that first messy draft and told me it was great even when it wasn't. I have always said that every girl needs a sister, and I am lucky enough to have three amazing ones. Our childhood inspired this novel, and our parents gave us a great one. Thank you, Mom and Dad!

Thank you, Erin McAnoy, for giving me that first positive critique and the motivation to keep going. I am certain I would have shelved this if it weren't for you. Thank you to my writing group, Julia Nusbaum and Kyla Najjar, for helping me polish and carry it over the finish line. Thank you to my agent, Ann Leslie Tuttle, who understood this book from the very beginning and championed it every step along the way. Your enthusiasm for this project has fueled me through each round of edits, and your experience has proved invaluable. Thank you to Alicia Clancy at Lake Union Publishing for your patience with me and for taking a chance on a newbie writer.

Thank you to my daughters, who inspire me every day to be a better person and remind me daily that I can do hard things. It is because of you that I took a chance and queried this work.

Lastly, thank you to my husband, who encouraged me to write in the first place. I am 100 percent certain this book would not exist without you. Thank you for never making me feel guilty about all those hours I spent on the couch, for letting me bounce ideas off you, for baking me dozens of chocolate chip cookies, and, most importantly, for knowing when to order out for dinner. I love you.

ABOUT THE AUTHOR

Photo © 2021 Emily Murdock Photography

Laura Barrow is a former teacher and a lover of books. She received her bachelor's degree in music education from Centenary College in northwest Louisiana, where she grew up. She now resides in northeast Texas, just outside Dallas, with her husband, three daughters, and a houseful of pets.